Nia, **Jessie** and **M**... that there's a lo... Because **Jake**, **Li**... decided to laur... *don't* mean one of the corporate kina! For these three couples, business is just about to get very, *very* personal…

NINE TO FIVE

Colleagues by day…lovers by night

An exciting collection of short stories by favourite Mills & Boon® authors,

Kim Lawrence, Sandra Marton and **Cathy Williams!**

NINE TO FIVE

BABY AND THE BOSS
MALONE'S VOW
ASSIGNMENT: SEDUCTION

MILLS & BOON®

*MILLS & BOON and MILLS & BOON with the Rose Device
are registered trademarks of the publisher.
Harlequin Mills & Boon Limited,
Eton House, 18-24 Paradise Road, Richmond, Surrey, TW9 1SR*

NINE TO FIVE © by Harlequin Enterprises II B.V., 2001

The publisher acknowledges the copyright holders of the
individual works as follows:

Baby and the Boss © Kim Lawrence 2000
Malone's Vow © Sandra Myles 2001
Assignment: Seduction © Cathy Williams 2000

ISBN 0 263 82839 5

118-0401

*Printed and bound in Spain
by Litografia Rosés S.A., Barcelona*

CONTENTS

BABY AND THE BOSS
by
Kim Lawrence

Kim Lawrence lives on a farm in rural Anglesey. She runs two miles daily and finds this an excellent opportunity to unwind and seek inspiration for her writing! It also helps her keep up with her husband, two active sons, and the various stray animals which have adopted them. Always a fanatical consumer of fiction, she is now equally enthusiastic about writing. She loves a happy ending!

Look out for
A CONVENIENT HUSBAND by Kim Lawrence
in Modern Romance™, May 2001

CHAPTER ONE

NIA was breathless by the time she reached her desk. The connecting door was open and to her relief her boss unusually wasn't back from lunch yet, either. She glanced at her watch, two minutes late. Hastily pushing her packages under the desk, she slid into her seat and adopted her best cool, unflappable expression.

It wasn't that the cool capable part was an act, it was just that her present boss always looked as though he thought it was.

Working as a temp had made her adaptable, but some employers were a lot easier to adapt to than others. Jake Prentice wasn't the most difficult boss she'd ever had to work for, but he was, she reflected tightening the barrette that was meant to hold back her rich auburn curls, right up there in the *awful* category.

It was nigh on impossible to build up a good working relationship with someone who didn't appear to think she was capable of breathing without being given detailed instructions on the process!

She didn't think his antipathy was actually personal, despite his initial reaction—one she now knew was *extremely* uncharacteristic. She suspected he had her in the same mental file as office furniture. She'd always known a successful temp had to be a bit of a chameleon, but you had to draw a line somewhere. She wasn't about to start wearing a wig even for the sake of industrial harmony!

'You've got red hair.'

The awkward thirty-second aftermath which followed that startled accusation was the only time she'd ever seen Jake

Prentice display anything approaching embarrassment. The fact that her expression hadn't done much to disguise that she thought it had been a pretty stupid thing to say probably hadn't done much to improve matters.

He'd been treating her like a nasty smell ever since, but honestly what had the man expected her to do? It hadn't been a very imaginative comment for someone who was supposed to be one of the most brilliant, innovative architects of his generation. He must be good, he was young—early thirties— to be an architect with the sort of international reputation he had.

He didn't come across as her idea of a sensitive creative type, but he had a cupboard full of awards proclaiming he was, so she must be missing something. She hadn't missed the signs of Grade-A workaholism, though, nor his teeth-clenching unremitting attention to detail!

If she'd made any mistakes she'd have known about it, he'd have made sure of that! Without saying a word—one raised brow and a pained expression had done it—he'd made it pretty clear that the cluster of family photos and the dis-creet pot plant she'd brought in were unwelcome additions to the office.

She hadn't made a song and dance about it. He was a man heavily into the minimalist look, and he paid her salary. She'd taken it philosophically and had made no further at-tempts to personalise her space.

'Miss Jones, would you arrange coffee for my brother?'

She started and knocked a manila folder onto the floor.

'Brother?' She didn't have the faintest idea what he was talking about.

Fortunately mind-reading wasn't one of his talents, al-though with those eyes—who knew! There was something almost spooky about his grey eyes, really pale grey with a distinctive dark rim around the iris, fringed by lashes that were luxuriantly long and curling—they struck her as a frivolous detail in an otherwise austerely handsome face.

Not for the first time she wondered how he managed to enter a room totally silently. She sounded like a regiment when her heels clattered on the pale elm flooring that had been used throughout the building. The man must have been an assassin in a previous reincarnation. Yes, she decided, there was something sinister and predatory about those finely chiselled features. She looked at the uncompromising line of his square jaw and it clicked—*the man on the stairs!*

'Your brother has left,' she informed him confidently.

The interrogative quirk of one dark brow had her rushing on to explain herself. 'I bumped into him on the stairs. I didn't actually realise he was your brother at the time, but he looked…'

It wasn't the similarity, which now seemed obvious, that had made the incident and the stranger stand out in her mind, just the terrible haunted expression in his eyes. Well, that, and the fact he was the most sinfully gorgeous creature she'd ever laid eyes on. Didn't that mean he was the second most sinfully gorgeous creature…? The similarity was striking… She only conceded her employer's gorgeous status with the utmost reluctance.

Perhaps it was something to do with expressions, she pondered thoughtfully. She could never imagine anything about Jake making her want to run after him and ask if she could help. His brother had made her want to do just that.

Nia had been in the big city long enough to know you didn't follow a gut instinct to run after total strangers and offer help. No wonder she hadn't made the family connection, Jake Prentice was the least needy man she'd ever met!

Jake's lips tightened fractionally before he nodded abruptly. 'We're twins. Put the call from Stockholm straight through.'

Twins! Yes, the mental photo fit was an exact match.

So alike, but so *different,* she thought, letting out a gusty sigh as he vanished into his own room. She had developed the silly habit of holding her breath since she'd been working for this tiresome man. Would Jake Prentice really look like the man on the stairs with a couple of days' growth of beard and his neatly trimmed dark hair falling almost to his shoulders?

She mentally replaced the dull lank locks for something with a nice healthy sheen, her employer wasn't the sort of man you associated lank hair with. The first thing she'd seen on the stairs had been a pair of very long muscular legs coming towards her. The stranger's upper body had been just as impressive.

It naturally followed that his twin would be equally blessed—physically speaking. This wasn't a big shock, it had always been obvious that inside those conservative but beautifully cut suits there lurked a super-fit body. Vitality simply oozed out of every pore.

The intercom interrupted her private contemplation of her employer's physical attributes. Her cheeks were pink but her tone cool and composed as she responded.

'Miss Jones, there's an animal in my office.'

'Are you sure?' she asked doubtfully.

'Of course I'm damned sure! I can hear it. A cat. Is it yours?'

Someone who brought in a photo of her parents and loved ones was obviously capable of starting a farm in his office—especially if they had red hair!

'I'm allergic to cats. Now if you'd said dog… Shall I call security?' she asked politely.

'I think I can cope with a cat, Miss Jones.' She heard his startled intake of breath and then the shaken, *'Oh, my God!—I really don't believe this! Josh, you damn fool!'*

Men like Jake Prentice didn't sound that gobsmacked without pretty good cause! Nia leaped to her feet, her actions, it had to be said, impelled more by curiosity than a noble desire to be helpful.

Nia had a weakness for shoes, without the bank balance to compensate. The beautiful, impractical creations she wore today had been a sale bargain that she hadn't been able to resist, even if they were a bit on the tight side. She did a lot of clattering before she erupted breathlessly into the inner sanctum.

The inner sanctum had a glass wall, views to make your average estate agent break into spontaneous song, and individual pieces of furniture that were earmarked to be the collectible antiques of the next century.

Nia didn't have eyes for the interior decor, her attention was focused on the unlikely spectacle of her boss, all six foot five of him crouched on all fours on the floor in front of the vast curved blonde wood desk.

'What's wrong?'

As Jake lifted one unsteady hand to his dark head and spared her a fleeting look before shifting his stance slightly, Nia saw for the first time what he was staring at.

'Oh, my goodness! That's a baby,' she said, staring with disbelief at the tiny creature strapped into a car seat. 'It's not mine,' she added defensively as her employer's stunned eyes reached her face.

He looked at her as though she'd said something even more imbecilic than usual. 'I'm well aware of that, woman.'

'Then it's yours!' she gasped, leaping to the obvious conclusion. On closer inspection there was something very familiar about those darkly fringed grey eyes.

'No, it's not mine!'

'Are you *quite* sure?' she persisted doubtfully, looking from the small chubby unformed face to the forbidding mature version.

Holding the carrying handle of the baby carrier at arm's

length, as though the contents were contagious, Jake got to his feet.

'Miss Jones, I am one hundred percent sure that this baby could not possibly be mine.' He was trying hard to be patient, but there were limits and this female seemed determined to stretch them to the breaking point.

Comprehension flooded over her and Nia gave a grimace of sympathy. 'I'm so sorry, I didn't know.'

'Didn't know what?' he said in a measured tone that suggested he was trying desperately to retain his grip on reality in an increasingly surreal situation.

'That you're infertile. You shouldn't give up hope. You know, they're making the most amazing medical advances in that field. Why only the other week I saw this documentary…'

'*Miss Jones!*'

His bellow of rage cut through her helpful observations. Nia's rather full lips thinned to a line of disapproval and a militant light entered her green eyes.

Had this woman never heard of professional distance? Why couldn't she keep to normal topics like the weather? In a few weeks his office had become a sanctum for every love-lorn soul in the building. He found all that damned empathy uncomfortable.

He closed his eyes briefly and cursed the day his real secretary had decided to extend her family. When Fiona had been here there had been no babies or children of any variety left under his desk.

'Shut up…*please.*' He forced himself to smile patiently. Fiona didn't wear earrings that jingled in that distracting way, either. On her return he would give her an outrageously generous rise on the strict understanding she *never* left his employ again.

His attention was diverted to the infant he still held at arm's length. The baby's gurgles had become less contented and more urgent and its little face had deepened to an alarming shade of red.

'Babies don't like loud noises,' Nia observed, not without a certain degree of spiteful satisfaction. 'Neither,' she added pointedly, 'do I.'

'I am not sterile.'

'Of course not,' she agreed kindly.

The damned woman was humouring him! 'No *really,*' he insisted, speaking from between clenched teeth. 'I just happen to know for sure this baby isn't mine because it's my brother's.'

'Oh! I see.' Nia screwed up her nose and gave a frown. 'Well, actually, I don't. Why did your brother leave his…is it a boy or girl?'

'Boy.'

'Why did he leave his son under your desk?' That sort of carelessness went a bit beyond the forgetful.

'When we find him, you can ask him,' he promised grimly.

'*We?*' she queried suspiciously.

'Do I have much scheduled for this afternoon?'

'You might have the odd fifteen seconds to spare.'

He let this display of sarcasm pass, unfortunately he needed a bit of female cooperation right now. The baby let out an ear-piercing screech just to reinforce this fact at that precise moment.

'Reschedule my appointments,' he said hastily. 'I'll find Josh and you can watch the baby.'

The high-handed assumption of her automatic cooperation was so typical of the man, she thought indignantly. 'Me! Why me?' Why didn't he ask Victoria or Jasmine or who was the other one…? She stifled a grin at the thought of these ladies' responses if they'd been asked to babysit.

'You're a woman, aren't you?' He raised his voice to be heard over the baby's wail.

She was amazed he'd noticed. 'And that automatically

qualifies me to look after babies?' she suggested with a wide-eyed attentive look.

'I'm just asking for a bit of give-and-take here, Miss Jones. This is an emergency.'

He must be desperate, he was using that high-voltage smile that he reserved for Jasmine, Victoria and, of course, Selina. How could she have forgotten Selina? His smile made all of those pencil-slim, extremely tall beauties very understanding when he kept them waiting for hours.

Well, if he expects me to start panting to please him, he's doomed to disappointment. She'd been brought up in a male-dominated household and when the male of the species said give-and-take in her experience *she* was expected to do most of the giving!

'I did the giving when I came in two hours early three days this week, on the understanding, you recall, that I could leave promptly at three this afternoon. If you go off searching for your brother, who might very well not want to be found, what chance is there of that?'

'That's a very selfish view to take,' he observed regarding her with deepening dislike.

'If it's any comfort, my big brothers all share your opinion of my selfish disposition—all five of them. If you were looking for a temporary doormat, Mr. Prentice, you lucked out,' she told him frankly. 'I'm not about to sacrifice my personal life for your convenience, but I might make a rather obvious suggestion—why don't you just phone your brother's wife?'

'I would if I could—she's dead,' he announced expressionlessly.

This flat matter-of-fact statement wiped the superior smile clean off her face. She looked from his grim face to the tiny baby and felt the prickle of tears at the backs of her eyelids.

'That's…that really…' She swallowed, *dreadful* didn't really sound adequate to cover such a tragedy. The mystery of the distressed young man on the stairs was sadly solved. She wished now she'd obeyed her instincts and had approached him. Her tender heart ached and his disappearing act became more understandable.

'It is,' he agreed.

One solitary tear escaped her swimming eyes and Jake watched it progress over the smooth contours of her face before she flicked a careless finger to blot it.

'Does this work for you as a compromise?'

Compromise! Jake Prentice! She blinked, she was amazed the term was in his vocabulary.

'All three of us,' he glanced towards the baby, 'go to look for Josh, and when it's three o'clock you go and do whatever it is you so urgently need to do.'

'I suppose that might be all right,' she conceded, still not sold on the plan.

Jake didn't feel any more enthusiastic about the plan than she sounded. 'Do you think possibly you should change or feed him or something?'

'I thought this was a joint venture? I might come from a large family but my experience of babies is nil, I was the baby.'

And used to getting her own way from day one, he thought, eyeing that dimple in her right cheek with cynical suspicion. When she smiled, and he'd noticed she did so indiscriminately at everyone from the sandwich boy to visiting government dignitaries, it deepened in a very beguiling way. She didn't smile at him, a fact that was naturally a deep source of relief to him.

'Now, if you wanted me to strip an engine…'

'How hard can it be?'

Nia assumed he was referring to babies, not the internal combustion engine. She watched as he placed the distressed baby, still strapped in his seat, on one of the chunky leather sofas.

Nia bit her lip to stop herself grinning—actually she knew a lot more about babies than she'd let on.

'I do admire a confident attitude.' She bent over and picked up a large holdall emblazoned with big fluffy yellow rabbits. 'This looks promising,' she added, tossing it towards him.

Jake automatically caught it one handed. He had an enviable athletic coordination, which was probably why she found herself staring when he walked across a room.

'But…'

'I'll cancel your appointments,' she said, turning a deliberate blind eye to his stereotypical display of helpless male panic.

When she returned a few minutes later Jake was struggling with the plastic tags of a disposable nappy, several ruined ones lay on the floor beside him. The baby was kicking happily, enjoying his freedom.

He glanced around as she came in. His eyes moved upwards from her slim ankles, moving up the shapely curve of her calves before eventually reaching her face. His colour was slightly heightened.

'A very poor design,' he grumbled as she dropped down onto the floor beside him.

'Perhaps you don't have the gentle touch?' He'd used his folded jacket as a changing mat for the baby and through the fine fabric of his shirt she could make out the shadowy suggestion outline of dark hair across his chest.

Anyone would think the man was stark naked, she told herself impatiently. That neat jolt of inexplicable sexual awareness had been impossible to misinterpret even if she'd wanted to. Remember rule number one, Nia. Never, *never* get romantically interested in your boss. She'd seen too many friends take that particular path to disaster.

'Nobody has ever complained about my touch.' It was impossible to tell from his sardonic expression if any double entendre was intended. The mere possibility was enough to make her lower jaw drop. 'I thought you didn't know anything about babies?'

Hands flat on the floor, Nia leaned over the baby, making those unintelligible noises small helpless things inspired in the female breast. Half of her hair was loose again, he'd noticed it didn't usually last beyond midmorning no matter how she tried to restrain it. The swathe of pre-Raphaelite curls swung with a life of their own over her shoulders and brushed the floor. Jake could smell the fresh scent of her shampoo, and a muscle in his lean cheek jumped.

The baby watched the fiery cloud apparently fascinated—genetics had a lot to answer for, Jake thought drily. Then his nephew did something he'd spent far too long thinking about, either by design or accident, he reached up and wrapped his small chubby fingers in a handy strand. Nia let out a yelp and then a soft chuckle.

'Aren't you a strong boy,' she admired warmly, trying to loosen the tenacious grip with little success.

Jake doubted her response would have been as mild had *he* chosen to sink his fingers deep into that glowing mass that was composed of shades that ran the full length of the spectrum from gold to deepest Titian.

'What's his name?' A smile on her face, she turned her head and found that Jake was watching her with an odd, stomach-tightening intensity.

He didn't look away, just held her eyes. She didn't know why, perhaps just because he could? He could make female hearts—not to mention stomachs, go haywire, even if their owners didn't actually like him. Even if their owners were *supposed* to be happily engaged to someone else.

'Liam.'

'What a lovely name.' Nia didn't like the way her voice had dropped a husky octave. It had a worrying come-hither sound to it. She waited hopefully for her pulse rate to slow down.

'Bridie was Irish.'

'How did she…? Sorry it's none of my—ouch!' She winced and bent her head closer as the baby tugged.

'Let me.' With one hand he took some of the slack out of the long silky hank of hair to protect her scalp from sudden assaults and with the other he gently prized the tiny curling fingers from her hair.

It was just as well the task didn't take him long because she'd forgotten to breathe for the duration. The couple of deep restoring breaths she took to compensate had the middle two buttons on her shirt popping. She hastily pulled the two sides together to cover the pretty lavender lace of her bra.

Whilst she'd automatically adapted her clothes to blend in with the conspicuous conservative office dress policy she'd seen no need—until now—to extend that trend to her undergarments.

'Is he a toucher?' her flatmate Toni had sympathetically asked when she'd confessed she wished she'd never started this particular job. Nia had laughed—her laughter had been a little strained. The idea of Jake Prentice chasing her around his desk, or even hers, had been so ludicrous she couldn't even bring herself to think about it—you couldn't count one or two disturbing dreams as thinking, could you? The subconscious was a law unto itself.

She hadn't realised until that moment that he'd never touched her before, not even the casual touching of hands—she'd have remembered. She skipped swiftly over the worrying fact she was so certain of this. It was almost as if he had actively avoided touching her. With an impatient shake of her head, she dismissed this silly idea.

'Thank you,' she said huskily as, cheeks pink, she tried to refasten the buttons with clumsy fingers.

What would she do if he tried to help her out of that situation, too? She had a sudden mental image of his long clever fingers dextrously addressing the problem of her buttons—only he wasn't fastening them! She could feel the warm surge of blood that washed over her fair Celtic skin.

'I think he's hungry.'

'Is he bottle fed?' she wondered out loud.

'The poor little tyke didn't have the option.'

'Of course not,' Nia said, miserable that she'd been so

tactless. Then as she saw the direction of his oddly distracted gaze she glanced down to check that she was still fully buttoned.

When she raised her relieved eyes, they collided explosively with his. The impact shuddered through her body, awakening all sorts of embarrassing physical responses. Rather than draw attention to the most obvious of these, she didn't lift her hands like a shield over her tingling breasts.

Jake was astonished that his eyes had strayed as obviously as a schoolboy or some sort of pathetic lecher when he was speaking to the woman. The breast-feeding connection had just been too much for his self-control, especially after that tantalising glimpse of creamy cleavage.

'Perhaps there's a bottle in the bag?' Her voice was desperately normal.

'Why didn't I think of that?' Because you were too busy ogling your secretary is why, he silently replied with a self-derisive shrug. He had no intention of getting a reputation as a serial sucker in the workplace. Besides, she wasn't available…which was just as well because they had nothing whatever in common.

'Let me hold him.' The darkened damp patch on the lining of his jacket was pretty obvious as she picked up the baby. 'Oops.' Considering the name she'd seen hand-stitched into the lining, that was quite a costly accident.

To her surprise Jake gave a quick grin—the spontaneous nice sort of grin that she hadn't known he was capable of. Nia frowned, she'd felt safer when he was an inhumanly demanding boss; she didn't need any hints of niceness. Not when she had developed this worrying tendency to think lustful thoughts about him. Actually she didn't even think them—they'd been springing fully formed into her head all afternoon!

CHAPTER TWO

JAKE divided the list of anyone he thought might be able to locate his brother in two and whilst the baby, his stomach full, slept, they worked their way through the contacts.

'Any joy?' He pushed the intervening door open and leaned against the jamb, rolling his head slowly from side to side to relieve the tension.

Despite a work schedule that would have had normal mortals on their knees, this was the first time Nia had ever seen him display any physical tiredness. She shook her head rapidly when his quizzical expression brought home the fact she'd been staring a little too obviously.

'Then we'd better try his place. I don't know what the hell I'm going to do if there's no clue there. Are you ready?'

It wasn't a question or even a request. Nia resisted the temptation to salute.

'Isn't there anyone who could look after the baby? Grandparents…?'

Jake glanced rather impatiently down at her, adjusting his stride, rather belatedly, to accommodate the height of her heels and the disparity in their leg length.

'My mother's in the States where my sister's due to give birth to twins at any second, and Josh's in-laws would only be too happy to take responsibility. As far as they're concerned possession's nine-tenths of the law,' he said drily.

Nia watched as he clipped the baby seat into the back of the Jaguar saloon he drove and wondered where she'd have sat if he'd gone in for a convertible—the boot, probably.

'You can't think they wouldn't give Liam back.'

'That,' he said, holding the door open for her—coldly

courteous to the last, 'is exactly what I think. They've been trying to convince Josh to let them bring up the baby ever since Bridie died—subtly, and then not so subtly. They'd like nothing better than for Josh to prove himself an unfit father and Josh—being Josh,' he grated, his voice harsh with frustration, 'is going out of his way to prove their case. They never wanted Bridie to marry him in the first place.'

Something about the way he said that made her frown thoughtfully. 'Why, did they have someone else in mind?' she asked, responding to an intuitive flash.

Jake turned the key in the ignition and the car purred smoothly into life. He'd known it was a mistake to take her out of the office environment. Those big eyes were going to get all misty any minute now, and then she'd decide to personally sort out his life.

'Yes,' he said, turning his head to look at her. 'Me.'

'Oh!'

This astonishing revelation put an entirely new twist on matters. God knows what emotions were bottled up in that very impressive chest, she thought, unable to resist a furtive little glance at that general area of his anatomy.

He wouldn't be human if he didn't feel a bit ambivalent about his twin. On top of that, he was obviously grieving for a woman he'd once loved—still did, for all she knew. God, what a mess, she thought, feeling way out of her depth.

'*Oh* indeed,' he mocked, nodding to the uniformed guardian of the underground parking area. 'I was engaged to Bridie before she met Josh. If any aspects of my personal life fascinate you, just come right out and ask. The office grapevine has only recently become relatively quiet on the subject. I'd prefer nobody resurrected it.' His eyes were icily cold as they touched her face.

'I'm aware you don't think much of me as a secretary, Mr. Prentice, but I'm no gossip,' she responded huffily.

'Under the circumstances I think you'd better make it Jake,

and you should know how to keep a secret. I would imagine every soul in the building has confided their deepest darkest ones to you by now. Does it ever occur to you you've picked the wrong profession? You seem to think it your mission in life to sort out peoples' lives.'

'I've had no complaints about my secretarial skills until now—well, not many,' she conceded honestly. 'But that wasn't my fault. I don't like being groped,' she added darkly.

'I'll keep that in mind,' came the dry reply.

'I didn't mean you,' she said with startled dismay. 'I know *you* wouldn't dream…'

'We all dream, Nia,' he replied cryptically.

There was a really tight feeling in her chest as her racing mind delivered various versions of what the man beside her might dream—not about her, of course—he didn't like red hair and hers was very hard to ignore.

'I didn't know your brother lived out of town,' she said after they'd travelled for a short time in uncompanionable silence.

He flicked her a quick sideways glance that said he'd forgotten she was there. 'He does.'

'How far out?' She was doing some quick mental calculations. Just how long would it take her to get back from wherever he was taking her? 'It won't do me much good if you let me go on time if it's going to take me hours to get back to the city,' she added crisply when he didn't immediately respond.

'Oh, I forgot, your urgent appointment.' His mocking drawl made her eyes narrow angrily.

'I realise that my personal life fades into insignificance beside yours.'

'What is it that's so damned important, anyway?'

'I need to catch a train home for the weekend.'

'Oh, yes, the girl from the valleys.'

'Actually I live on a mountain, not in a valley, and your acccent's all wrong. I'm from North Wales not South.'

'Why would someone who lives on a mountain—the northern variety—want to come and live in a poky bedsit?'

'How do you know I live in a poky bedsit? Actually I share a flat—quite a nice flat.' Though that depended on what you were used to, and she suspected Jake Prentice was used to the very best—top-drawer houses, cars, she stroked the soft leather upholstery, and women, she decided with throwing him a sour look.

'And do you share this flat with the fiancé?'

Nia's eyes transferred to her lap where she self-consciously rubbed the antique garnet-and-pearl-encrusted ring on her left hand.

'Huw lives in Wales,' she said shortly.

'Hence the breathless eagerness to get back home.' His tone held a faint but definite impression of a sneer. 'I'm surprised he's happy to let you move so far away.' She was wilful enough, he thought, thinking of that square determined little chin, to go her own way regardless.

His quick glance, she decided, suggested he wouldn't have trusted her as far as he could throw her.

'There aren't many jobs to be had on mountainsides.'

'But…Huw, he has one?'

'His family's land adjoins Dad's farm,' she replied shortly, uncomfortable at the probing nature of his questions.

'I can't see you as a farmer's wife.'

Nia wasn't sure she wanted to know what he did see her as. She saw no reason to correct this shaky interpretation of the information, either. In one way Huw's family were farmers, they did own vast tracts of hill land and also a tidy bit of much more profitable lowland pasture and woods. The estate had at least a dozen tenant farms and a beautiful manor house with gardens that were open to the public on bank holidays.

These days the estate, which Huw ran, was almost a hobby, most of the family's money came from some very clever investments in the leisure industry. If she had still been engaged to Huw and wearing his ring, not the one she'd inherited from her grandmother, Huw might indeed have been unhappy about her decision to move to London. As it was, he probably felt relief.

She gave a quick glance over her shoulder at the sleeping baby—happily, he was still dead to the world—just as Jake slowed down to pass several people on horseback. It really was getting worryingly rural.

'Why didn't you tell me your brother lived in the back of beyond?'

'If I had, would you have come along?' He glanced coolly at her indignant face. *'Exactly.'*

'I'll miss my train. Not that you'd care,' she added wrathfully. 'Just so long as you're getting your own way.'

'You think I want to spend my afternoon with a crying baby and a…' He broke off suspiciously abruptly and continued in a reasonable voice she didn't believe for an instant. 'If you miss your train tonight you can have Monday off.'

'And a what?' she said in a dangerously quiet voice. 'A baby and a what?'

'Secretary.'

She gave a dismissive snort that went a bit wobbly because he was negotiating a rough bone-shaking mud track. 'That wasn't what you were going to say.'

'I thought better of it,' he admitted frankly as he drew up in front of a small but picturesque cottage. 'I have a healthy respect for red-headed tempers. Here we are,' he added unnecessarily. 'No signs of life that I can see,' he concluded gloomily after his initial inspection.

Nia followed his lead and clambered out of the car. 'I know you don't like redheads,' she shouted at him. Hearing the childish sound of her waspish accusation, she winced.

Jake's initial sharp glance held surprise and then, as she watched, amusement pulled at the corners of his mouth. Whilst he was still watching, she lurched inelegantly as one heel slid on the slippery cobbled surface. Go on, girl, give him something to laugh properly about, why don't you?

'Farmer's daughter did you say?'

Nia caught her breath and her balance. 'I thought I was dressing for the office today,' she replied with as much dignity as she could muster.

'Is that what you call it?' His eyes ran comprehensively over her pale green, soft faux silk skirt and matching blouse, they dwelt on the perilously high heels she wore.

'What,' she asked, her bosom swelling with indignation, 'is wrong with my clothes? First my hair, now my dress sense. Is there anything about me you do approve of?'

An expression flared in his eyes before the ebony lashes fell in a concealing cloak. 'Did I say I didn't like red hair?'

'You implied it,' she countered, annoyed that she was acting as if it mattered to her—which, of course, it didn't.

'It might be better if you take those things off—the shoes,' he added as she continued to stare up at him.

'I knew that,' she countered. He wouldn't be asking her to take off anything else, would he? Reluctantly she did as he suggested. Without the benefit of heels she had sunk back down to way below his shoulder height again.

'What are you waiting for?' he asked when she didn't fall into step beside him. 'Do you want me to carry you?' he enquired with offensive sarcasm.

'Haven't you forgotten something?' Her voice held an extra acid sharpness to compensate for the bizarre route her imagination had taken.

She'd have walked across hot coals before she'd have admitted her sweaty palms and shaking knees had anything to do with the image of herself being lifted effortlessly by strong masculine arms—when you considered the person the

masculine arms were attached to it made her derangement all
the more serious!

'What?' He gave her an impatient look.

'The baby.'

In his urgency to find his brother that small but all-
important detail had for a second slipped his mind. At the
crisp reminder, he lifted a harassed hand to his brow. His
eyes went automatically to the occupied back seat and Nia
saw his shoulders square both mentally and physically.

'Or do you intend leaving him outside in the car?'

'If you're not too busy scoring points, do you think you
could bring in some of that paraphernalia?' he asked, nodding
to the inevitable clutter that accompanies infants as he lifted
the baby carrier clear of the car.

Nia resisted the temptation of having the last word and
followed him into the picture-postcard cottage.

CHAPTER THREE

'DIDN'T you have any hint that your brother might do something like this?' Nia couldn't keep the edge of criticism from her voice. She pushed aside a pile of newspapers from a small armchair and sank wearily into it. 'He looked pretty, well...*desperate* when I saw him.'

Jake looked across at her just as, elbow bent, she used her forearm to impatiently brush back the heavy swathe of loose curls that were tickling her face. His eyes faithfully followed the rippling red curls as they settled in place. Nia blew the last few wisps away and he turned abruptly.

Toe tapping on the floor, Nia waited for him to respond, his broad back looked angry as he brushed the dust from a pretty chintzy sofa before following her example.

He scowled unappreciatively at the pile of prettily embroidered cushions stacked up behind his broad shoulders before nudging them out of the way.

'What are you grinning about now?' That damned dimple was very much in evidence.

'I didn't know I was grinning,' she responded, a little bemused by the depth of antagonism in his voice. 'We don't all ration our smiles, you know.'

'You could smile for Britain,' he observed broodingly. Her smile had, he decided, a dangerous combination of innocence and seductiveness. He was just surprised she managed to keep the prowling office romeos at bay—maybe she didn't.

'You make it sound like a crime to be cheerful.' She preferred to have the odd laugh line rather than the deep frown lines that had appeared over the bridge of his hawkish nose. On him, she conceded, they were attractive.

'If you must know, you look funny sitting on that thing—wrong scale,' she explained. 'Your legs are too long.' Her glance flickered to his long legs and she gulped—why was she visualising those legs minus the expensive packaging?

The furniture was in scale with the entire cottage, which was compact; it had only taken Jake a few frustrating moments to confirm it was empty. Probably hitting his head on a low beam hadn't improved his temper, she concluded, trying to focus on something less distracting than the muscle-packed power of his thighs.

Inside the cottage the signs of neglect were even more pronounced than a few weeds growing in the stone-flagged path. The place looked as unkempt and neglected as the man she'd seen on the stairs. A small frown of worry appeared between Nia's brows as she thought about him.

'I shouldn't have let him go,' she fretted, catching her full underlip between her teeth.

Jake seemed to have no problem defining who she was talking about. 'My brother's only half an inch shorter than me. I doubt if you could have stopped him,' he responded drily. He wouldn't have been surprised if his own hands could span her very narrow waist. Suddenly he had the strongest impulse to prove his theory...

'The all-important half an inch,' she mused, kicking off her tight shoes for the second time.

'Meaning...?'

She shrugged. 'I suppose it gives you that slight edge—like being born five minutes earlier. It makes you top dog—dominant twin.' He was successful enough to give any sibling an inferiority complex.

'I'm rendered speechless with admiration by this startling display of perception. Hate to ruin your psychological profile, but Josh was the firstborn, and don't let the dinky cottage throw you off track. He lives here by choice, not necessity—

they were big into the whole self-sufficiency thing. If you collected modern art…'

'It was the art collection or the private jet—something had to go.' She gave a soulful sigh. 'Decisions, decisions…'

'You'd know,' he continued, ignoring her sarcastic interjection. 'My brother is one of the most bankable artists in the country—Europe, probably,' he elaborated. 'Even the critics love him. Just for the record, he wouldn't be starving in any rat-invested garret even if he never sold a painting.

'He starting playing the stock exchange when we were eighteen. You could say he has a certain talent for it. What am I saying…? You probably already know this. After all, you must have seen him for at least—what?—thirty seconds on the stairs—long enough to give you a deep insight into his mental state.' Jake's distinctive winged eyebrows shot sarcastically upwards as he stretched his long legs in front of him. 'I'm impressed,' he drawled, sounding anything but.

'Don't get nasty with me just because you feel guilty.'

Nia saw the shock chase across his disgustingly perfect features. She remained unrepentant; if he'd wanted to keep their secretary/boss relationship intact he should have kept her in the office. The problem was, she didn't *feel* like a secretary here, she'd left her tact and discretion along with her sensible walking shoes—back in the office. She could do with those shoes now, her feet were killing her.

'Why the hell should I feel guilty?' he barked.

'Well, when was the last time you saw him?'

Jake Prentice looked to her like one of those dark, brooding types who held a grudge. Even if he had been of the turn-the-cheek school, when your brother pinched the woman you wanted to marry, just how long did it take for you to forgive him?

'I've been carrying the can for my brother running away from responsibility all his life,' he grated. 'But I'm damned

if I'm going to do so this time!' Jake instantly regretted the
reply she'd goaded from him.

Face dark with anger, he sprang to his feet and began to
pace the room, pausing only to kick a dirty dinner plate out
of his path.

Guilt. She had it right there! Guilt was like a lead weight
around his neck. Did she think he needed telling his twin was
more volatile, deeper, too sensitive for his own good.

She was right, he should have seen this coming. Perhaps
he'd even precipitated it when he discouraged Josh from
handing over the baby to his in-laws. It had seemed to make
sense at the time, a baby—*their* baby—would give Josh the
incentive to carry on. That had been the theory, anyway.
What do I know? He was appalled at his own arrogance. I
haven't lost a wife!

He automatically glanced to the place on the mantel shelf
where the smiling picture of Bridie sat—it was turned face
down. He could imagine Josh sitting here in the cottage he
and Bridie had loved, unable to stand the emptiness and re-
minders of what he'd lost—God, Josh, *where are you?*

Five days ago, when he'd been here, Josh had seemed to
be coping. God knows what had happened to the nanny. And
this place hadn't seen the tender care of the part-time house-
keeper he had arranged—for days, by the look of it.

With the advent of Bridie, Josh had become really focused.
She'd been his redemption, a fact Josh had drunkenly confessed that night Bridie had put them both in a room and told
them they weren't coming out until they sorted out their dif-
ferences—she'd actually locked the door!

Jake could still see the determined expression on her face
with complete clarity. His pain-filled eyes went to the sleeping child and the hard lines of his face deepened.

'Don't go all moody on me.' That stopped him in his tracks
quite literally. 'This isn't about you,' she reminded him as-
tringently before scooping up an armful of dirty crockery and

walking past him into the kitchen before he had a chance to respond.

'What's that supposed to mean?' His voice followed her out into the small passageway. 'Are you trying to imply I'm some self-centred...' She pushed the door closed with her foot so she was spared the rest of his indignant tirade. Her reprieve didn't last long.

'What do you think you're doing?'

Nia knew before he spoke that he'd followed her into the room. His physical presence was making the hairs on the nape of her neck stand on end and her sensitive nostrils had immediately detected the elusive fragrance of the masculine cologne he used.

She took a small steadying breath before she turned and tried to meet his accusing glare calmly. It wasn't easy—he looked mad as hell. In the narrow room he seemed very close, the cold edge of the Belfast sink was chilly through her blouse as she pressed backwards in a futile attempt to increase the distance between them.

'I just tell it the way I see it. Sorry, did I speak before I was spoken to?' Just what was he mad at, anyhow?

'Are you trying to provoke me?' he ground out.

'I do that without opening my mouth,' she responded without thinking.

Jake's eyes widened fractionally and the dark band of colour that stained the sharp curve of his high cheekbones made it pretty obvious she'd made a direct hit. It was hardly news! She knew he didn't like her; despite the lack of a shock factor, she had to swallow several times to clear the constriction in her throat.

'I had no idea you were so moody.'

'I have a very even, easygoing temperament.' This statement was ground out from between clenched teeth; she doubted he'd appreciate the irony even if she had pointed it out.

'And I'm a blonde,' she muttered. 'It's very difficult to act like a disinterested observer when you've been hauled into the middle of a family crisis.'

His gaze collided with hers and abruptly the hostility seemed to drain out of him. One corner of his sensual mouth quirked, and he lifted his shoulders in a gesture that conceded her statement had validity. The response surprised Nia and the half smile frankly bewitched her.

'I wasn't really thinking when I dragged you into this, was I?' Rueful regret and apology? Nia hadn't been prepared for either.

'Well, there wasn't anyone else to drag, was there?' Be still my silly heart, she silently berated—it's not even a proper smile—basically he's not frowning, or looking as if he's just caught me slurping my coffee.

'I doubt if anyone but you would have come.'

Nia gave a dry chuckle. 'I doubt that! Everyone I've spoken to whispers your name in slavish adoration.' In fact, the wholesale admiration had surprised her.

'He can be brusque' was the closest she'd ever heard to a complaint. When she'd tentatively mentioned how cold and distant he was, they'd acted as though she was talking about someone they didn't know.

Not a muscle in his enigmatic lean face had moved, but somehow Nia felt something indefinable but very important had changed. Perhaps it was his very stillness that alerted her to the subtle difference in the atmosphere.

'And how do *you* whisper my name…?' His deep voice had a texture, an abrasive texture that feathered along her nerve endings.

'I don't.' In pure panic she turned her back on him.

'What are you doing now?' He sounded disgruntled and resentful; an elbow propped with unstudied elegance against the Welsh dresser top, he watched her burst of frenetic activity.

'Washing up,' she said, rolling up her sleeves to illustrate the point. From now on she was going to concentrate exclusively on such mundane practical tasks. Leave the pleasingly sensual outline of his lips to the Selinas and Jasmines of this world.

'That should keep me amused for the foreseeable future, don't you think?' she predicted drily. 'Is there any hot water?' She pulled her finger from under the stream of steaming water. 'Yes, there is,' she confirmed, sticking her stinging fingertip in her mouth.

'Very scientific.' His voice was harsh.

Her lips were pink and lushly full; it wasn't the first time he'd noticed. Noticing always made his body act independently of his will, now was no exception. Lush could have been equally accurately applied to other aspects of her person from that glorious mass of hair to the hourglass curves of her figure.

'You don't have to do that.'

When he'd heard a junior member of his team refer to the lovely Miss Jones as 'Sex on a Stick,' he'd had a few choice words to say that had left that particular young man in no doubt as to his opinion of the fine line between office romance and sexual harassment. He had personal reasons to frown on the former and he had no tolerance for the latter.

'I know, but in times of stress I need tea and I seriously doubt there's a cup in the place that isn't a breeding ground for something fatal. What are you going to do?' she added, her brow puckering in a frown as she dipped her hands in a bowl of steaming suds.

'I think the next move is Josh's,' he admitted reluctantly.

'Do you think he'll come back here?'

She felt a deep empathic wave of sympathy. At this moment Jake looked almost as strung out as his brother had. His short cut hair was spiky on top where he'd rubbed his fingers through it, that muscle in his taut cheek was silently ticking away.

Dreamily her eyes strayed to his neck. A good strong neck and what lovely olive skin he had—given a bit of sun he'd probably turn deep brown... What would it be like to touch...?

'I think he'll find me.'

The sound of his voice fractured her hot little daydream. Dear God, girl, you're *drooling?* Dismay and embarrassment sizzled through her body.

Jake didn't bother explaining that a lifetime's experience made him confident that Josh would find him. Josh always found him when there was nowhere else left to go.

'But then, he thought he had found me, didn't he?' He gave a harsh laugh. What's happened to my life when my own brother has to make an appointment?

Looking at his arrestingly attractive profile, it was obvious to Nia that he was tormenting himself with dark thoughts.

'Don't blame yourself.' Her voice was gruff, but her emerald eyes were luminous with soft sympathy.

'You've changed your tune. I thought that's what I was meant to do. I thought my callous attitude had driven my brother away...?'

'Guilt isn't very constructive, some people might say it smacks of self-indulgence.'

Jake took a steadying gulp of country air—he still wanted to strangle her—or kiss her...? Where the hell had *that* thought come from? He felt his body stir hungrily as he watched her vividly expressive face. Abruptly, her eyes widened in alarm.

'He wouldn't do anything...*anything* foolish? *Would* he?'

When Jake froze and went remarkably pale, she wished she'd kept her concerns to herself—or at least phrased them more tactfully. There was a long nerve-stretching pause dur-

ing which the suds from her fingers dripped down her skirt
and his skin lost that terrible grey tinge.

'I think he just needs time—time to himself.' He ran a
tongue over his dry lips and focused once more on her face.
'Josh is a lot stronger than people give him credit for,' he
said firmly. 'You ever seen those old movies where they do
a ''bad cop, good cop'' routine?' His smile was mirthless.
'We've been playing reliable, sensible twin and volatile, erratic twin since the day someone first attached the labels—
in our cradles, most likely. Nothing in life is that black and
white, including our respective strengths and weaknesses.'

Nia had curved her hands around his forearms; it was only
the direction of his gaze that made her aware of her foolishly
spontaneous action. Even as she let go she registered, at some
level, the sinewed strength under her fingers. The warm flut-
tery movement deep in her belly became impossible to ignore.

'Sorry,' she mumbled, making a clumsy dabbing attempt
to remove the damp fingermarks that were dark smudges on
the expensive shirtsleeve.

'Did you resent it?' she couldn't resist adding. The scent
of his body had lodged firmly in her nostrils and she couldn't
shake it. Neither could she prevent her body pulsing with a
bone-deep dangerous awareness.

'What?'

'Forget it, it's none of my business,' she responded with
a lofty sniff.

He laughed and she watched the crinkly lines that fanned
out from the corners of his lustrously lashed eyes.

'We both know that insignificant fact has never stopped
you poking your nose in where it's not wanted, so spit it
out.'

Her expression grew indignant at this unjust criticism. She
had no desire to be as cynically clinical as he was. What was
so wrong with wanting to help? *As if she didn't know…!* It

wasn't so much the desire to help, but the person who needed the help that was the problem. Getting to know the man outside the office, discovering he was human—granted, an awkward human—was an emotional minefield!

'I wondered if you ever get tired of playing the good twin,' she confessed defiantly.

'I stopped *playing,* Miss Jones, a long time ago.'

'How boring.' Nia didn't like being patronised by anyone, but he'd developed the activity into an art form! The *Miss Jones* was a pretty pointed reminder she was only the secretary. 'I hope I'll never forget how to play.'

She continued to glare at him, blissfully ignorant of the chain of thoughts her innocent mark had set in motion in his less than innocent mind.

Jake didn't think she had *those* sorts of games in mind. If she had…? Some very interesting pictures flickered through his head. With a sharp inhalation, he brought this line of sensual speculation to an abrupt close. Hell-fire! Are you here to indulge in debauched fantasy or to find your brother? He was disgusted at how easily he was being distracted—not to mention how much he was enjoying being distracted!

'And I've seen how worried you are about your brother, so you don't have to keep up the emotionless man-of-steel pose.'

'The concerned brother pose might be more accurate.'

Head on one side, she regarded him thoughtfully for a moment. 'No,' she said, shaking her head slowly. 'I don't think so.'

'Do you always think the best of people?'

'Don't you?'

He gave an exasperated sigh. 'You'll like Josh.'

'I will?' she echoed suspiciously.

'You're alike in some ways, non-conformists. Josh has that dangerous quality of a man who's well aquainted with the wild side.' Nia had dangerous qualities of her own. He wondered whether she had a wild side, too. 'Irresistible to the sort of woman who believes all a man needs is the love of a good woman.'

Nia refused to rise despite the provocation and just inclined her head in an attitude of silent understanding, which she knew would annoy him. Jake wasn't into understanding, sympathy or sharing—not with secretaries, anyhow.

'Actually I was only offering sympathy, not my body,' she told him gently. 'I expect it often seemed like it would be more fun being the bad boy,' she surmised with genuine sympathy.

Privately she was amused to discover how amazingly in-accurate his idea of the image he presented to the world was. She'd seen both brothers, one admittedly briefly, but if you were talking dangerous auras she knew which one had her vote!

When he frowned, as he was doing now, the sharp angles of Jake's face became even more pronounced—bones to die for, she thought with a silent wistful sigh. Jake Prentice was your original Iceberg Man—you always had the impression nine-tenths of his passions were intriguingly just below the surface.

She only let her mind dwell for one breathless heartbeat on what it would be like to explore those hidden depths. The carnal slant of her reflections sent a slow shiver up her spine and she was painfully conscious of the wave of heat that abruptly engulfed her from head to toe.

'I didn't employ you as an agony aunt, Miss Jones,' he grated harshly. He didn't encourage his staff to stroll casually around his subconscious—especially when they unearthed a petty jealousy he wasn't proud of!

He regarded her upturned face with smouldering resent-ment.

'True.' Her soft, lilting voice had an attractive husky qual-ity. 'But I don't recall nanny being in the job description, either,' she reminded him in a firmer tone. 'Speaking of which, Liam will be awake soon and he'll want feeding. I only saw one bottle in the bag…' She paused and he didn't contradict her. 'I suggest you look around for some formula and sterilizing equipment.'

'When it's anything to do with babies, why do all women feel obliged to talk to men as though they're intellectually challenged?' Despite his complaint he did begin to systematically ransack the kitchen cupboards above his head. He gave a grunt of triumph as he extracted a tin of formula milk.

'I can't speak for all women, but personally the opportunity to treat *you* like an idiot for a change just appealed irresistibly to my baser instincts.'

'Are you saying I'm an unfair boss?' he demanded stiffly.

'Not unfair…' she assured him sweetly. 'Just inhumanly demanding and overbearing.'

'Whilst you're the perfect secretary?'

'God!' she exclaimed, her expression comically horrified at the thought of what Jake's perfect secretary would be like. *'I hope not.'*

'You can rest easy,' he assured her drily.

'Perfection is so boring.'

'You're not that,' he conceded grudgingly.

Nia was encouraged by the flicker of amusement in his lean face.

'I think that's probably the nicest thing you've ever said to me,' she told him as a warm infectious grin spread over her face. 'The *only* nice thing probably.'

'I'm surprised you stayed.' He observed the dimple with studied disinterest.

'Put it down to natural-born cussedness.' She gave a sigh and her slender shoulders lifted. 'I hate to admit defeat.'

The least said or even thought about how much an unhealthy fascination with the man who was her reluctant boss might have contributed to her decision to tough it out, the better.

'Besides, I'm not sure how well your *perfect* secretary would cope with all this.' Her sweeping gesture encompassed the devastated kitchen and sent a stream of soapy water across his face. 'Oops, sorry.'

She grabbed the clean tea towel she'd tucked into the waistband of her skirt and reached up to mop his face.

'At least I'm adaptable…'

'Leave it alone.' He caught her wrist and pulled her hand away, his voice was unexpectedly harsh.

'Don't worry,' she responded, unable to keep the hurt confusion from pooling in her eyes. 'I'm not contagious.'

'From where I'm standing you're…' he began in a hard angry voice she didn't understand—not unless…? She instantly rejected the idea that the distracting lustful thoughts weren't entirely one-sided. *Get real, girl,* she silently jeered.

His fingers were still curled manacle-like around her wrist. Nia raised her eyes warily to his level and saw he had closed his eyes, his lips were moving, silently forming a string of harsh expletives.

'I can't help it if I'm a tactile sort of person.' She moved her wrist gently just to remind him he was still constraining her in a viselike grip.

His eyes snapped open. *'I can imagine.'*

He inhaled deeply and his nostrils flared as his eyes swept over her face. No prizes for guessing what he was imagining. This time there was no question of the sensual appreciation being a product of wish fulfillment. The scorching heat in his appraisal was explicit.

Nia heard the whimper but knew it hadn't emerged from her throat—she wasn't a whimpering sort of girl. She tried to focus on his dark face but the unnatural heaviness that had invaded her limbs seemed to extend as far as her heavy eyelids, which drooped over her eyes.

Her stunned brain supplied the pictures that went with Jake…imagining her touching him…

The sensory overload left her in a stupidly catatonic state. What, she wondered, would she do if he actually did more than grab her by the wrist? Was he going to…? Of course he wasn't, you idiot—barring bizarre blips, he didn't even like redheads.

He was rubbing his hand, the one which had been in contact with her skin against his thigh, as if it was contaminated. She could still feel the imprint of his fingers circling her wrist, a perceptible tingling was all that remained of the pulsing electrical sensation. Soon that, along with her lustful fantasies, would fade, also.

'Perhaps we should get busy before he wakes.'

His voice didn't suggest anything deep and meaningful had just occurred. It suggested mild exasperation, which was something she seemed to inspire in him frequently. It would account for the increased tempo of that muscle twitching in his lean cheek.

He always used that impersonal tone with her, why should she resent it so much now? It was depressing in the extreme to acknowledge that whatever he had felt—if anything—he had been able to switch it off like a tap. Whereas she…

'If it makes you happier to think it was your idea—fine!'

He didn't respond, which was just as well. She felt a lot crankier than her sharp tone implied. She felt the sort of seething frustration that she'd always thought was something reserved for less emotionally robust individuals than herself.

By the time Liam did wake, a frenetically energetic Nia had cleared the fridge of many suspect items long past their sell-by date. Several prepared bottles of formula were neatly lined up on the freshly disinfected shelves and the clean dishes were neatly stacked on the work counter.

Jake had stiffened when she'd placed the warm, squirming and very hungry baby on his lap, but he hadn't protested. A nasty part of her had wanted to see him disintegrate, but another part had got all warm and mushy seeing him feeding the hungry baby—at first tentatively, and then with a growing confidence. They presented a deeply poignant picture. Shaken deeply, she had watched greedily the growing fascination visible in Jake's eyes.

It was on the tip of her tongue to ask him did he want children when she realised that might reveal her unhealthy interest in the subject. Besides, she didn't want to remind him of the last time she'd brought up the subject of his fertility.

Her feelings had been strong and disturbing enough to send her outside—a few lungfuls of fresh air might help her regain some semblance of sanity. When she eventually returned, her pockets and hands were full of eggs courtesy of the hens that ran free in the adjoining meadow.

'Omelette?' she suggested, holding up a glossy brown egg. There were some promising-looking herbs in pots on the sunny patio. 'Even if you're not hungry, I am,' she added prosaically, blowing a piece of straw off the egg she was proudly displaying. 'And the cupboard is quite literally bare. What's wrong with you?' she added as Jake continued to look at her with a peculiar expression.

She knew she sounded grumpy but the unexpected sight of her usually immaculately clad, sophisticated boss gently patting a baby which was draped over his shoulder was doing some very worrying things to her heart.

She tried conveniently to file her gut reaction away— hunky big man, small baby—every publicist's dream, enough to get anyone's heartstrings working overtime. Despite her best efforts her cynicism remained very lacklustre. *Maybe* her heartstrings were just a bit too susceptible where this particular hunky man was concerned!

'I thought you were sulking.'

'Men sulk, women keep the wheels turning.' Her cheeky

grin peeped out spontaneously for a moment. 'About that tea…' Nobody would have guessed from her brisk tone that she'd finally admitted she'd fallen for the wretched unattainable man!

CHAPTER FOUR

MALT whisky might have been better, but the collection of empty bottles he'd found in every room had revealed all too clearly to Jake that his brother had emptied all available alcoholic stimulants from the premises.

'A good idea.' The soft burp and warm trickle down his shoulder made Jake hope his brother had at least one clean shirt in the place—he wasn't hopeful!

'There's no milk,' she told him solemnly, 'but there is a goat tethered in the garden who badly needs milking.' Her expression carried the condemnation of anyone who would neglect an animal whatever the circumstances.

'And you're a farmer's daughter—perfect. I knew I fetched you for some reason.'

Not for the pleasure of my company, she thought gloomily. 'Don't get excited,' she advised drily. 'My father's one of the old school who classes goats right up there with ramblers who leave gates open. He considers them evil, smelly creatures kept by hippies.'

'The tolerant open-minded type.'

'I knew you reminded me of someone,' she shot back with defensive acid. 'I'm just warning you not to expect too much. I'll do my best.'

'I feel sure you will.'

It amused him to imagine how several people in the air-conditioned building he sometimes thought he might as well call home would stare if they saw 'Sex on a Stick' rolling up her sleeves to milk a goat! He found himself smiling as she swept purposefully from the room—he hadn't thought this day would elicit any smiles.

41

The tea tasted strange but drinkable, the omelette was fluffily delicious. They ate in silence, if you discounted the steady ticking of the grandfather clock and the contented snuffly snores of the baby.

'What time's your train?'

'It doesn't matter. I'll never get back in time.' She buried her nose in the teacup and regarded him warily over the rim.

Monday it would be business as usual in the office, she thought forlornly. Given the emotional turmoil raging in her breast, not to mention her head, she doubted she could cope with business as usual. Completely clean break. It was the best way to go—the *only* way to go, she decided with bracing practicality. The enthusiasm she managed to work up for this plan was tepid at the best.

'You will—*just*, if I ring straightaway for a taxi to take you to the local station.' He frowned as he deciphered a timetable placed conveniently by the phone.

'Why didn't I think of that?' she said hollowly. He enjoyed her company so much he was almost falling over himself in his haste to get rid of her.

'I'd take you myself but I'm loath to wake up Liam transferring him to the car seat.'

'Don't do that!' Nia responded immediately. It had taken a long, *long* time to get the fretful child to sleep. 'What about you?' she asked as he picked up the phone. 'What are you going to do now?'

'Josh is likely to head back here, so I'll be staying. Besides,' he said, glancing at his nephew asleep in the wicker crib, 'my place is even less equipped to cope with babies than I am.'

'Actually I think you've done really well,' she assured him warmly. Then, because she was aware her tone had been *too* warm, she opened her mouth to dilute the implied admiration. 'For a...'

'Inhumanly demanding male?'

'If the cap fits…'

'I don't know about the cap, but this shirt is feeling a bit damp not to mention ripe.' He inhaled suspiciously and grimaced as he touched the shoulder. 'The number's here,' he added, tapping the memo pad. 'I'll go and see if I can dig up something of Josh's.'

He'd only been gone for seconds before there was a knock on the front door. Nia put the receiver down, and one wary eye on the sleeping baby, leaped to hush the imperative rapping.

She struggled for several seconds with the unfamiliar locks before pulling open the door.

'You must be the nanny.'

Nia didn't have to deny or confirm this statement as the prosperous-looking couple pushed past her into the cottage.

'Where is my precious darling?' the smart silver-haired woman enquired in a voice that Nia feared would wake the precious darling for sure.

The loving grandparents, she realised in horror, recalling the alarming things Jake had told her about them. Perhaps Jake had been exaggerating; he was obviously very overprotective of his twin. They didn't look like people trying to deprive a father of his child. They just looked *nice*.

'We tried to ring, but you were engaged,' the man announced. 'We haven't met. I'm Donal Fitzgerald, you must be Natalie.'

'Nia,' she responded in a daze as her hand was enfolded in a firm clasp. If you discounted the dusty corners, the room was tidy enough after her whirlwind attack to now pass the couple's covert but distinctly critical scrutinisation.

'I was sure he said Natalie, didn't he, Maeve?' he appealed to his wife with a frown. 'You're younger than I thought,' he added, looking her up and down with a frown.

If Nia had been the nanny, his expression would have made her feel totally inadequate to the task, but as she wasn't, she just felt a twinge of irritation at being examined like a piece of livestock on the auction block.

'It wouldn't surprise me if Josh got it wrong, things being as they are,' his wife contributed helpfully in a warm confidential manner. 'You must have your hands full. I don't expect Joshua is much help,' she added sympathetically.

They were fishing, very discreetly, but their motivation was nonetheless obvious, they wanted her to dish the dirt on Josh. Her reply was all important. *Help!* She was slap-bang in the middle of a family war.

'I wouldn't say that,' she responded carefully. She wouldn't say *anything* if she had her choice. Where the hell was Jake when you needed him?

'Is he still drinking?'

'There's not a drop in the house,' she responded honestly. They hadn't asked about empties and she wasn't about to mention them.

It occurred to her that her actions had transformed her from an objective observer to a participant in this particular war. She hoped she wouldn't regret her action.

'Was that Jake's car outside? Is he here, too?'

'Yes…no!' They were staring at her with what her frantic mind interpreted as suspicion. 'He was here, but he's gone. His car broke down,' she improvised wildly as she silently apologised to the aforementioned piece of high-class engineering for this slur.

'Did I hear…?' Jake emerged from the direction of his brother's studio buttoning a clean but paint-splattered shirt. Several inches of muscularly defined washboard-flat belly were visible.

Her own undiscriminating belly chose this moment to dissolve into a molten pool of irrational craving. He always looked rampantly male enough to make every female in sniffing distance sigh appreciatively.

In his beautifully cut designer suits he had represented an

unattainable peak of male perfection, now with his hair ruffled and his shirt creased it seemed—very misleadingly, she knew—as if for once he walked in the same world as she did. She ripped her eyes away and took a deep, steadying breath. At least, that had been the idea; actually she still felt breathless and shaky. Pull yourself together before someone notices you're drooling, woman!

'Yes, *Josh,* it's Liam's grandparents.' To her ears she sounded maniacally bubbly but the Fitzgeralds didn't appear to notice anything amiss. Their attention was focused on the tall figure in the doorway—so was Nia's, she held her breath.

'So I see,' Jake responded without a flicker as he held her eyes.

She gave a tiny sigh of relief. 'I was just telling them *Jake's* car broke down. I hope he caught his train.' There wasn't much chance she would now.

'This is a surprise, Maeve, Donal.' He walked forward with his hand extended, after a startled pause the older man returned the gesture, but his wife pointedly withheld her hand. She regarded Jake with thinly veiled resentment.

'No, well, we were just passing.'

'And you thought you'd drop in. How nice.' Discovering there were no buttons on the cuffs of the cotton shirt Jake rolled up the sleeves before tucking the shirt hem into his trousers.

Nia found herself staring at the dark sprinkling of hair on his strong sinewed forearms. With a self-conscious flush she withdrew her gaze only to discover that Maeve Fitzgerald was watching her with a very unpleasant knowing expression.

'You're looking a lot better than when we saw you last, isn't he, Maeve?'

'It'll take more than a shave and a haircut to make him a fit father for my poor baby's child!' She picked up Liam who began to cry in sleepy protest. 'If she'd married Jake and not you, she'd be alive today! *He* wouldn't have got her pregnant. She was always too frail to have a baby!' She hugged Liam tighter and his cries grew more insistent.

'Now come along, Maeve, you promised,' pleaded her husband, looking distinctly uncomfortable.

'Bridie was a fit, happy young woman, Maeve, and you know it,' Jake said in a slow careful voice that didn't seek to justify or accuse. 'There was no way the doctors or anyone else could have predicted what happened,' he added sombrely. 'We should all be thinking about Liam now, not assigning blame.'

Jake's response startled the grandparents and Nia could imagine that his bereaved twin had responded quite differently previously when they had thrown similar accusations of blame at him.

Nia translated the slight inclination of Jake's head and gently took the baby from the weeping woman who after one angry glance into her sympathetic face relinquished her hold.

It was a warm unexpected moment of understanding when Jake's glance shifted from the baby and he smiled at her. Nia found her eyes inexplicably fused with his—she couldn't look away. A flood-tide of emotion engulfed her.

'It's easy to see why *he's* looking so well,' Maeve hissed viciously, shrugging away the comforting pressure of her husband's arm from her heaving shoulders. 'He's already got a replacement for our Bridie. *Sleep-in* nanny! How *convenient.* Have you seen the way she's been looking at him? Like a cat after a canary.'

Nia froze, her eyes still melded with Jake's. There was a disturbing gleam in those grey depths she didn't like the look of. Who are you kidding, girl? You like the look of everything about this man, she told herself, giving a delicate, self-derisive shudder and shutting her eyes tight.

Rocking slightly on the balls of her feet, she hugged Liam closer. The safety he afforded was illusory. With a few well-chosen words, his grandmother had blown her cover good and proper!

'Don't let Jake hear you say that, Maeve.'

This dry, almost-amused comment made Nia lift her head from the baby's downy head.

'You mean…?' Donal Fitzgerald was looking at her with renewed interest.

Jake nodded. 'They've been together for almost…six weeks, is it, Nia?'

'Seven,' she managed, throwing him a look which nobody could have interpreted as anything but loathing. Jake seemed unperturbed by her hostility.

'She's been counting the days. Isn't that sweet?'

He looked like he was actually enjoying himself, she decided, her bosom swelling with righteous indignation. She hadn't expected him to enter into the role with this much enthusiasm, or this much creativity.

'The ring?' Donal joked.

Nia's eyes rested warningly on Jake's face—he *wouldn't*. He did!

'No public announcement yet, while Mum's out of the country.'

'So Anna doesn't know yet.' The older man nodded understandingly and his wife looked stunned. 'We won't tell a soul. This,' he lifted his broad shoulders wearily, 'it was a mistake,' he confessed frankly.

Not the only one, Nia thought, wondering if anyone would notice if she, too, dissolved into hysterical tears.

The two men exchanged firm masculine handshakes. 'You're welcome to see Liam anytime, but it might be an idea to ring next time, Donal.'

CHAPTER FIVE

'DO YOU think they bugged the place?' Jake lifted up a vase and examined the underneath. 'Or did they make do with hidden cameras?'

He looked so damned pleased with himself, Nia could have strangled him! 'How *could* you?' she hissed. She pulled the cover over the baby she'd just managed to soothe back off to sleep. She, on the other hand, didn't feel soothed at all.

'I thought I rose to the occasion magnificently,' Jake observed in an unconvincing confused tone. 'Besides, you set the scene, I just improvised the role you gave me.'

'You know what I mean! Why did you let them think you and I...we...' His politely expectant expression and mocking grey stare reduced her to stuttering incoherence. Cheeks red-hot, she broke off.

'Hush!' he admonished, holding a finger to his lips. 'If you're going to screech,' he said, taking firm hold of her arm, 'let's get out of here.'

Quietly smouldering—the quiet part was in deference to the sleeping baby not his uncle—she resentfully allowed herself to be led into what looked like a studio. Shrouded paintings were stacked against the walls, but despite the layer of dust, unlike the rest of the cottage when they'd arrived, order reigned here.

'Josh's studio,' he said, pushing her into a low leather sofa set against one wall. He pulled off a cover and stepped back to admire the brilliantly vivid landscape beneath. 'God, but he's good!' he exclaimed with warm admiration.

Nia agreed, but wasn't to be distracted. 'Why did you make up that story?'

48

'Would it be better to let them think Josh is sleeping with the nanny?' Arms folded across his chest, one fist tapped rhythmically against the muscled biceps.

'Nobody's sleeping with the nanny—me, that is!' she responded crossly.

'Long-distance relationships are doomed to failure,' he agreed sympathetically.

She self-consciously covered her beringed finger with her opposite hand. 'Leave Huw out of this.'

The sardonically amused light was snuffed out of Jake's eyes. 'I wasn't thinking of inviting him,' he responded in a hard voice. 'What does the man expect, letting you work the other end of the country?' he snorted with scathing contempt.

Nia wasn't entirely sure who the contempt was aimed at, herself or the absent, much-maligned Huw. Either way, she couldn't let this brazenly sexist remark pass unchallenged.

'*Letting?* I didn't request permission.' A small worried frown disturbed the smoothness of her brow. 'I wouldn't worry, the sort of women you attract don't seem the type who are likely to develop any urgent need to acquire new skills that will take them outside yelling distance.' she gave a sudden worried frown. 'What is it exactly you're *not* inviting him to?'

His slow smile sent her pulse rate totally out of control.

'I hope you didn't take what Mrs. Fitzgerald said seriously…' She gave a particularly unconvincing laugh.

'What particular part did you have in mind?' His dark brows rose in the general direction of his hairline.

'I don't want to play games.'

'That's not what you said earlier,' he reminded her, pouncing on this display of inconsistency with obvious relish. 'I had to do something to distract them from your lustful gazes in my direction, you know. It worked, too,' he finished on a callous self-congratulatory note. 'I don't like to complain, but you weren't being much help.'

His words made Nia abandon all pretence of being in control of the situation. With a groan, she buried her face in her hands. To think she'd imagined she'd have the upper hand outside the office! She felt totally inadequate to cope with this off-duty Jake.

'*I wasn't!*' She lifted her head in protest and pushed her hair impatiently from her face.

'No, that's what I said,' he agreed.

'I mean, I wasn't looking…lustful.' She gave an inarticulate grunt of frustration as she met the confident gleam of his bold stare. 'The woman isn't rational, you know that.' She's not the only one!

'True, but she always did have a fine eye for detail. It was nice to have a second opinion.'

He *had* noticed! 'Are you accusing me of *ogling* you?' She was plumbing new depths of humiliation.

'Not accusing, just congratulating you on your natural good taste.'

'You got a buzz from the risk of being caught out!' Nia gasped, looking at him hard. She was astonished to interpret the light in his eyes as pure, reckless exhilaration.

His head inclined thoughtfully to the side as one dark, strongly delineated brow rose to a quizzical angle. 'I think you're right. Perhaps I donned more than my brother's clothes?' he suggested thoughtfully.

The casual flick of his long fingers against the orange fabric—the Jake she knew would *never* wear that particular shade—popped several of the buttons and she was treated to an excellent view of his lean, deeply muscled torso.

'But then, I often wonder just how much of our behaviour is just conditioning,' he brooded. 'I mean, Jake and I share an identical genetic blueprint, but he would never waste an opportunity like this.'

'Like what?' she asked hoarsely. In her head excitement and fear were fighting for supremacy in much the same manner as her lungs were fighting for air as Jake unexpectedly dropped down onto his knees beside the sofa—he was doing a lot of unexpected things!

She shrank back as he placed one arm on the back of the sofa behind her head. 'What do you think you're doing?' she croaked.

'Stroking your face. You have the most incredibly soft skin,' he reflected as the pad of his fingertip lightly grazed the curve of her jaw.

'I know that.' She desperately wanted to close her eyes and enjoy to the full all the delicious whispery sensations that were travelling down to her curling toes.

'I'm sure you do,' he reflected wryly.

'I didn't mean...' She immediately forgot what she did mean because, elbows bent, both his arms were placed beside her head now and his face was only inches away from her own. As her wide startled eyes met his, his thumbs pressed softly in the gentle hollow of each temple and his splayed fingers snaked deeply into the springy softness of her abundant hair. He made a greedy sound in his throat.

'You can't pull it off, it's not a wig!' Her hoarse tone didn't carry the flippant note she'd hoped would defuse this explosive situation.

'I don't want to remove it, just wrap myself in it.' A smokily thoughtful expression flickered into his eyes. 'Or better still, wrap both of us in it,' he said, smiling hawkishly at this improved version of his private fantasy.

Nia saw his chest lift in a deep soundless sigh. 'The contrast of your creamy skin against that hair...' His husky words dripped like warm chocolate.

'You've got a hair fetish,' she accused hoarsely, feeling the hot fingers crawl all over her skin as a picture of the decadent scene he'd just described floated into her feverish mind.

'Just a Miss Jones fetish,' he reassured her, smooth as silk.

'Since when?' she croaked.

'Since the first time I saw you smile. It wasn't at me.'

Nia's head spun, she hadn't been expecting a reply that specific. Even allowing for poetic licence, if he was actually telling the truth, that put a different complexion on a lot of things.

His body curved closer and she held out a hand to protect herself from the morally destructive influence of his closeness. The resistance her hand encountered was the bare flesh of his chest.

'No!' he commanded firmly, trapping her fingers in his. 'Keep it there. I like it.'

Nia saw his long fingers wrap themselves around her smaller digits. She saw him uncurl them and spread them very deliberately against the lightly tanned skin of his chest.

The image was mind-blowingly erotic. His skin had a satiny quality she hadn't expected, even the liberal sprinkling of dark hair was surprisingly soft. The tongues of flame low in her belly grew molten and delicious shivers chased each other down her spine until she was one continual tremor.

'I can feel your heart beat,' she whispered wonderingly as she raised her eyes to his.

'I want to share more than that with you. You've been driving me insane from the first time I set eyes on you,' he growled, taking her delicate jaw between his fingers.

'You didn't like me.' She was mesmerised by this frank admission, but uneasy and not quite willing to believe this was anything but a waking dream. Was he just taking roleplaying to its ultimate conclusion? If she was going to be seduced by a Prentice, she wanted to know for sure which one it was!

'You distracted me, I couldn't concentrate. I've already done the office romance thing with Bridie—been there, done that and got the T-shirt.'

'I didn't know that.' She felt suddenly uneasy. Had Bridie been his secretary, too?

'You don't know everything about me, Miss Jones. Beautiful, sexy, heavenly Miss Jones.' It took a long time for him to complete this homage because he punctuated each word with a kiss.

Nia had never suspected kisses had such infinite variety; each one was perfect, each one devastating. Gasping she let her head fall forward onto his conveniently placed shoulder.

'You taste marvellous,' she gasped with rapturous approval.

'My thought exactly.' He laughed, hooking a finger under her chin and forcing her chin upwards. 'God, what a fool I've been. I was determined to prove it would take more than a soft laughing voice, a heavenly body and the most kissable lips in the universe to get between me and work. I'd vowed to never mix business and pleasure again. God, but this is pleasure,' he groaned as his teeth closed over the soft flesh of her earlobe.

'It is!' she agreed with shaky fervour. His breath was warm against her neck. She was overpoweringly conscious of the heat from his body, the sharp, spicy male odour that was his—and she loved it—just as she loved him.

'I don't agree with office romances, either,' she assured him.

'But this is an exceptional case.'

'Compartmentalise…' she murmured vaguely.

'My thought exactly.'

For once they seemed to be in complete harmony. His nose nudged the side of hers and his mouth was tormentingly close. All she had to do was open her mouth and… 'Did Bridie work for you?' That wasn't what she'd intended to do with her tongue at all. Why had she asked that?

'Not me. Alan,' he said thickly, identifying the senior partner. 'Are you going to stop talking and let me kiss you?'

'Do I remind you of Bridie?'

He placed a firm hand against her spine and applied enough pressure to bring the peaks of her aching breasts in contact with his bare chest. His expression was thoughtful.

'I've never met *anyone* like you, Nia.'

She had to be satisfied with his reply.

He looked at the quivering line of her slightly parted lips and he clamped his lips together to suppress the sharp pained gasp that emerged from his dry throat.

The slow predatory grin that curved his beautifully sensual mouth ought to have made alarm bells ring in her head, but it didn't.

'To hell with self-control!'

Nia discovered that when Jake abandoned something he did the thing wholeheartedly! The first tentative movement of his mouth against her own lulled her into a false sense of security. One second, it was slow, languid, an almost-reverent exploration. The next, it had been transformed into raw rampant hunger! She'd never experienced the pure sensual thrill of such unadorned raw desire before. She wasn't a victim of the erotic storm, she was part of it—the centre of it.

She let out a low moan as his tongue thrust repeatedly into the warm sweet interior of her mouth. Her arms slid up and over the warm skin of his back. Jake shifted his weight and she was dragged inexorably off the sofa until she lay on top of him on the floor.

'I'll squash you.'

'Yes, please.'

He raised his knees and planted his feet flat on the floor. She slid into the hollow between his legs and felt the full force—well as much as the irritating layers of clothes would permit—of his brazen arousal.

Nia decided it was time to do something about the clothes

situation. She sat up suddenly, a circumstance which made
him give a low groan. Nia was immediately contrite.

'Did I hurt you?' she asked, unbuttoning her blouse to
reveal the frothy confection of lace and satin beneath. She
felt the heat of his scalding gaze and enjoyed it. She felt
intoxicated by a wild elemental surge of feminine power. He
wanted her, she was making this blissfully beautiful man
ache.

'Huh?' This wasn't Jake at his articulate best, but Nia
didn't mind. The glittering light in his half-closed eyes, however, was *extremely* expressive as he watched her slow deliberate movements. His powerful chest rose silently in sync
with his deep, rapid inhalations.

Her emcrald eyes burned with sultry invitation. Her body
swayed slightly as she continued to slowly slide the blouse
off her shoulders. Her movements had an almost feline grace.
Nia's eyes didn't leave his for an instant, not until the last
second.

'My God!' he breathed almost reverently as she unhooked
her bra and flung it to one side. Her full rounded breasts
peaked by rosily engorged nipples swayed gently. 'You are
just—'

The unmistakable sound of a baby's cry drowned out his
next words completely. They both froze and waited for a
hopeful split second, but then the angry noise erupted once
more and put paid to optimism.

Nia felt one deep powerful shudder move through his body
before Jake raised a clenched fist to the bridge of his nose
and closed his eyes. There was a light covering of sweat over
his face that extended over his bronzed beautiful torso.

'I'll go.' His voice sounded tense as he rolled to one side.
'My God,' he reflected grimly, getting to his feet in one
graceful movement, 'babies must be one of the world's
greatest forms of contraception. Speaking of which, have
you…?'

Nia didn't feel capable of anything graceful, she felt clumsy, awkward, and intensely conscious of her dishevelled half-naked state. She ached. *God, but she ached.* The sense of deprivation went bone-deep.

Still breathing as though she'd just completed a marathon, she retrieved her blouse and held it in front of her, feeling nothing like the wild, wanton creature of seconds before and very much like the embarrassed virgin she was. What was I doing?

'Have I what?' she asked in a vague distracted voice. Belatedly she caught the drift of his words and she blushed deeply. 'No,' she choked.

'Me, neither.' He gave a wry twisted smile and dragged a hand through his hair before tucking his shirt back into his waistband. 'Under the circumstances, Liam might just have done us a favour.'

His dry parting shot finally brought home to her the enormity of what she had just done—*almost* done. There were consequences to what they had been about to do—and she hadn't even given them a thought. She'd wanted to be possessed—totally possessed—nothing else had mattered.

Her thoughts didn't recoil from all that would mean. She'd always imagined she might be a little sexually inhibited so the hot ache between her thighs as she thought of Jake being inside her was all the more shocking—and exciting.

She could hear Jake through the open door talking to the baby whose cries began to diminish. Her body was afflicted still by cramps and tremors that were quite alien to her. She wanted quite badly to weep—she hardly ever did that—tearing her hair out wasn't entirely out of the question, either.

She'd have to explain about Huw, of course. It worried her that Jake thought she was the sort of woman who would sleep with him whilst she was engaged to someone else. She was assuming a lot. What if he didn't care about Huw? For him this was sex without involvement. Taking her seemed to be almost an act of rebellion—perhaps her unsuitability was part of the attraction. She dwelt miserably on the disturbing thought.

It was even possible that the fact she was engaged—at least as far as he knew—was an added frisson. She certainly couldn't make any demands on him if she already had a man, and from what she'd seen of Jake and the women who decoratively hovered on the perimeter of his life, he was good at avoiding demands! She couldn't be one of those women— she wasn't nearly decorative or docile enough, for starters.

Did she really want to get any more deeply involved with a man who was still such a dangerous enigma? The answer was blindingly clear—the only definite unassailable fact in a sea of uncertainty and doubts. Yes, she did!

She wished Liam hadn't woken; she wished Jake was making love to her now. Jake seemed to be able to read her thoughts with uncanny precision because when he strolled back into the room he stood quietly beside her and took her face between his hands.

'I feel cheated, too. I'm afraid...' he added heavily.

'That you have to meet Mr. Bergen at the airport. He arrives from Stockholm later this evening. I would have told you.' *Eventually.* At least, she hoped she would have.

'What a marvellous secretary you are.'

She gave a sniff and a watery grin. 'It took you long enough to discover that.'

'I haven't been concentrating on your secretarial skills.' The stark message in his taut face was some compensation for the fact that he was leaving. Nia felt the sudden sting of emotional tears prickle her eyelids and she turned abruptly from him.

'If I had a choice, I wouldn't go, you know that.' His voice was warm and soothing as he came up behind her. His arms weren't so gentle when they closed possessively around her, across her ribcage just under the swell of her breasts. Nia was drawn back against his hard solid length of muscle and bone.

'But you know Mats Bergen has to fly out to Vancouver first thing in the morning.' He pushed aside her hair and kissed the side of her neck, sending sharp arrows of pleasure shooting through her tense body. 'Considering he's making the stopover at my request, I can't not appear,' he told her huskily.

'I know that.' She didn't have to like it, though.

'I'll contact the nanny agency and see what they can do for me, but if they can't come up with the goods by tonight, I'll just have to take Liam with me. God knows what Mats'll make of that.'

She'd assumed he would ask her to help. Isn't that what friends did? Only they weren't friends, they weren't even lovers!

'I don't think Mr. Bergen will mind,' she suggested, swallowing the lump in her throat. She walked out of his arms and with a puzzled frown, Jake's arms fell to his sides. 'After all he's got four children himself, and the little one, Eric,' she recalled the name with a frown, 'he's only eighteen months.'

'And how the hell do you know that?'

He'd been working on a joint project with the man for the past three months. Their e-mail correspondence had been bulky, but he didn't even know if Mats Bergen was married let alone the number, age and sex of his family.

'Well, he's rung you several times, and we got talking. He's a lovely man,' Nia added with a touch of defiance.

'My God, your Christmas card list must stretch from here to Cardiff!'

His sneering sarcasm brought an angry sparkle to her eyes. 'At least I write mine personally. When was the last time you did that?'

'My friends know I don't send Christmas cards or buy into

that whole over-commercialised thing.' Something about her reproachful wide-eyed innocence made him overplay the jaundiced cynic role.

'Scrooge is alive and well!' she breathed, appalled by his cynical outlook. 'I hope for this little one's sake your brother isn't as joyless as you!'

'I hope for this little one's sake my brother is here by Christmas,' he grated harshly.

Nia's antagonism melted away. 'Try not to worry, and remember that you can't be too hasty when it comes to choosing a nanny,' she added with a worried frown. 'You need someone who's compatible.'

'I'm not choosing a mate.'

That hurt. Did he think she needed any heavy-handed warnings not to mistake his physical fascination for her with anything more serious?

'The way I hear it, that's a lot easier.' Not if her personal experience was anything to go by, though.

'It'll be up to Josh to make any permanent arrangements.' Considering how well his last piece of interfering had turned out, Jake was going to be very cautious about the type of advice he gave in future!

'Why don't I stay here and look after Liam tonight? You could go off and meet Mats Bergen then, without dragging him along. If your brother turns up, I'll ring you. It's the ideal solution and you know it.' She could tell from his expression he was tempted. 'I'd have offered even if you hadn't seduced me.'

'If I'd actually got to do any real seducing I wouldn't be feeling the way I do now,' he reflected with feeling.

'You must have known I wouldn't mind.'

'You have pointed out earlier that your job description didn't include baby-sitting duties.'

'It didn't include sleeping with the boss, either, but I'm…'

'Going to,' he concluded with steely certainty. '*Going to,*

Nia,' he added in an even harder voice as her eyes dropped from his. 'You want me?'

'Yes,' she confessed rawly.

Satisfaction flared in his eyes. 'And I'll be back in the morning,' he said, taking her by the shoulders. 'Will you be all right here alone?'

'I won't be alone,' she reminded him. 'And if you were the sort of boss who required initiative in a secretary you'd already know I'm a great problem-solver.'

'I'm not as blind as you think, Nia…'

Oh, God, he knew she loved him!

'I know you engineered the wedding everyone in the building is talking about.'

'Oh, that.' She gave a small self-conscious flush and felt almost disappointed the truth wasn't out. 'I didn't engineer it—everyone knew they were crazy about each other. They just needed a little push.'

'Which you supplied.'

'I just listened.'

CHAPTER SIX

NIA was forced to reassess her boastful claim of being experienced with babies. Experience of baby-sitting neighbours' children back home had not prepared her for the full horrors of a small child that wouldn't sleep, and a body and brain that craved sleep. She didn't know which of them was more exhausted by the time Liam eventually settled. The last time she'd glanced at her watch it had been 3:00 a.m. When silence finally reigned she'd been too weary to update this depressing time check.

Emerging from a deep sleep, she experienced a few panic-stricken seconds' total disorientation as she blinked hazily at the wall of the unfamiliar room. Then it all came flooding back to her.

Liam was awake, too. His chubby legs were kicking and when his big eyes came to rest on her, she smiled automatically.

'Hello, beautiful,' she crooned.

'Whad ya say?'

Nia froze, the reply had come from the same region as the squeaking bed springs. Jake was back! And he was in bed with her? Had she *really* decided at some point last night she was going to tell him the whole thing had been a bad idea? Sleep deprivation made you think crazy things.

The welcoming smile faded on her parted eager lips.

Just for a split second, Josh thought... The anticlimax he always felt when he saw someone in a crowd who reminded him of Bridie was leavened by the first curiosity he'd felt for several months.

'Look who's been sleeping in my bed,' he said slowly, raising himself up on one elbow.

The sheets slithered down his body, giving the very definite suggestion that he was wearing nothing underneath. When...how...? What to do next? The questions were jostling for position in her confused brain.

'That's by the way of being a question—*who's* been sleeping in my bed?' The girl's knuckles had turned white against the sheet she still clutched.

'I'm Nia.'

Jake's twin seemed to be taking a strange woman's presence in his bed very casually. Had she led a sheltered life? Perhaps this sort of thing happened often?

'I'm Josh.'

'I know.'

'Should I know you?'

'Not really. I work for your brother.'

Her nose had emerged from under the covers and he could see it was a nice one.

'In the bedroom or boardroom?' Had Jake sent her to take his mind off his troubles? No, he couldn't bring himself to believe his twin could have dreamt up that one.

Nia flushed darkly. 'I'm his secretary, temporarily.'

Half the story, in light of that welcoming smile on her lips—the one that had faded ludicrously when she'd realised he wasn't Jake. But if she wanted to play it that way, fine.

His eyes travelled thoughtfully over her tumbled auburn curls.

'He always did have a thing about red hair—we both did.' There was nothing personal in his matter-of-fact observation. 'Borderline fetish,' he continued candidly, uncannily echoing her accusation of yesterday. 'Women are odd. My wife actually used to complain about being a carrot top.' His throat worked as he closed his eyes briefly.

Nia felt her jaw drop. Swallowing, she consciously closed her mouth. 'She was a redhead.'

The office romance with a redhead! History repeating itself. That explained Jake's over-the-top reaction when he'd first seen her. It could also explain a lot more if you had a nasty suspicious mind. The connections she'd have preferred not to make persisted on clicking into place in her head. What if he was just using her as substitute for Bridie—the love he'd lost? Nia went cold all over but she couldn't shake the nasty intrusive thought.

The palpable pain of the man beside her made her own dilemma seem petty. There was time later to brood over her feelings for Jake—and more importantly his feelings for her. The waves of distress emanating from Josh were almost tangible.

'You must think it's a bit strange finding me here in your home—in your bed,' she began tentatively.

'I don't, but I should, shouldn't I?' His smile was weary. He rubbed the stubbly dark growth on his jaw. 'Can you give me a sec before you begin the full explanation? I don't think my brain's in gear just yet.'

At that moment Liam let out a loud gurgle. She felt the man beside her freeze.

'*Liam?*' he asked in a choked voice.

There was a mingled longing and pain in his voice that made Nia's eyes mist.

'Yes.' She flipped back the sheets, scrambled hastily out of the bed to lift the baby from the cot. Kneeling on the bed, she held her full arms out to his father.

Almost greedily he reached out to accept the baby. 'He smells good, doesn't he?' he asked as he looked down into his son's solemn eyes. 'Do you forgive me, champ?' he asked huskily. The child looked trustingly back up at him.

Nia sniffed loudly and he glanced back towards her.

'You looked after him last night?'

She nodded her head.

'I hope he wasn't any trouble.'

'Not a scrap,' she lied enthusiastically.

'I never had any trouble running away before to avoid an awkward situation,' he remarked wonderingly to nobody in particular.

'You never had Liam before.' Maybe she was poking her nose in where it didn't belong but…

'I thought he deserved better.'

'He deserves a father.' And from what she could see he had one—a loving one, and in her book that was what mattered.

Josh didn't say anything but his eyes were filled with wry warmth. 'Where's Jake?' There was a detectable wariness in his suspiciously husky voice.

'He had to go up to London, that's why I offered to stay. He'll be back this morning.' What time was it, anyway? she wondered, trying to recall where she'd left her watch when she'd taken it off.

'Was he…?'

'Worried about you—yes.' He probably wasn't ready to hear about his in-laws' visit.

Josh slumped back against the pillows and lifted the baby up to eye level. 'I always dump on good old Jake, and he always rides to the rescue.'

'I expect you'd do the same for him.'

'I expect I would, only Jake doesn't need rescuing very often.'

Nia couldn't quite decide if it was resentment she could hear in his voice. The twins certainly had a complex relationship, falling in love with the same woman had obviously not simplified matters.

'Limped to the rescue on this occasion.'

Josh looked across at Nia's tone. She folded her legs underneath her and gave a small conspiratorial grin.

'Have you ever seen your brother change a baby's nappy?'

She was glad to see an answering sparkle of humour in Josh's eyes, which on closer inspection weren't identical to his brother's at all. She could see how some women would find the naughty-little-boy look in the man appealing—fortunately she wasn't one of them. It was bad enough she'd gone all mushy about one twin!

'A poor design concept,' she explained, shaking her head with mock solemnity.

'I can hear him. Poor, Jake!' To her delight, his twin began to laugh.

'You had to be there,' she agreed.

'Care to share the joke? Jake's voice was soft and expressionless. His relaxed posture as he leaned against the doorjamb was highly deceptive, his eyes were cold grey steel. 'Or is that me?'

The sight of his tall, fully clothed figure several feet away did what being within inches of his naked identical twin had not. Every muscle in her body tensed as a hot shocking ball of sexual craving unfurled itself deep in her belly. Her nerve endings all started screaming in agonised unison. Lips slightly parted, dragging air into her oxygen-depleted lungs, she waited for the explosion of *feeling* to subside. How could she react so differently to two physically identical men? How could she react like this to *any* man?

By the time she had regained control of her breathing, Nia had registered the scathing contempt in Jake's eyes as they swept over the cosily intimate scene on the bed. His derision made a ridiculously guilty flush rise to her cheeks.

Why should I feel guilty? Her chin went up and a light of angry defiance began to sparkle in her eyes.

Anyone would have thought he'd be glad to have found his brother. Nothing about Jake suggested he was overflowing with filial compassion—quite the contrary!

'Long night, bro?' A thoughtful light in his eyes, Josh eased his son onto his shoulder.

Nia noticed for the first time that Jake wasn't looking his usual pristine self. He didn't appear to have changed his clothes since the previous night and the dark shadows under his eyes didn't suggest much sleep. He could even look haggard stylishly, she thought gloomily.

'I could ask you the same question, but I won't.' His icy-cold eyes rested pointedly on Nia before he turned sharply on his heel and walked out of the room.

'He's the rudest man I've ever met. What did he mean by that, anyway?' she demanded angrily, still puzzling over his cryptic parting shot.

'I think maybe he might think that we…' Josh's smile was sympathetic as he met the clear-eyed indignant frown of the young woman beside him. 'Jake thinks I can't help trying to pinch his women.'

Nia didn't see the relevance, but the subject intrigued her enough to pursue it. 'And can't you?'

'The truth be known, more often than not I got his leftovers,' he told her with engaging candour. 'Jake never quite mastered the concept that women like to think they're the most important thing in the world to a man.'

'Even if they're not?' Nia found this frank insight into the male mind was fascinating.

Josh grinned, and for a second she had a glimpse of the devilish—possibly ruthless—charmer he'd once been.

'Don't feel too sorry for Jake. There were plenty who were ready to take him despite the fact they had to do all the running. You can see how it did my reputation no harm at all to let him think I'd poached them if he wanted to. We were always on the competitive side.'

'I can imagine.' She could, and despite the humorous acceptance in Josh's voice now, she suspected his attitude hadn't always been so relaxed. Two high achievers constantly battling for the upper hand seemed an exhausting situation to her.

'The only thing I was really good at was getting into trouble and winding Jake up.'

Having had an unscheduled tour of his studio, Nia didn't take this statement too seriously. It had been a mistake to think of that dusty studio, the memories it revived made it hard to concentrate on the rest of his words and ignore the fact every strand of downy hair on her body was standing on end. The burning sensation in her nipples was pleasurably distracting.

'He thought that's what I was doing with Bridie,' she heard Josh muse as he rested his chin gently on the top of his son's head, his expression faraway. 'All it took was a look,' he said simply. 'Have you ever felt like that?'

Had she? Nia swallowed and avoided the issue. 'I don't see what that's got to do with…' Her frown deepened. 'It's not as if he thinks you…we…?' Her eyes grew saucer-like. Not even Jake could jump to such a preposterous conclusion. Did he think she slept with anyone with the right initials!

'Uh-huh, that's *exactly* what he thinks.'

'The disgusting, sleazy-minded snake!'

'We are sharing a bed.' Josh felt impelled to defend his absent twin from this volcanic display of red-headed fury. 'I am naked,' he added, confirming her suspicions. 'And you're wearing my T-shirt. Keep it,' he added as she slid out of the bed and marched purposefully towards the door. 'It looks much better on you than me,' he added to an empty room.

He let out a silent whistle and quickly forgot about the drama unfolding elsewhere in his house as he began to talk to his son who was satisfyingly receptive, hanging with flattering interest on his every word.

*　　*　　*

'How *dare* you!' Nia didn't waste any time with the prelim-inaries. Bare-footed, she stepped out onto the cobbled yard outside the kitchen door.

Hands resting firmly on her hips, she stalked up to the tall figure who was silently contemplating a stray hen who was fossicking for food amongst the clumps of wildflowers that had seeded themselves in the tiny crevices of soil.

Jake turned around slowly. His unhurried negligent manner only served to fuel her fury.

'You're scaring the wildlife,' he observed as the hen flut-tered noisily away. If he hadn't gotten out of that room he'd have throttled his own brother! Looking at his hands now, he was still deeply shocked by the depth of his response.

His eyes moved expressionlessly over Nia's angry flushed face, sparkling eyes, heaving bosom and bare length of shapely leg before coming to rest on her pink-painted toe-nails.

'I should watch where you step if I were you.'

He didn't sound concerned for her welfare one little bit. His smile was as thin and unpleasant as a razor. Nia didn't know whether this warning was just what it sounded, or if it had a veiled sinister significance—she didn't care!

'You know where you can stick your advice, don't you?' she hissed, eager to be presented with the opportunity to elab-orate on the theme in Technicolor detail. She jabbed a finger in the general direction of his chest, but didn't actually make contact—she didn't need that sort of distraction right now.

'I could hazard a guess,' he responded drily. 'You don't look happy.' She did, however, look magnificent, but he wasn't about to mention this.

'Josh said…he said…' Her cheeks almost put her hair in the shade as she tried to force the words past her reluctant tongue.

'Spare me the details. I'm sure he responded most satis-factorily to your own unique form of *therapy*. Was Josh by way of a trial run? Or did you just forget to include part-time sex therapy on your C.V.?'

Nia drew herself up to her full height and let her scornful eyes roam freely over him. It was horrifying that even now at some basic level she registered a wistful sigh of appreciation—he was quite simply the most beautiful man she'd ever seen.

'Are you just being sarcastic?' she enquired, her voice soft and deadly. 'Or is your own sex life so predictable you actually want the details of mine?' Just as well he didn't know what a perfect cure for insomnia that was!

'I knew you were a bleeding heart, but I didn't know just how far you'd go. Tell me, does your fiancé know you offer more than tea and sympathy to your strays?'

'This concern for Huw is very touching. Strange I didn't notice it stopping you trying to get me into bed yesterday.'

'Not bed. We were on the floor, if you recall.'

Nia's wild rose colour faded dramatically. She recalled, all right—every minute detail and she was sure she always would.

'It didn't bother you I had a ring on my finger at the time,' she reminded him in a hard voice.

'What can I say?' His impressive shoulders lifted expressively. '*Mea culpa*... When a man's offered it on a plate he's inclined not to think too deeply about the moral correctitude,' he observed, cynically dismissive. 'Of course later he might feel a bit queasy about it, but we're shallow creatures on the whole.'

The insult viciously found its mark. Nia took a step backwards and her bare foot came down on a sharp jagged stone which dug deep into the vulnerable flesh of her instep. Even though the blood immediately started seeping out of the deep wound, the pain didn't begin to compare with that inflicted by his crude, insulting words.

'Shallow,' she echoed shakily. 'You said it. Don't touch

me!' she cried, punching out wildly and connecting with air as he swayed sinuously to avoid the blow.

'You've hurt yourself,' he grated.

'That should make you happy,' she accused self-pityingly. 'You *actually* do think I made love to your brother.' Her voice trembled with disbelief.

'Didn't I say you'd like him?' Jake's iron self-possession wasn't flawless, he couldn't control that maverick nerve in his cheek.

'I do!' she cried. 'Unlike you, he's not some anal-retentive prig!'

'I'm sure the poor sod was more than happy to forget everything in your arms for a little while,' Jake reflected grimly. 'You're very good at making a man forget,' he ground out bitterly.

'So, Josh was the victim of my libidinous desires. I couldn't have you, so he'd do?' she suggested, driven to the edge of hysteria by the image he painted of some femme fatale.

'Did you know the difference?' He sounded politely surprised.

'I can't compare notes when I haven't actually experienced your full repertoire!' And never would now.

'If that was a request, I'm definitely not in the mood.'

Her even white teeth grated against one another as she smiled back at him with a scornful lack of concern.

'You must be so pleased to find something about me you can despise other than my dress sense, my hairstyle and my skirt length. Yes!' she jeered, shaking back her hair and sniffing haughtily. 'Yes, I've seen you looking to check I'm not exceeding the two inches above the knee rule!'

'That wasn't why I was looking,' he retorted thickly. The thick veil of his lashes lifted and his eyes collided with hers. 'And you know it. I was looking at your legs,' he told her.

'…like now.' The words emerged as a low throaty growl as his glance dropped to the hem of his twin's black T-shirt.

The suggestive sweep of his eyes, his hard audible intake of breath, had Nia quivering. Her brave contemptuous smile faded. She felt weak and exposed.

'You've got a nasty, smutty little mind. Well, I'm sick of you looking down your superior nose at me!' Especially when the look was as broodingly expressive as his was right now. Those remarkable eyes of his had stripped the skimpy garment clear off her back.

'Unless you grow several inches, I'll have to carry on looking down at you—even when you wear those ludicrous heels.'

'I'm perfectly well aware of my physical deficiencies,' she snapped, thinking of Victoria, Selina, Jasmine, and their uniformly long legs.

'From where I'm standing, you don't have any!' he yelled.

This totally unexpected statement becalmed her fury midflight.

'What did you say?' she squeaked. Her knees felt distinctly wobbly as she tried to focus her scattered thoughts.

'I was making a reference to your physical perfection. I appreciate these things are subjective but…' His eyes suddenly narrowed. 'You expect me to believe you *didn't* sleep with my brother? *Look at you!'*

She glanced quickly down at her scantily clad figure. 'What's wrong with the way I look?' she enquired mutinously. She didn't think he could come up with any insults worse than the ones he'd already levelled at her.

'Nothing!' he snarled, apparently gaining little pleasure from her supposed perfection. 'That's my point.' The resentful expression in his eyes was hunger at its most savage and basic.

The hormone cascade that slid through her body in response to that expression almost obliterated her resentful fury.

'Unlike you, your brother isn't trying to replace his wife with a substitute.'

Jake was getting seriously worried by her waxy pallor, but at her derisive jeer, his eyes jerked from the sticky dark stain around her injured foot to her face.

'It's just coincidence we're redheads, I suppose,' she added, feeling inexplicably defensive in the face of his glowering white-lipped silence.

'I thought Bridie and I were compatible in every way. We spent six months slowly getting to know one another, and then Josh came back from Italy.' His shoulders lifted expressively. 'They *should* have been wildly incompatible—' His lips curled in a self-derisive smile. 'They were total opposites.'

'Like you and me.' Nia flushed when she realised she'd spoken her thoughts out loud.

'I'm not still in love with Bridie.' Even when he'd thought he was, he'd never experienced a mindless desire to injure his brother. The disturbing memory of how difficult it had been to walk out of the room was still fresh in his mind.

'I thought I might be in love with you…how's *that* for a joke?' His laugh had a hollow ring. 'But although Josh and I share a lot of things, we've never shared our women—hell, we've never even compared notes!' he jeered.

He didn't even try to avoid the impact from the wide, arcing sweep of her hand. The crack as it connected with his lean cheek reverberated around the yard. Before her horrified eyes, the livid imprint of her fingers developed.

'For your information, I didn't even hug Josh, but I think perhaps his brother should,' she added shakily. Jake's narrowed eyes were still as sharp and contemptuous as knives. *In love with me!* Had he *really* said that? She hadn't missed the significant past tense, either.

'You must think I'm simple, Nia. You're a very physical woman. When I left you last night you were as frustrated as hell. You almost ate me alive. You expect me to believe that you didn't…!'

'Eat your brother?' she suggested tightly. His insanity knew no bounds.

'I know what I saw, Nia.'

Which meant he hadn't listened to anything she'd said and from his closed, stubborn expression he wasn't going to! Of all the pigheaded stupid males…! Well, she was going to make him listen even if she had to hit him with a large blunt instrument to get his attention!

Actually aggravating him worked just as well as brute force. The mocking little trill of laughter did the trick.

'And I know jealousy when I see it!'

'And you like that, do you? You like men to fight over you.'

'Of course not,' she responded with a shudder of genuine distaste. 'I'm trying to point out that you're allowing your inbuilt rivalry with your brother to cloud your judgement. Even if I'd wanted to sleep with him, I wouldn't have had the energy! Have you any idea how long it took me to get Liam to sleep last night? Well, this morning, to be more accurate. I'm not telling you this because I give a damn what you think of me,' she continued angrily. 'I just don't think now's the time for you to be fighting with Josh. He needs your help and support,' she said earnestly.

'You didn't sleep with Josh?'

'That's what I've been trying to tell you. He got as much of a shock when he woke up this morning as I did.'

'He didn't look too traumatised when I walked in,' Jake reflected grimly.

Nia gave a sigh of exasperation. 'You'd prefer it if he was a basket case?' she snapped impatiently.

'Perhaps it's my jealousy speaking?' His hard words had a reckless edge.

Nia swallowed. 'You've *both* lost the woman you loved. I would have thought that should bring you closer—it could if you let it.' It was sick, she told herself in disgust, to feel jealous of dead women.

CHAPTER SEVEN

JAKE looked down into her earnest heart-shaped little face. 'You think I'm talking about Bridie, don't you?' He shook his head and placed a finger under her tilted chin. 'Put your compassion away, Miss Jones. I envy my brother because he woke up beside you. Because he had the opportunity to do this…' Her gasp of shock was extinguished as his hot, marauding mouth covered hers hungrily.

As one strong arm fastened just under her ribcage her body was drawn upwards in a tight arc until she stood on tiptoes. Her breasts were crushed against his hard masculine chest and the dizzying pleasure of this, combined with the sudden suggestive surge of his body against her, made her hover momentarily on the brink of losing consciousness—it was just so *intense*.

The thrust of his tongue sent an electrifying shock juddering through her hot, receptive body.

His lips had a bruising quality without being remotely brutal. As his fingers sunk deep into her luxuriant hair his tongue entered the equally lush region of her warm inviting mouth.

His hands were on her body and hers, clumsy and eager, were on his. The scalding heat of his hard-muscled body fed the hunger that imploded in her head.

The closest Nia had come to this was in her dreams; but dreams didn't sear you to the bone and deeper. Dreams didn't leave your lips feeling bruised and tender, and her lips as she pressed the back of her hand to them were both—plus they were trembling. Correction, *she* was trembling full-stop—all over.

When she blinked she had her own private firework display going off behind her eyelids, brilliant splashes of chrysanthemum against velvety black. She tugged fretfully at the baggy neckline of the black cotton T-shirt she wore—it was hard to breathe, especially when she recalled how his hand had smoothly slid underneath it following the line of her thigh to the curve of her bottom. His fingers had spread out, sinking possessively into the firm flesh.

With a low agitated moan she pulled back. *'Don't!'* She pushed her hair behind her ears with shaking fingers. Her entire body was burning from his touch.

His smouldering glance held a sensual belligerence as it rested over the outline of her taut, heaving breasts. 'I want you…you want me.' His attitude said clearly, What more is there to say?

'I don't think it's appropriate for you to kiss me.' The outline of her full lips was blurred and slightly swollen; there were tiny beads of sweat along the upper curve.

'Appropriate!' he mimicked savagely. He withdrew his hungry gaze with apparent difficulty from her flushed, aroused face. 'Because of your fiancé.'

'No, there is no fiancé,' she responded almost absently. 'When I make love to a man, I want it to be someone who trusts me,' she told him bitterly. 'So far this morning you've virtually accused me of being a nymphomaniac. From where I'm standing, that's not the best foundation for a relationship, but you don't have relationships, do you? No, nothing so complicated. You have *appointments.*'

As much as her body craved for his touch, she knew there was no future without trust, and Jake had proved beyond doubt that he didn't trust her. He didn't even seem to like her very much. His words had been calculated to cause the maximum pain and they'd succeeded. You didn't try and injure the person you loved! Did you?

Uneasily she recalled that some of her gibes hadn't been intended to soothe and charm.

He'd spent half the night sitting in his car wondering how she'd respond when he told her she had to choose between him and her farmer, and now she calmly said he didn't exist! He'd known it was a risky thing to do—what would he do if she didn't respond to the ultimatum the way he wanted? But he needed exclusivity. He'd actually worked out the exact wording!

Now she was telling him there was no boyfriend and she didn't want him anyhow—after kissing him back like *that!* His hands balled into fists at his sides as he fought to retain control of his erratic breathing and his sizzling temper.

'*When* makes it sound as though you haven't done so yet.'

He had to say something, he couldn't just stand there like an idiot. If his desire had been reduced in direct proportion to his mental capability, he wouldn't be feeling as though he was going to explode out of pure frustration any minute.

'That's right,' she responded simply.

For the second time in minutes Jake felt as though someone had punched him in the solar plexus—hard! 'Are you trying to tell me you're a…a…*virgin?*' His healthy colour fled, leaving his skin the colour of marble.

She gave a defensive sniff. 'What if I am?' He was looking at her as though she'd done it—or not in this case—deliberately, just to annoy him. 'And I didn't make up Huw. We were engaged, only I decided…'

'He didn't reach your high expectations. What man could?' he breathed, dragging a hand through his already tousled dark hair.

Nia wanted to smooth it down so much it hurt physically not to reach out.

'No, it was me,' she confessed with a sigh. 'I didn't love him enough—not in *that* way. That's why I came to London. We live in a small village, and it wasn't very nice for Huw to bump into me all the time. I haven't been going back very often. I was really looking forward to this weekend.' She recalled the presents she'd bought for her family still under her office desk. Her lower lip quivered and she bit down on it so hard she tasted blood. At a time like this, a girl needed her mum!

'You can talk about trust when you let me think you were engaged. You didn't tell me you were a virgin!' His tone had acquired an outraged lecturing twang she deeply resented.

'I don't really see what it had to do with you,' she announced truculently.

'If Liam hadn't woken, you would be an ex-virgin, that's what it had to do with me!' He gave an incredulous shake of his head.

'And you'd be none the wiser.'

'If you think that, you really are…'

'I wouldn't have mentioned it if I'd known you were going to take on so.'

His eyes narrowed to slits. 'I can't decide if you're being deliberately obtuse.'

'As for the engagement, I wore my grandmother's ring on this finger after a couple of bad experiences with amorous bosses. It was more tactful to produce a large jealous rugby-playing boyfriend than a left hook—unless of course all else failed.'

This matter-of-fact explanation did not appear to have soothed Jake's ruffled feelings.

'I didn't notice you throwing any left hooks when I got physical,' he goaded.

'That's because I wanted you to,' she confessed gloomily.

Jake breathed deeply and swore. 'Make up your mind, woman,' he growled, reaching out to greedily encircle her slim waist.

'I have,' she gasped, giving a sinuous little twist to evade capture—capture her whole treacherous body wanted more than anything else in the world. 'I need more than you can offer, Jake,' she threw over her shoulder as she limped back into the kitchen.

'How would you know?' he yelled after her, 'you don't begin to know what I can give you!'

'Hurt yourself?' Josh queried, popping the lid on a steaming pot of tea. He was dressed in a black towelling robe that reached midcalf and gaped to show a lot of chest. Nia could be completely objective about his body, which was way better than marvellous.

Why, she wondered, when I can't stop fantasising about one twin's body do I keep getting full frontal—or very nearly—of the other one?

'I stepped on something.' It was probably better this way. If Jake had started peeling off his clothes she might just forget how impossible it would be to build anything on a relationship without mutual trust.

'Not Jake?' he enquired. 'No, not Jake,' he added in mock regretful tones as his brother entered the room. 'Nia's hurt her foot, Jake.'

'I know.' He caught her from behind and, ignoring her squeals and struggles, sat her on the top of a work surface. 'The foot needs cleaning and dressing. If you can't bear my touch,' he snarled, aware of his twin's interested eyes, 'Josh will do it.'

'No, he won't,' his twin contradicted firmly. 'The sight of blood makes me feel faint,' he explained apologetically to Nia.

'Since when?'

Josh met his twin's brooding distrust with a sunny smile. 'The first-aid kit's second drawer down. I'll take my tea back to bed, if nobody minds.'

'Wait, Josh!' She was conscious of two similar pairs of eyes fixed expectantly upon her. 'Have you got a pen?'

'Pen!'

'Or pencil. I feel the urgent need to tender my resignation. It's no great loss, you're a terrible boss.' The second spiteful observation was addressed to Jake.

'No need for that, you're sacked.'

'I'll tell the agency you sexually harassed me. They'll blacklist you!' she threatened wildly.

'I'll tell them you sexually harassed me back.'

'You're *unbelievable!*'

'So I've been told,' he responded modestly as he tipped the contents of the first-aid chest onto the work surface.

Nia threw him a look of frustrated dislike. 'Don't you think trust is the most important thing in any relationship, Josh?' she appealed to the silent twin who was unobtrusively backing out of the room.

A cloud passed over his face, leaving a sombre shadow in its wake. 'Yes I do,' he said before disappearing.

'Oh, no, look what you've made me do!' she cried, wringing her hands in agitation at her tactless choice of words. *'Poor Josh.'*

'*I* made you do?' He took hold of her foot and lifted it to examine the deep puncture wound. 'Keep still!' he added brusquely as she automatically twisted her foot away as his fingers closed over her ankle. 'I need to clean it. It might hurt.'

Since when did that matter to you? she wondered, caught up on a fresh wave of self-pity.

Actually he was gentle but firm. The fire in her belly started to glow once more as she watched the skilful movements of his incredibly elegant hands. He doesn't love me, he just *wants* me, she told herself, wanting to hate him but not succeeding.

'How's that?'

'Better,' she murmured miserably, without meeting his eyes. She flexed her toes experimentally.

The fact she had rejected her need of him verbally didn't

stop the small room seething with a tense sexual atmosphere. Nia was finding it hard to breathe. The sudden violent shudder that rippled through Jake's lean body communicated itself through his fingertips, which rested against the shapely curve of her slim calf, making it obvious he wasn't immune.

'I was wondering if you needed a lift up to town, Nia? Liam and I need to stock up on supplies.' Josh breezed in, tucking his shirt into a pair of loose-fitting combat-style trousers.

He recoiled slightly at the dark scowl his brother threw in his direction. 'Shall I go out and come back in? Or not come back in?'

'No!'

'Yes!'

They both replied simultaneously.

'Please, Josh, I'd appreciate a lift.' Nia eased herself slowly down off the counter. 'After all, I'm unemployed. I need to watch the pennies.'

If she was going to recover from this stupid mindless infatuation, it was about time she started acting positively.

'Don't worry, I'll pay you overtime for this weekend's work.'

'And don't think I won't take it!' she yelled as he slammed out of the room.

'Wow! You certainly took the civilised out of the man!' Josh breathed admiringly.

Nia began to cry very noisily.

CHAPTER EIGHT

'HAVE you been waiting long? The train was delayed.' He wasn't Jake, but it still hurt to see the familiar shared features. The constant ache in Nia's chest threatened to become full-blown agony.

'No problem,' Josh said, picking up her bag and kissing her cheek casually. 'It's really good of you to step into the breech like this.'

'He's grown,' Nia whispered, glancing at the sleeping baby cocooned in the nursing sling across his father's chest.

'Baby's do that. You've lost weight—a lot of weight,' he announced, neither congratulating or commiserating with her over this circumstance.

'Do you always say exactly what you're thinking?' she wondered out loud. She wasn't sure quite where frankness tipped over into rudeness, but he was definitely cutting it fine!

'Unlike Jake, you mean.' He didn't comment when Nia almost tripped over her own feet. 'That's me, an open book, whereas Jake…well, I don't need to tell you Jake doesn't always say what he's thinking. The car's over here,' he nodded to a Range Rover as he led her across the car park. 'This is really very kind of you.'

Nia was already beginning to suspect her compassion had been misplaced. 'You sounded desperate.'

Looking at him now, she could see no sign of the end-of-his-tether stress that had been in his voice when they'd spoken on the telephone. In fact, he looked a thousand times better than when she'd last seen him six weeks previously.

'Did I really?' he replied, looking so startled she felt embarrassed at her interpretation of their conversation. 'Actually for the most part Liam and I are coping pretty well without a nanny. But then, I'm lucky I don't have to punch a time clock nine to five. I'm working around Liam.'

'You're working?'

His brows shot up. 'Expecting to find an emotional wreck?' He grinned as he smoothly transferred the baby to his bucket seat and clicked the restraint into place. 'Actually, I do have bad days,' he told her frankly as he climbed into the driver's seat.

The slightly purplish smudgy shadows under his eyes suggested his nights weren't all plain sailing, either.

'I find work therapeutic. And are you working?'

'Yes.'

'A more amenable boss than Jake?'

All expression was abruptly wiped from Nia's face. 'I don't want to talk about...' she began stiffly.

'Don't blame you...' To her relief he let the subject drop. For one awful second she'd thought he might have engineered this acting as some sort of go-between on Jake's behalf.

You mean, you'd hoped he was. A small self-derisive smile curved her lips as she leaned farther back in her seat—it seemed Josh had a nasty habit of taking hairpin bends in fourth gear. Jake probably hadn't even given her a second thought!

'What time does your exhibition start?' She couldn't help but notice he kept glancing at the clock on the dashboard.

'Early,' he responded vaguely. 'Liam's really adaptable, but he had a bit of a cold last week and I didn't want to drag him all the way up to town. It'll be a long evening.'

'He looks fine now,' Nia responded, craning her neck to look at the sleeping baby in the back seat.

'We Prentices are a resilient bunch.'

*   *   *

The lawn and flower-filled borders were looking as neat as their owner's freshly trimmed hair. Nia frowned. Speaking to Josh on the phone, she'd had the impression of chaotic disorganisation—his last-minute plea for a baby-sitter had seemed representative of this.

Now that she could see how well he'd pulled things together, it seemed a little strange. She couldn't put her finger on it, but something wasn't quite right.

'Go through to the small sitting room and I'll fetch you some tea.'

'I'll help. Was that a car I heard?' she asked, moving towards the window.

Josh stepped in her way. *'No!'* He smiled to take the edge off his terse refusal. 'I'm expecting a delivery. I won't be a sec.'

He was more than that, but not much. Nia lifted the lid of the small upright piano set against one wall and depressed a key.

'Are you sure I can't help?' she asked, lifting her head as she heard the footfall against the creaky old oak boards. She saw the distinctive grey eyes set beneath a pair of dark, arched satirically brows, and her belly dissolved into a warm aching pit of nothingness.

'You! What are you doing here?' Outrage stiffened her slender figure as she glared at the tall casually clad figure in the doorway.

'If you're not in cahoots with him, I think we might just ask my interfering brother that,' Jake said heavily.

Cahoots! The cheek of the man. He had the unmitigated gall to even think she would conspire to have the dubious pleasure of his company.

He turned towards the latched door just as it closed gently in his face. Before he reached it there was the unmistakable sound of bolts sliding into place.

'Josh!' he yelled, dark colour seeping up beneath the

smooth olive tones of his skin. 'Open this damned thing!' He banged his fist on the unyielding wood.

'Sorry, no can do,' came the cheerful but muffled reply. 'Not until you two start behaving like grown-ups.'

'What is it? What's happening? Why…?'

'That's exactly what Bridie said to us the day she locked us both in my study…*grown-ups*. We were fighting…'

'When are you not fighting?' Nia asked, in no mood to share his nostalgia over past imprisonment. Panic was coursing through her veins. She *couldn't* be locked in here—she looked wildly around the room—not with Jake!

'Come on, Josh…'

'If you get thirsty you'll find refreshments in the bureau. Liam and I are just going out. An afternoon at the zoo I think…'

'*Josh!*' Jake's furious roar was greeted with silence.

'They're locked!' Nia panted as she turned from leaded windows. 'What are you doing?'

Jake extracted a bottle from the ice bucket he'd discovered inside the small walnut bureau. 'At least he's got excellent, not to mention expensive, taste,' he observed ripping off the foil and twisting the cork on the champagne bottle.

'Are you mad?' she asked blankly as she watched him fill the two glasses provided. 'You're both mad,' she continued—insanity would explain a lot. 'I don't want to drink champagne!'

'If you can think of a better alternative, I'm open to suggestions.'

Was he thinking what she thought he was thinking—wishful thinking? What was it absence was meant to do? It had made her more appreciative of his incredible good looks, more susceptible, not less, to the whole charismatic persona of the man. She cursed her delinquent heart and tried to look scornful.

He raised his glass to her in a sardonic salute and drained

it in one swallow. 'There's no point getting emotional about this.'

Easy for him to say. 'I *am* emotional about this. Call me peculiar, but I don't like being locked in a room against my will with a man I...'

'Loathe?' he suggested.

'I don't loathe you.'

'That sounds promising.'

'I'm completely indifferent.' Would that were true! She rubbed her sweaty palms nervously together.

'I'm dashed.'

He didn't look it, she noticed resentfully.

'When do you think Josh'll let us out? What time does the exhibition finish?' she asked, avoiding his fabulous grey eyes.

'Nia, haven't you caught on yet? My pet, there is no exhibition—this is a put-up job,' Jake explained pityingly.

'There's no need to patronise me, he suckered you, too, remember.'

'I haven't forgotten,' Jake remarked drily.

'He sounded so convincing on the phone,' she fretted resentfully.

'That boy kissed the blarney stone—we both did—only he must have had better suction in his lips, because he's been a chip off the old block ever since.'

There was nothing wrong with Jake's lips. In fact, he had the most sensually perfect lips, she thought dreamily, allowing her eyes to dwell overlong on their firm outline.

'What is this meant to achieve?' she asked quickly, her colour heightened because he'd been watching her looking...

His dark brows shot upwards. 'I would have thought that was obvious. Champagne,' he crunched the bottle viciously in the ice bucket, 'enforced intimacy. I'm just surprised he couldn't swing a partial eclipse to improve the ambience. The scene is set for seduction, Nia. I should explain that Josh is a true romantic at heart.'

'That's better than being a sneering cynic.'

'You want romance?' He made a sudden movement that made her overstimulated reflexes respond automatically. She stepped hastily backwards. 'That's what I thought.' His lips twisted into a cold derisive smile. 'We just have to sit here and wait.'

'I can't.'

'Why not?'

'*Because...*' Nia glared at him with frustrated loathing. How was she meant to explain that being near him was pure undiluted agony—that every individual fibre of her being ached for his touch? That all she could think about was the texture of his warm lips, the hardness of his lean body...the musky warm male smell—

'You must have said something to make Josh think this charade would be welcome!' she accused.

'I'd hardly burden my brother with the boring details of my failed relationships at the moment, would I?'

'If we're talking boring, perhaps you should take a good long look in the mirror. At least your brother isn't short in the imagination department—though a bit misguided,' she added awkwardly, just in case he got the idea she approved of the situation.

'Is that an invitation to prove how imaginative I can be?' The tormenting gleam faded from his eyes as Nia swayed. 'Are you all right'

Nia put out a hand to steady herself. 'You can ask that? If you must know, I think I'm developing claustrophobia.'

'Don't think about it.'

'How...?' she began, not overly impressed by this insensitive advice.

'Make conversation.'

He wanted conversation—fine, he could have it!

'Is your new secretary good?' she responded inanely after a long strangulated pause.

'*He* is. And your new post?'

'Challenging.' Withdrawal symptoms had made her less than her usual super-efficient self, but so far nobody had noticed—she hoped. 'You didn't complain about me to the agency.' She perched nervously on the arm of a small armchair. 'They said you gave me a glowing reference.'

'I was afraid you'd counter complain.'

'I wouldn't have…'

'I know that.' The warmth in his restless glance as it moved over her made Nia shiver. 'Tell me, Nia…' There was no disguising the urgency in his harsh abrupt words.

She'd been so busy trying to disguise her feelings that until this moment she hadn't seen that underneath that almost-languid acceptance he was strung out with tension every bit as debilitating as her own.

'Yes?' she encouraged a little breathlessly.

'It doesn't matter.' His tone was clipped and dismissive.

She let out a gusty sigh and her shoulders sagged. 'Yes, Jake, *it does!*'

His eyes fastened onto hers with laser-like intensity. 'Are you trying to tell me…?' he asked warily.

'I'm not trying to tell you anything until you tell me first,' she told him candidly.

He nodded slowly then emptied the second glass of champagne in similar fashion to the first.

'Would the something you're not going to tell me have anything to do with feeling as if something vital is missing from your life?' he enquired tersely. 'Food tasting of sawdust and a total inability to concentrate?'

'The worst six weeks of my life,' she added thickly, raising misty eyes to his.

'I've missed having you around, Nia. What do you want me to say? *I love you?*' He might have intended it to contain a humorous ambiguity but by the time the words had emerged from his throat the intonation was raw appeal.

Her eyelashes fluttered almost as wildly as her heartbeat. Now she knew the meaning of bated breath!

'That would be nice for starters,' she finally managed.

'I came to your flat.' His eyes were devouring her. 'I was in the hallway when he came out.'

'*He?*' She felt impatient, not curious; she'd wanted to hear more on the love theme.

'I saw him kiss you.' A pretty pathetic affair it had been, too, he decided scornfully. 'I heard him.'

The musical accent had been the male version of her own. The worst part had been living with the fact she wouldn't have gone running back to her old love if he hadn't been fool enough to let her get away in the first place.

He had been arrogant enough to think she'd be waiting when he finally got around to admitting he needed her—it had been a sobering experience to realise she might just not need him at all. Josh was right—he was pigheaded and stubborn.

Sudden comprehension wiped away Nia's frown of confusion.

'You shouldn't settle for second best,' Jake announced grimly without a trace of the humility he'd decided to display.

'That makes you…?' She pretended to puzzle over the problem. Some devil in her couldn't resist this opportunity to tease him.

Fire flashed in his eyes. 'The only man you need,' he declared outrageously.

Nia didn't feel outraged—she felt a wild surge of lust in response to this smug statement and the accompanying predatory intent that was stamped on his lean, intense features.

'It wasn't Huw you saw…'

Jake bit back a blistering response with difficulty. How

many were there, for God's sake? The Welsh valleys were obviously crawling with men slavering over his Miss Jones.

'It was Dervel, my brother. He works in Brussels. He likes to keep an eye on me.' All her brothers did, and it was a circumstance that had been the kiss of death to her social life over the years. The sight of her brawny brothers hovering protectively had put a damper on the ardour of many a prospective suitor.

'*Brother,*' he echoed in strained voice. 'I wanted to kill him,' he announced hoarsely.

'Just as well you didn't try, he's black belt in karate.'

'I boxed for my college.'

'Did you win?'

'Naturally.'

'Well, now we've established your murderous credentials, could you get back to the point?' she pleaded huskily. 'If you can remember where you were before that detour…'

'Let me think…' The teasing quality faded dramatically from his voice as his expression hardened into something much fiercer and intense. 'Beautiful, infuriating, Miss Jones, I love you.' The impetus of his lustful lunge had tipped her backwards into the chair which was totally inadequate to contain two people, even if they were tangled up.

Despite the elbow in his ribs, Jake managed to kiss her with desperate need until she was breathless and trembling.

'I missed you so much,' she breathed, pressing feverish kisses to his neck and his cleanly shaven cheek as his hands skilfully unfastened with remarkable speed a variety of buttons, clips and zips. Nia cooperated as much as her shaky coordination would allow.

Nia gave a gasp of relief as his hands found the aching flesh of her taut aching breasts. His thumb toyed expertly with the unfurled rosy peaks until her whole body was at fever pitch.

'You're just perfect,' he told her, weighing one quivering

mound of receptive flesh in his palm. 'I want to touch your skin, it's so incredibly smooth,' he groaned, crushing her lips under his. 'I shouldn't have let you go.' He wrapped his fingers in her hair and tugged her face closer. 'You've no idea how badly I need you,' he growled, his features stretched in a tense mask of pain.

Tongue tucked between her teeth, she let her glance drop to his lap. 'I've got an inkling,' she confessed with cheerful loving-eyed crudity.

Sitting astride him, her knees squashed between the sides of the chair and his long muscular thighs, she leaned forward a little farther and with a sensual little wriggle looped her arms around his neck. His shirt was open and her breasts grazed against the hard hair-roughened expanse of his chest. The sensation was so sensational that she did it again, half closing her eyes as she squirmed.

The tormentingly flirtatious look she cast him through the silky fringe of her lashes made him swear. 'If I don't have you now,' he growled, tightening his grip on her and standing up, 'I'll go quietly mad. I think I've been a little mad since the first moment I saw you.'

'Let's go mad together, darling,' she whispered.

They did.

It felt wildly decadent to be curled up naked on a rug sipping champagne. All they needed was a log fire, but the copper bowlful of full-blown late summer roses set in the old-fashioned inglenook was an acceptable substitute. One thing there was no substitute for was the man beside her.

She let her eyes run greedily over his lean naked body. He was relaxed now, but a few moments ago his body had been tense with raw need, each muscle pumped up to the limit of endurance. Though his skin was cooling, there was still a faint sheen of moisture that gave extra definition to each sinew and muscle. She ran a hand lovingly over his flat belly, allowing her fingers to playfully rest against the dark hair that cradled his now relaxed—well, almost—manhood.

Her action made him smile with slow lazy approval. She liked the intimacy and promise of that smile almost as much as the frenzied determination in his face as, teeth clenched, he'd tried to resist her pleas to be taken until the last possible moment.

He'd wanted her to be ready, so he'd said. Nia had thought she was dying—and what a way to go, she reflected, laying her head against his chest. Her relief had been as savage as his exultant cry when he'd finally plunged into her.

'Happy?' he asked, letting his fingers gently tangle into the burnished mass of her hair.

'Blissfully. I really enjoyed it, Jake.' She gave a languid sigh and stretched voluptuously.

'You mentioned that—once or twice.' If he was half as wonderful as she'd declared, he was quite a man! To think he'd once found fault with the warm generosity of her passionate emotional nature!

'Are you laughing at me?' she demanded with mock ire.

'Only in the nicest possible way,' he promised, catching hold of her free hand and kissing it. The glow of uncomplicated love in his eyes made her throat close over.

His body curved over hers. 'I'm not much good at showing my feelings, Nia.'

'Try.'

He laughed. It was a deep, warm, uninhibited sound, but then, she recalled he was a pretty uninhibited sort of lover.

'I've always thought it was a crazy concept, but it's true what they say, opposites do attract.'

'I think we complement each other—even when we're having a…frank exchange of opinions.'

One dark brow quirked satirically. 'Would that be short-hand for fighting?'

'It would be boring if we agreed about everything.'

'In that case, perhaps we ought to put the arrangement on a permanent basis.' He cleared his throat noisily.

If she hadn't known better, she'd have said Jake Prentice was blushing!

'Is that some sort of proposal?'

'Sorry. I'm not great with words.' Jake silently cursed his clumsiness, mistaking her stunned disbelief for criticism.

'You are when you hate me,' she reminded him drily.

'I'd spent that night after meeting Mats sitting in the car thinking—about you, about how I felt about you. I knew I wanted to be with you and I thought you were engaged. I'd decided to lay it all on the line for you, tell you how I felt, ask you to choose between me and the boyfriend. Then I walk in and find you in bed with *Josh* of all people. I was almost *crazy* with jealousy! I wanted to hurt Josh—that's a terrible thing to come to terms with…' he admitted with an expressive groan.

'But I *never* hated you!' he denied, pressing his lips to the pulse point beside her collarbone. 'Infuriated, enraged, entranced and bewitched by you…yes! But never hate, Nia. I love you and I always will.'

The simplicity of his declaration brought sparkling tears of pure joy to her eyes.

'And I love you, cariad,' she declared fervently.

His hands tightened around her shoulders. 'And you'll marry me?' It wasn't a request.

'I probably should…'

'*Should…?*' He didn't like the dutiful sound of that.

'Well, there was one thing your brother failed to supply…'

'There was?'

'I'm not sure how my family would take to their daughter being an unmarried mother.'

'*Oh, God!*' Jake rolled onto his back and covered his mouth with his open palm. 'You must think I'm the most irresponsible idiot ever. I've never *not* before…'

'It was another sort of first for me,' she reminded him gently. 'And my dates make it unlikely…so we don't have to get married on that account. That just leaves the other,' she mused, propping herself up on one elbow.

'Which is…?'

'That I love you madly, you daft man!' she cried joyfully as she covered him with her warm pliant body.

'Thank God for that!' he whooped as his hands curled possessively around her firm femininely rounded bottom. 'We're going to cook my brother the best meal ever by way of a thank-you. Have I told you I'm a great cook?'

'Nice idea, but we're locked in here.'

'See that wooden panel over there.'

Nia looked towards the wooden-panelled wall he'd indicated and nodded.

'It's not a panel. It's a door.'

'You mean, we could have left at any second?'

Jake nodded brazenly, not displaying any shame for his duplicity.

Nia stared down at him in open-mouthed amazement and suddenly began to laugh. 'You're a bad man!' she declared lovingly.

'For you I can get badder,' he growled with an outrageously lecherous grin.

'I'm looking forward to it.' She was looking forward, forward to the rest of her life with this glorious man. She gave a sigh of blissful contentment as Jake started to behave very badly indeed.

MALONE'S VOW
by
Sandra Marton

Sandra Marton is an American author who used to tell stories to her dolls when she was a little girl. Today, readers around the world fall in love with her sexy, dynamic heroes and outspoken, independent heroines. Her books have topped bestseller lists and won many awards. Sandra loves dressing up for a night out with her husband as much as she loves putting on her hiking boots for a walk in a south-western desert or a north-eastern forest. You can write to her at PO Box 295, Storrs, Connecticut, USA (please enclose SAE).

Look out for
THE ALVARES BRIDE by Sandra Marton
in Modern Romance™, August 2001

CHAPTER ONE

SHE WAS A BEAUTIFUL WOMAN, but not the kind a man should even consider marrying.

Not a man like Bill Thornton.

Liam Malone knew it the minute he saw her.

Bill wasn't her type. He was too good, too gentle, too trusting. He didn't stand a chance at being able to handle a woman like Jessica Warren. She was all quicksilver heat, while Bill was a glowing ember.

Hell, Liam thought as he stared out the window of Bill's study, past the rolling green lawn to Lake Washington glittering in the distance. He wasn't much given to thinking in metaphors, but that was what he'd thought of last night, at the rehearsal dinner. One look at his oldest friend's fiancée and he'd known Bill was making a big mistake.

Bill, of course, was clueless. He'd never been able to read women worth a damn. Liam always could. Jet-lagged as he'd been after the flight from Singapore to Seattle, one glance at his old friend's bride-to-be had told him everything he really didn't want to know.

"Wait until you meet Jessica," Bill had written in the letter that had followed Liam halfway around the world. "This is like a fairy tale, Liam, with me as the frog the beautiful princess turns into a prince. I still can't believe Jessica is going to be my wife."

Liam could. He'd spent enough years on the fringes of what most people called polite society to know that men and women married for lots of reasons, and hardly any had much connection to anything as banal as love.

More than one woman had called him a cynic, but Liam didn't agree. He was simply a realist. He understood that "love" was a catchall word people used instead of less poetic terms, especially in the rarefied strata of the very rich. Successful men married beautiful women as a balm to their egos. Beautiful women married successful men for the security of their wealth. He'd never sat in judgment on such arrangements. The tradeoff was fair enough. It could work, assuming both parties to the deal were still willing to settle for those things a year or two into the marriage.

The men usually were. Arm candy was arm candy, after all. But the women often became restless. They wanted both jewels on their fingers and pleasure in their beds, and they went looking for it. One glance at Jessica Warren and Liam had known that Bill wouldn't satisfy her for very long. She'd need more than his kindness and money to keep her happy.

It would take more than that to keep her at all.

But the poor bastard didn't know it. He was marrying for love, and in his case, ''love'' really did mean a bucketful of syrupy clichés. One man, one woman. Forever after. Until death do us part. Bill was ready to swallow all of it, hook, line and sinker.

And that was the problem.

Give it a couple of years and Bill would still be crazy about his wife but she'd be bored to tears and looking for greener pastures. For all Liam knew, she was bored already. The flash in her eyes last night, when she'd caught him watching her, had said it all. She'd managed a nice girlish blush and a quick downward sweep of her lashes, but that hadn't changed anything. She'd been interested. His best friend's bride-to-be, interested in another man, the night before her wedding.

Interested in him.

Liam's mouth thinned.

It wasn't the first time a woman with a rich man in her life had given him that kind of look. Not all that long ago, he'd been the guy with the looks that turned women on and the empty pockets that turned them off. He'd lived by a combination of luck and his wits, but even so, he'd refused those invitations. He wasn't into playing games with women who belonged to other men. At best, he'd found that kind of come-on amusing.

Not this time. A single glance from Bill's fiancée, and he'd felt himself respond.

"Damn," Liam muttered. He swung away from the window, tucked his hands into his pockets and paced the length of Bill's study.

Of course, he'd responded. What man wouldn't? The message in those eyes had been clear, a promise of satin sheets and silken skin, of heated whispers and sizzling caresses. In one swift instant, his brain had stripped away the expensive suit, undone the classically styled hair…

Well, why not? He wasn't a saint. He was a healthy, heterosexual, thirty-four-year-old male. Yes, she was Bill's fiancée but a man's hormones had a way of ignoring the niceties. He knew that just as surely as he knew that a woman who was signing on for a happy ending with one man shouldn't look at another the way Jessica Warren had looked at him.

The trouble was, he had no idea what to do about it. He couldn't collar Bill and say, "You can't go through with the wedding this morning. The marriage won't work.''

Bill would laugh in his face. As far as he was concerned, Jessica was the only woman in the world. As soon as she'd gone to the powder room, he'd leaned in close and confided that he'd never been this happy in his life. Jessica was all the things he'd ever wanted. She was beautiful and good-natured; she was bright and charming. And when Liam had cautiously hinted that she was getting a good deal, too, that marrying a guy with an old family name and money wasn't exactly a bad thing for a woman, Bill had happily agreed.

''Everything Jessica has, Liam—her education, her career—she got on her own.'' His smile had turned soft and loving. ''It's going to be a joy to spoil her—if she lets me.''

She'd let him, Liam knew. She was, already. The rock on her finger, the expensive watch on her wrist…oh, yes, Jessica Warren would let her husband spoil her. The sad part, or maybe the good part, depending on your point of view, was that Bill's gifts would make both of them happy, he to give them and she to receive them. The question was, would the jewels, the furs, the cars, be enough to keep the lady faithful?

Liam doubted it. He knew how this particular fairy tale would end, and he was helpless to do anything about it without telling Bill the way Jessica had looked at him…and the way he'd looked at her.

A muscle ticked in Liam's jaw. He picked up a decanter of brandy and poured some into a crystal snifter.

There had to be some way to protect his oldest friend. They'd met at Princeton, where they'd made a strange pair. Bill had probably been enrolled the day he was born. Old-line money and a family that had come over on the *Mayflower* tended to do that for a man. Liam, on the other hand, was at Princeton courtesy of a glib tongue and money from the U.S. Army. His great-great-who-knew-how-many-times-great-grandfather had come to America either to escape the Irish potato famine or the long arm of the law, depending on who was telling the tale. Money and status weren't exactly part of the Malone family history.

Liam smiled.

Still, he and Bill had clicked. They'd fallen easily into an older brother, younger brother relationship, especially after Bill lost his parents in a plane crash in his sophomore year. Bill had financial consultants but it was Liam, the man of the world, who'd counseled him about Life. Bill, for his part, had saved Liam's tail more than once.

Liam had been plagued with something an endless succession of advisors had called "an attitude problem." Put simply, it meant he'd have been kicked out of college half a dozen times, if it hadn't been for Bill and his connections.

It was time to return the favor.

"It's good to see I can still read your mind at a hundred paces, Liam, my man."

Liam swung toward the door. Bill, resplendent in his morning coat and striped trousers, grinned at him.

"Can you?" Liam said, and managed a smile.

"Sure." Bill walked to where Liam stood, reached past him for the decanter and poured himself some brandy. "'What's Malone doing now?' I asked myself a minute ago." Smiling, Bill lifted his glass to Liam's. "'He's stalking around my study,' myself replied, 'fortifying himself with brandy while he works up to telling me I'm on the verge of making the biggest mistake of my life.'" Bill laughed at the look on Liam's face. "I'm right, aren't I?"

"Absolutely, as long as you've asked."

"I knew it. What else would a confirmed bachelor like you think on my wedding day?" Bill downed half his drink and grimaced. "I needed that. My stomach's been going up and down like an elevator all morning."

"Bill." Liam put down his snifter. "Look, I know you think you're in love with this girl…"

"Woman," Bill said, and grinned. "Jessica has very definite opinions on the male-female thing."

"Yes," Liam said coolly, "I'm sure she does."

"Wouldn't go out with me at all, even though we'd been working together almost a year. Said it wasn't right for a woman to date her boss."

"But you managed to change her mind."

Bill didn't seem to hear the sarcasm in Liam's tone. "I did," he said, and gave a lopsided grin. "Bet you didn't think I could talk a woman who looks like that into dating a guy like me, huh?"

Liam's brows lifted. "This isn't your first brandy today, is it?"

"It's my first in this room," Bill said, and chuckled. "Hey, you'd be edgy, too, if you were about to take a wife."

"You don't know what you're doing," Liam said bluntly, and felt better for finally having spoken the truth.

Bill sighed, sank into his favorite leather armchair and sipped his brandy. "I wondered how long it would take you to get around to that."

"Well, dammit, what choice do I have? You're about to make the biggest mistake of your life—"

"See? I even got the wording right."

"Bill, I'm serious."

"So am I, Liam. I love Jessica and she loves me."

"You know nothing about her."

"I know everything about her. I told you, she's had to make her own way in life. Her father never managed to hold on to a dime. He died when Jess was eighteen and she lost her mother only a year later. She's never been married, she has a degree in business studies—"

"You know nothing about her," Liam insisted. "You've only been dating her for, what, four months?"

"Only because she wouldn't go out with me sooner."

"Are you sleeping with her?" Liam said brusquely.

Bill blushed. "Direct, as always, Malone. Why do you want to know?"

A good question, Liam thought, and came up with what wasn't quite an answer. "It's normal for a man and woman who love each other to share a bed."

"So?"

"So, if you haven't slept with her, maybe you should consider why."

"Liam, I know you've been with a lot of women but Jessica is—"

"Different. Yes, I figured you'd say that. Look,

you have to know that there are women who use sex to snare a man.''

"Well, Jessica hasn't. Not that it's any of your business, but she hasn't slept with me yet. I haven't asked her to. She's not that kind.''

Liam snorted.

"She isn't, dammit!''

"There are all kinds of ways to use sex, Bill. Withholding it is only one of them.''

"Oh, for…'' Bill shot to his feet. "Listen to me, Liam. Jessica is about to become my wife. Keep that in mind when you talk about her.''

"Dammit, Thornton, haven't you grown up at all? You're as naive as you were when you needed me to save your skinny tail from the weird babe with the purple hair. You were certain she was the love of your life, too, remember?''

"Oh, give me a break! I was eighteen, not thirty.''

"And not much smarter, from what I can see.''

Bill's mouth thinned. "Back off, okay? I love Jessica, and she loves me.''

"What if it's your money she loves? Your name? The step up you'll give her by marrying her?''

"It isn't.'' Bill walked to Liam's side, smiled and clapped a hand lightly on his back. "She loves me for myself, hard as that may be for you to believe, considering that it's you, with your black Irish good looks, the ladies always drool over.''

''Dammit, hear me out.''

''No.'' Bill threw an arm around Liam's shoulders. ''No, for once, Malone, *you* hear *me* out. This is love. The real thing, and don't judge it by your need to bed every good-looking female in sight, or by figuring a man with a bank account is always a hostage to his money.''

Liam looked at his old friend. He thought of telling him he'd changed that attitude when he'd finally decided there were better ways to indulge a love of risk than on the fall of the cards, but then he'd have to explain more than that, and this wasn't the time to do it. Not on Bill's wedding day, and it looked as if this really was going to be his wedding day.

Hell. Maybe Bill was right. Maybe the marriage would work. The bottom line was that there was nothing more he could do, except hope he was around to help pick up the pieces if, and when, the time came.

''Liam?''

Liam looked up.

''You could, at least, try and look happy for me.''

"Sure." Liam sighed. "I hope it works out. You know that."

"It will," Bill said solemnly. "Jess is the best thing that ever happened to me. Once you get to know her, you'll think so, too. Come on, get that sour look off your face and admit the truth. You're just jealous 'cause I've found the perfect woman."

Bill smiled. Liam tried to, and wondered if he'd succeeded. "I hope you're right."

"I know I am. Now, drink up, wish me luck and then get out there and do your duty. I fielded half a dozen phone calls after the rehearsal dinner last night, every last one from a lady aching to know more about my best man."

Liam grinned. "Only half a dozen?"

"All right, a dozen." Bill grinned, too, and touched his glass to Liam's. The men finished their brandy, put down the snifters and walked to the door together. "You know how come you're such a cynic, my man? It's because the ladies let you get away with murder."

"The Malone charm," Liam said lazily. "Love 'em and leave 'em, that's me."

"Yeah, well, sooner or later, you'll meet a woman like my Jessica and you'll change your tune."

"Sure," Liam answered, because an intelligent

man always knew when it was time to admit defeat. "Maybe in the next century."

Bill laughed. "Go on out and charm the ladies."

Liam strolled through the house to the music room, where the ceremony would take place. Pink and white roses filled the air with their perfume, and strains of Vivaldi drifted from the library. A pair of bridesmaids, ethereally lovely in gowns of palest pink, flashed him welcoming smiles.

Welcoming smiles to what he knew was going to end in disaster.

Liam turned on his heel and made his way through the house and out a side door to a garden with narrow, hedge-lined paths winding through it. He'd done what he could to convince Bill he was making a mistake. He was his friend's best man, not his conscience.

From this moment on, everything was up to fate.

UPSTAIRS, in one of the guest suites of her fiancé's home—the home that would soon be hers—Jessica paced restlessly from one wall to the other.

She'd longed for a perfect wedding day, and she had one. Blue skies, bright sun, not a single cloud to obscure the silhouette of Mount Rainier on the horizon…rare things in Seattle, but then, this was a special day. She was marrying the man she loved.

"Fate has really smiled on you, Jess," her maid of honor had said just a little while ago.

It was true. Jessie had never put much stock in fate, but how else could she explain all the wonderful things that had happened in the past few months? She and William had gotten to know each other. Their mutual respect had become friendship, and friendship had become love.

Jessica looked at her reflection in the mirror and smiled. How could the day be anything less than perfect? Not just the weather but everything. The music she and William had selected. The menu they'd planned. The vows they'd written together.

I, Jessica, do solemnly vow that I will love you, William, for the rest of my life, that I will always be at your side…

Her stomach did a slow, dangerous roll.

She was nervous, that was all. And that was normal. Everybody said so, from the seamstress who'd put a couple of quick darts into her ivory satin gown to the stylist who'd plaited tiny pink tea roses into her hair. Even Carrie, her maid of honor, had said the same thing when she saw Jessie's hands trembling.

"Butterflies," Carrie had assured her. "All brides have them."

Where *was* Carrie, anyway? How long could it take to look for a bridal bouquet? Jessica glanced at the platinum-and-diamond watch William had given to her last night at the rehearsal dinner. "Something new," he'd said softly. The "something old" was the emerald-and-diamond engagement ring on her finger, which had belonged to his mother and grandmother.

The watch had caught her completely by surprise.

"Oh, it's too much," she'd blurted when she opened the long blue box and saw the wink of diamonds. William had laughed, kissed her gently and said that nothing was too much where she was concerned.

"I love you, Jess," he'd said softly.

Jessica swallowed dryly. She loved him, too. Her fiancé was a kind, generous, wonderful man and she was the luckiest woman in the world, and yes, the day really was going to be perfect...if she could just stop trembling.

"Butterflies," Jessie whispered to her image in the mirror. "All brides have them."

Was that true? She didn't know much about brides, perhaps because she'd never thought she'd be one, not after watching her mother endure a marriage to a man who'd made a mockery of the word. Jessie's father had been a handsome rogue. He couldn't stay in one place for very long or, as it turned out, be faithful to one woman, but her mother had adored him anyway.

Jessie grew up knowing she'd never be that kind of fool. Why would a woman have to be blinded by passion to fall in love? Love could be something that happened slowly and gently. That was the best way, the way that would last.

She smiled.

That was the way she'd fallen in love with William.

She'd worked for him for almost a year before he'd asked her out and even then, she'd turned him down. She knew that dating your boss was never a good idea, but he'd been gently persistent and, at last, after a late night at the office, she'd agreed to dinner. Saying no under those circumstances would have been silly. Soon they'd begun spending all their time together. When he'd proposed, saying yes had been the most natural thing in the world.

Now she was less than an hour away from becoming Mrs. William Thornton the Third. It was hard to believe it was happening.

One man, one exchange of vows, for the rest of her life. Maybe it wasn't fashionable to believe in forever-after anymore, but Jessie did. It worried her a little that she'd never yet wanted more than William's tender good-night kisses, but she was sure that would change. Given time, her skin would tingle when he touched her. Just looking at him would make her breathless. She'd feel the way she'd felt last night, when she'd first laid eyes on Liam Malone.

Jessie took a step back, felt the bed hit behind her knees and sank down on the edge of it.

"Oh, God," she whispered, and shut her eyes as if she could block out the memory. What was she doing, thinking about another man on her wedding day? She hadn't even been looking forward to meeting Liam. William had talked about him endlessly, until she'd been weary of hearing the name and the stories that went with it. How Liam traveled the world. How he made fortunes and lost them on the turn of a card. How he went through women. She'd been appalled by some of the stories, fascinated by others and aware, almost immediately, that her sweet, sensible William was wistfully envious of Liam's free and easy life.

She'd come up with a picture to go with the tall tales. Liam would be sexy as sin, gorgeous as the devil and twice as persuasive. In other words, he'd be the kind of man she most disliked.

As it turned out, she'd gotten it almost all right.

The rehearsal dinner had been in full swing; William had been holding her hand and telling her how happy they were going to be. Suddenly he'd dropped her hand, leaped from his chair and said, "Liam, my man, you made it!" She'd looked up and there, in the doorway, she'd seen Liam Malone for the very first time, exactly as she expected: tall, broad shouldered, with a handsome face, a shock of silky black hair and emerald-green eyes.

What she hadn't expected was the jolt of electricity that slammed through her when those green eyes met hers. Her heart had gone into overdrive and a pervasive heat had slipped under her skin. She'd felt all the reactions she'd sworn she'd never feel for any man, and she'd felt them for her fiancé's best friend.

She'd wanted to bolt from her chair and run. Instead, she'd torn her eyes from Liam's, stared blindly down at the table, and hoped, prayed, that the floor would open up and swallow her.

"Jessica, sweetheart," she'd heard William say, and she'd forced herself to look up and smile. William had his arm slung around Liam's shoulders and he was smiling, too, but Liam hadn't smiled at all. He'd just watched her through narrowed eyes set in a face that might have been chiseled from granite.

Somehow she'd stood up, said all the right things, extended her hand and tried not to jump at the tiny spark that leaped from Liam's fingers to hers.

"Static electricity," she'd said with a forced laugh.

"Indeed," Liam had replied, and the slightest smile had curved his mouth, a smile that said he knew exactly what she was feeling. "It's a pleasure to meet you at last, Jessica."

And that had been the end of it.

Jessie let out a breath she hadn't realized she'd been holding.

What was the matter with her? That *had* been the end of it. The moment had come and gone. Liam pulled up a chair, William settled in beside her again, and she'd listened while the two friends talked about old times. Her gaze had met Liam's once again but she'd looked quickly away and, before she knew it, the evening ended. Come stay with us, William had said, and she'd found herself fearing the answer, but Liam had thanked him politely, said he already had found a place and went off to wherever it was.

"A hostel, for all I know," William had said cheerfully, "or a penthouse. It depends on whether his luck's been good or bad."

Good, Jessie thought now, remembering the expensive cut of Liam Malone's gray suit. Or maybe bad, considering the longer-than-it-should-have-been, black-as-midnight hair that curled over his collar. She thought, too, of what William had told her, that Liam liked to gamble. Poker was his specialty, William said, but Jessie knew that women would be Liam Malone's specialty, women who were willing to trade one night in his bed for a lifetime of hot memories.

She stood up quickly and smoothed down her skirt. Where was Carrie? Better still, where was William? She needed to see him, put her hand in his, feel the warmth of his smile.

"Got 'em!"

Jessie swung around. Her maid of honor stood in the doorway, holding a bouquet of tiny pink roses, trailing baby orchids and lacy-white stephanotis in her hand.

"Would you believe the kid who delivered the flowers left your bouquet on a table in the—"

"Have you seen William?" Jessie hadn't meant to sound so shaky, but the look on Carrie's face told her she hadn't succeeded.

"What's the matter, Jess?"

"Nothing. I just want to see him, that's all."

"You can't see him. It's bad luck for the bride and the groom to see each other before the ceremony."

It was worse luck to think about another man before the ceremony, but Jessie knew better than to say that.

"That's just a silly superstition."

"Maybe, but do you really want to tempt fate?"

"No." Jessie gave a choked laugh. "That's the last thing I want to do."

"Jess." Carrie's voice softened. "Honey, I keep telling you, all brides are jittery."

"I know. And I'm not jittery. I just—I need some fresh air." Jessie gathered up her skirt so the hem wouldn't drag. "I'm going for a walk in the garden."

"What?" Carrie stared at her as if she'd lost her mind. "You can't! It's only half an hour until the ceremony."

"That's plenty of time."

"What if someone sees you?"

"Nobody will. I'll go down the back stairs."

"But—but you'll get grass stains on the hem of your gown."

"I won't. See?" Jessie hoisted the gown higher.

Carrie sighed. "Well, who am I to argue with the bride? You want to go for a walk? Fine. We'll go for a walk."

"No!" Jessie swallowed hard. "No," she said,

more calmly, "really, I need a few minutes by myself."

"It's cold outside," Carrie said worriedly. "At least take a jacket."

"It's okay," Jessie said, "I know what I'm doing."

But she didn't. And the enormity of the lie scared the life out of her.

THE GARDEN WAS QUIET. All the hullabaloo was taking place inside the house. Liam was glad he'd decided to go for a walk where he could escape the necessity for social niceties.

He felt a lot better, too. For all he knew, Bill was right. Maybe he'd misread everything. The newlyweds would settle into a pleasantly dull marriage. A couple of years down the road he'd look at Jessica and know that he'd been wrong about her.

But if he was, then what was that invitation he'd seen in her eyes last night? What would she have done if he'd taken her up on it, if he'd walked straight across the room, pulled her out of her chair and kissed her?

Slugged him, probably, because whatever else the lady was, she wasn't a fool. Bill would have slugged him, too, but at least he'd have learned if that soft, pink mouth tasted as sweet as it—

There was a whisper of sound just behind him. Liam drew a breath. Even before he turned around, he knew she'd be there.

"Miss Warren," he said with deliberate courtesy.

Her chin lifted, her cheeks pinkened. Could she possibly know what he'd been thinking?

"Mr. Malone," she said, just as courteously. "I didn't expect to find you here."

His smile didn't reach his eyes. "Is it customary for brides to wander around, alone, moments before they wed?"

"I might ask you the same question about groomsmen. What are you doing in the garden?"

Liam looked at the woman who was about to marry his best friend, into the smoky blue eyes that had haunted him through a long and sleepless night.

"Looking for you," he said, and before she could respond, he reached for her.

CHAPTER TWO

PEOPLE ALWAYS TALKED about time standing still or going too fast, but in Jessie's experience, time was more like a treadmill. It moved at a steady, predictable pace.

Now she knew she'd been wrong. Liam reached for her and time hung suspended by a silken thread. She had all the opportunity she needed to anticipate what was about to happen. He was going to take her in his arms, gather her close and kiss her. And she'd let him do it. The dreams that had kept her awake half the night because, yes, she'd dreamed of him, yes, she'd imagined this happening…those dreams would come true.

She sighed, lifted her head, closed her eyes, waited to feel the hardness of Liam Malone's body, the race of his heart…

Waited to betray William.

She took a quick step back, her hands upraised. ''No,'' she said, but it didn't stop him. Liam caught her hands, drew them down. "Liam," she said sharply, "think of William!"

He lifted his head and stared at her through eyes that were dark and hot. Slowly, like clouds receding after a storm, the wildness in his eyes faded. A shudder racked his body, and his hands fell to his sides.

"My God!" He spoke in a choked whisper. "We must be crazy."

Jessie opened her mouth, then closed it. The truth was ugly, but she couldn't deny it. She'd been a part of what had almost happened.

"Nothing happened." Panic lent her words harsh urgency. "Nothing," she repeated, as if saying it again would make it so.

"No." Liam nodded. He turned his back to her and she saw the rise and fall of his shoulders, heard the sound of breath being dragged deep into his lungs. "Nothing happened. And anyway, it didn't mean a…" He swung toward her, anger etched into his face. "The hell it didn't! I'm Bill's best man. You're his bride. And we almost went at each other like a pair of—of sex-starved teenagers. And you say, nothing happened?"

"Mr. Malone…"

"Oh, that's great. That's terrific. Another minute, we'd have been down on the grass and you're calling me 'Mr. Malone'?"

Jessie stiffened. "There's no need to be crude."

"Crude is you not remembering that you're marrying my best friend this morning."

A breeze rustled through dried autumn leaves still trapped in the hedge. Jessie shivered and wrapped her arms around herself.

"I remembered it, and so did you. That's why nothing happened."

"I came within a breath of betraying my friend. You came within inches of violating the promises you've made him. Seems to me that something happened."

The wind lifted a strand of Jessie's hair. Her hand trembled as she smoothed it back. He was right. They'd almost kissed. Pretending they hadn't wouldn't change the fact, but there had to be an explanation. She'd never hurt William. Never.

"All right." Her voice quavered. "But—but it's been a stressful week."

"Now, why didn't I think of that?" Liam said coldly. "You're stressed. I'm jet-lagged. And that makes it all…" He paused, then blew out a ragged breath. She was right. Nothing they could do would erase that one moment but, the truth was, they hadn't done anything. The best solution was to shove the memory into a dark corner and forget it was there.

"Okay. We made a mistake. Let's leave it at that."

"That's what I've been saying." Something in his eyes—contempt, perhaps, or a suggestion of it—stirred Jessie's anger. "And if you want to be specific, Mr. Malone, we didn't make a mistake. You did. I'm not the one who—who…"

"Do us both a favor, okay? Let's not waste time lying." His mouth twisted. "You and I both know what's going on here. You looked at me last night exactly the way you did a couple of minutes ago."

"I don't know what you're talking about." Jessie gathered up the skirt of her bridal gown. "And I have better things to do than stand here and talk nonsense."

"Yeah," Liam said coldly. "You have to step up to a judge, take Bill's hand and promise to love, honor and cherish till death—"

"I know the vows I'm going to take, Mr. Malone."

Liam's eyes narrowed until there was just the barest flash of green. "I thought you were all wrong for him. Now I know it."

"Is that what this—this little episode was all about? The Liam Malone quality control test?"

Jessie said, trying to keep her tone as cold and even as his.

"Bill deserves better than you. A man deserves a woman who loves him without reservation."

"And that's just the way I love William," she said heatedly. "He knows that."

"Right." Liam smiled tightly and rocked back on his heels. "I'm sure he'd agree that the last few minutes prove it."

"You can't tell him! You'd break his heart!"

"I know that. No, I won't tell him. Neither will you. You're right. Nothing happened." He paused, and a seductive softness crept into his voice. "But it could have."

Jessie knew what he was thinking. How it would have been, if they'd kissed. The mingling of breath. The taste. The feel of his arms around her, the heat of their bodies pressed together.

"This is a pointless conversation," she said, and some small part of her mind gave a brisk nod of approval that she could sound so calm when she was shaking inside. "William is waiting. The wedding—"

Liam caught her wrist as she began to turn away. "Why didn't you slap me?"

"Mr. Malone. Liam. I thought we just agreed—"

"It's a simple question. You knew what I was

about to do. How come you didn't haul off and slug me?''

"Is that how the women you come on to generally react?'' She smiled sweetly before her lips hardened into a thin, accusing line. "I don't understand how William can think of you as his best friend. You're not like him at all.''

"No,'' Liam said softly, "I'm not.''

He took a step toward her; she retreated, but the bench was behind her and she was trapped. Her heart pounded. She'd been right about Liam Malone. He was sexy as sin and gorgeous as the devil. Why hadn't she realized he'd be as dangerous as the devil, too?

"Keep away from me!''

He smiled, a quick glint of white teeth against his tanned face. "Maybe that's what appeals to you, Jessie.'' Lazily he ran a finger over her cheek. "Maybe you know there's no way you could wrap me around your little finger, or buy me off with a smile and a promise.''

"You're right. I should have slapped you. You're a horrible man.''

"I must be,'' he whispered, his fingers curling around the back of her neck, "because I'm going to finish what I started a few minutes ago. What you want, despite all your self-righteous protests.''

He watched her face as he drew her to him and told himself he was only doing this because she was twisting things, making it sound as if he were the only one who'd wanted the kiss. One whisper of dissent, just one, and he'd back off. But when she looked up at him, he saw that her eyes had gone from blue to the color of the sky just before sunrise in the mountains, and not all her protests or his excuses could keep those eyes from telling him everything he needed to know.

"Jessie," he said softly, and she sighed, tilted her head back and met his descending mouth with hers.

It was a gentle kiss, only the brush of his lips over hers. It was the kiss a man gives a woman when he knows he can never claim the taste of her again. And because the kiss was gentle, because Jessie knew that there would only be this once between them, because she could no more have stopped the rotation of the earth than rid herself of the need for it, she let it happen. She let him draw her closer, and when he did, she laid her palms flat against his chest, rose on her toes and parted her lips to his, let him slip his tongue into her mouth.

A wave of white-hot flame consumed her. She moaned, curled her fingers into the lapels of Liam's morning coat and let everything she'd spent the night dreaming about happen. His kiss was all the poets said a kiss could be. It was more. It was turning her inside out, dissolving her flesh, melting her bones. It was…

She lifted her arms, wound them around Liam's neck and stopped thinking.

The wind scurried through the garden again. Jessie trembled, but not from the cold. Liam drew her, hard, against him. His hands swept down her back, cupped her bottom, lifted her against him, into him. Sounds drifted on the air. Music from the chamber orchestra. The distant buzz of conversation.

And, from somewhere nearby, Carrie's voice.

"Jessica? Jess, where are you?"

Jessie tore her mouth from Liam's. Panic raced through her blood. "Liam!"

His arms tightened around her as she tried to pull away. "Come back here," he said thickly.

"Liam, for the love of God, someone's coming!"

He blinked, shook his head, whispered a word that might have been a blessing or an oath and stepped back, as if putting distance between them could change what had happened.

"I didn't…" He stopped, cleared his throat. "Jessie, I never meant—I never meant this to happen."

"Then—then it didn't," she said frantically. "Do you hear me? This never happened." Her lips felt dry. She touched them with the tip of her tongue, tasted Liam and felt as if she wanted to die. "William must never find out. Do you understand?"

"Dammit," Liam said harshly, "don't you think I know that? But we can't just forget. We—"

"Jess?"

Jessie spun around. Carrie stood a few feet away, staring at them. "Everyone is waiting," she said slowly. "The judge. The guests. William."

"Of course." Jessie gave in to the temptation to touch her hand to her hair. She could feel some strands that had come undone, but the wind could have done that. Only the wind. She'd simply been out here, having a pleasant chat with William's best man. Nobody had to know the truth, not ever. Nobody but Liam. And she. Oh God, she would know, she'd always know. "Certainly," she said, and smiled. "I'm ready."

Carrie cleared her throat. "I think—why don't you just let me fix your makeup, Jess? Your lipstick. And your hair. The, uh, the wind must have…" Her voice trailed away as she hurried forward and clasped Jessie's arm. "Come on up to the house, okay?" She smiled brightly. "A bride should look perfect on her wedding day. Isn't that right, Mr. Malone?''

Liam nodded. It was the best he could manage.

''Why don't you go tell William we'll just be another five minutes? He can wait that long for the woman who's going to be his for the rest of his life, don't you think?''

The message might have been subtle, but the way Jessie's maid of honor looked at him wasn't. Could what they'd done be so obvious? Liam cleared his throat and decided to see if he could get out something more than a croak.

''Yes,'' he said, ''I'm sure he can.''

''Good.'' Carrie wrapped an arm around Jessie's waist. ''Now, come on, honey. This is your big day. You don't want to spoil it.''

''No,'' Jessie said. ''No, I don't.''

Her eyes met Liam's, and the terrible secret they shared burned hot between them.

''Jess?'' Carrie said, and Jessie smiled brightly and let her maid of honor hurry her toward the house.

Liam waited until they were out of sight. Then he let out a breath that was almost a moan and ran his hands through his hair. How could he let her go? He'd only had one taste of Jessie, only held her in his arms for a moment.

''Stop it,'' he said in a harsh whisper.

He walked deeper into the garden, found a bench, sank down on it and put his face in his hands. How could he have done this? She was to be Bill's bride. Bill, who was the best friend he'd ever had. If only there were a way to wipe away what had happened.

But there wasn't. And the longer he thought about it, the more he knew that nothing could have stopped him from kissing her, or make him regret the kiss. Now he knew how soft Jessie felt. How sweet her lips were. How it was to take her sigh into his mouth as she opened to him.

How right he'd been in his assessment of her.

Damn Jessica Warren to hell, and himself along with her! How could he let her marry Bill? And yet, he had to. He couldn't tell Bill what had happened, not if saving him meant destroying him. Time slipped past as he tried to find a solution but, at last, he knew he had to admit there was none. He had to play his role in this farce. There was no other choice.

At last, Liam sat up straight. He had no idea how long he'd been sitting there but it was time to put a smile on his face and do what was expected of him.

Liam stood, smoothed down his shirt, took a couple of deep breaths.

"Liam?"

Bill was hurrying toward him, his face tense, and for one awful moment, Liam thought he'd found out what had happened. But Carrie was trotting alongside him, looking just as bad.

"What is it?"

"It's Jessica," William said. "She's—she's gone."

"What?" Liam eased an arm around Bill's shoulders, led him to a bench and sat him down. "What do you mean, she's gone?"

Carrie knelt on the grass and took Bill's hands in hers. She spoke to Liam, but her eyes never left Bill's pale face.

"She wrote a note," Carrie said, "and left it on the bed with her engagement ring and watch."

Liam shook his head. Maybe he wasn't crazy. Maybe it was the rest of the world that had gone insane. "Bill?" He squatted down beside the bench. "Talk to me. How can she be gone? Gone where?"

Bill took a piece of paper from his pocket and handed it to Liam. "You can see how upset she must have been," he said shakily. "Just look at how she scrawled the words."

Upset? Oh, yes, Liam thought as he took the note, yes, indeed, the lady would have been upset. Beside herself, was more like it, afraid—no, terrified—that he'd break his promise and tell Bill what had happened.

Dearest William: I'm sorry. So terribly sorry. You're a wonderful man. A fine man. That's why I can't marry you. You deserve more than I can ever give you. Forgive me, please.

He read the note again and again, until anguish blurred both his anger and the words Jessie had written. He had done this. He'd given in to a moment's desire and this was the result.

Slowly Liam rose to his feet.

"Carrie? You took Jessie back to the house. What happened after that?"

"I started to fix her hair, but she said she wanted to do it herself. She asked me to go downstairs and make sure everything was ready. When I got back, she was gone." Carrie gave Liam a look filled with loathing and accusation. "She was fine before she went out to the garden. Just bridal jitters, that was all. She was fine!"

Liam nodded. There was a bitter taste in his mouth. He'd come back to Seattle to join in a happy celebration. Instead, he'd kissed a woman who wasn't his to kiss, and now his best friend was behaving as if his life had ended. Like it or not, he knew what he had to do.

"Bill?" He squatted down again, put a hand on Bill's knee. "Bill, you have to go after her."

"Go where?" Bill looked up, his face tear-stained. "She gave up her apartment when I asked her to move into the guest suite here."

"Well, what about family? Friends?"

"Jessica has no family. And her friends are all here, at the…in the house."

"Call the police," Carrie said. "Hire a private detective."

"No. No, I can't do that. Jess isn't a fugitive. She's my fiancée and if she's run away, it has to be my fault. I must have done something to make her—"

"You didn't," Liam said, so sharply that Bill stared at him. "I mean, there's no reason to think that. You'd know if you'd done something to drive her away."

"The only thing I know is that I have to get her back." Bill clamped his lips together, bowed his head. Seconds passed before he looked up again. "Liam? You have to find her for me."

Liam shot to his feet. "No. Not me."

Bill stood up slowly, looking as if he'd aged five years in the past five minutes. "She'd run if she saw me. She has no reason to run from you."

"Bill," Liam said, "Bill, please—"

"And you know something about running

away. You used to talk about it, remember? About how you'd run away all those times when you were a kid?''

''Yeah, but that was—''

''Let's be honest, okay? I'm—what's that phrase of yours? I'm a desk jockey. If I were going to run away, I'd probably tuck a couple of credit cards in my pocket and ring for the chauffeur to bring the car around.'' Bill gripped Liam's arm. ''I'm afraid for her. I can't imagine where she'll go. Carrie says she didn't even change her clothes or take anything with her. What will she do for money?''

''She took her car,'' Carrie offered excitedly. ''A white Civic. It's not in the driveway anymore.''

''Well, then, she'll drive until she runs out of gas.''

''Who knows where she'll be by then?'' Bill's hand dug into Liam's flesh. ''I'm begging you, man. You're like a brother to me, you know that. You've got to do it.''

There'd been times in Liam's life when he hadn't much liked himself. He'd thought that those times were all behind him. But as he looked into the pleading eyes of his oldest friend, he knew he'd never hated himself as much as he did at this moment.

"All right," he said slowly, "I'll find her for you."

Bill expelled a breath. "Thank you."

"Don't thank me until this is over."

"I know you, Liam." Bill put out his hand. "You'll find my Jessica, and you'll do the right thing."

Liam looked at his oldest friend's outstretched hand, clasped it and forced a smile to his lips. "I'll do the right thing," he said softly. "I promise you that."

CHAPTER THREE

LIAM SAT BEHIND THE WHEEL of his rented Corvette as Bill leaned through the open window.

"Call me as soon as you find her, okay?"

"Look, I can't guarantee—"

"Tell her I love her, that whatever's wrong, we can work things out." He gripped Liam's shoulder. "I don't know how to thank you, man."

"Don't," Liam said quickly. "Not until I've brought Jessie back."

"Jessica." Bill's voice broke. "Her name is—"

"Sure." Liam shifted into gear. "I'll be in touch."

Bill said something else but Liam didn't wait to hear it. He stepped on the gas and the Vette's tires squealed as he shot down the long driveway. Another couple of minutes listening to Bill talk about Jessie and how he couldn't think of a reason in the world she'd have done this, and he'd have blurted out the truth.

"I know the reason," he'd have said. "It's because I violated our friendship and my principles over a woman I don't even know."

"Hell," he said softly, and clamped his hands more tightly on the steering wheel. If there was one thing he'd learned, it was that there was no percentage in reliving the past. You made a mistake, you set it right and you moved on. That was exactly what he was going to do. Find Jessie, make her see reason, return her to Bill and move on.

He drove fast, slipping in and out of traffic, heading for his hotel so he could trade his morning coat and striped trousers for something that wouldn't make him stand out in a crowd. The only thing as noticeable as a woman driving around in a bridal gown would be a man pursuing her rigged out in a silly suit. Besides, who knew what story Jessie might tell if people asked for explanations? The last thing he needed was interference from some helpful soul who might take him for the groom she was fleeing.

Liam dressed quickly, trading his formal wear for faded jeans, an ancient Princeton Tigers sweatshirt, sneakers and a leather bomber jacket he'd had so long that it felt like an old friend. Then he got into the Vette, doubled back toward Lake Washington and got on the road Jessie would have taken. An excited guest had told him she'd headed toward the city, but where would she go? No apartment, no credit cards, no cash…well, not exactly. Carrie had remembered that Jessie kept a fifty-dollar bill and her driver's license in the glove compartment of her car.

"Mad money, she called it," Carrie had explained, while Bill clutched her hand like a lifeline. "I always told her that was just making it easy for a thief, but—"

"It's okay," Liam had replied. "She won't get far on fifty bucks."

Now he tried putting himself in Jessie's place. What would she use the money for? Like him, she'd want to get out of that bridal regalia. And she'd want a place to go to ground, but in a city like Seattle, how could anybody afford clothes and a hotel room on fifty bucks? That was the question, although the bigger one was what he could possibly do or say when he found her to make her see that kiss for what it really was.

Liam glanced in his mirror, gave the Vette a little more gas and switched lanes.

It was simple, really. What had happened between them was lust. That good old male-female, down-and-dirty,   I-want-to-get-you-between-the-sheets thing called lust. They'd been sexually attracted to each other, she'd been all nerves, and he'd taken advantage. End of story.

He wasn't a gentleman like Bill. And he couldn't let a moment's stupidity and weakness on his part ruin what Bill wanted. A wife, a couple of kids, a dog and a cat.

Some people were made for fairy tales.

Liam looked at the speedometer and eased his foot off the gas. He was driving too fast, and he could just imagine trying to explain this to a cop.

''Well, you see, Officer, I came on to my best friend's bride maybe ten minutes before the ceremony, and she ran away.''

Oh, yeah. That would go over big.

Dammit, where had she gone? Forget the change of clothes. She was upset, probably close to hysterics by now. Her first priority would be a hotel room, but without money…

A horn blared as Liam shot across two lanes of traffic and made for the exit ramp. He looked in the mirror, saw the guy he'd cut off tell him what he thought with a universal gesture, and fought back the urge to respond. The guy was right. There was no need to be angry at him. Jessie, dammit, she was the one who'd made him lose control, made a mountain out of a molehill, ruined what should have been the best day of Bill's life, and for what?

"For a kiss," Liam said, with a snort of disbelief. Just a kiss. Just a moment torn out of time, when he'd held her in his arms and never wanted to let her go....

There she was!

He stood on the brakes, made a hard turn into a lot dominated by a huge Kmart, and brought the car to a jolting stop. A slender figure in ivory satin, little pink roses braided into her honey-gold hair, was marching—there was no other word for it—straight toward the store entrance, her satin train sweeping behind her.

Liam eased the car forward a safe distance, pulled into a space, shut off the engine and watched. Someplace between her car and the door, she'd picked up a gaggle of followers. Kids, a few housewives, a guy in coveralls, all of them shuffling after her, grinning at each other, peering around as if they suspected they might be on *Candid Camera*. Well, he couldn't blame them. A bride in full regalia, going into a store that sold everything from aspirin to zippers, was definitely not an everyday sight, even in a city as sophisticated as Seattle.

Jessie had to know she was drawing a crowd, but her chin was up and her spine was as straight as it had been when she'd faced him down in the garden.

He got out of the car, pocketed his keys and started after her. He knew he'd have to approach her with caution. She might bolt or even scream. Given the insanity of the world, he'd probably end up trying to convince the crowd and then the cops that he wasn't a mugger or worse. So he followed her into the store at a discreet distance and asked himself what a bride on the run could possibly want in a Kmart?

Everything, it turned out.

Jessie grabbed a shopping cart and sailed down the aisles. Her cheeks glowed with color, so he knew she wasn't as oblivious to the gawkers as she tried to appear. She moved from counter to rack, snatching things only when there was a sale sign on view and dumping them into her cart. Jeans. A T-shirt. A desperately ugly lime-green nylon jacket whose claim to fame had to be the big sign that said not just Sale but Fifty Percent Off. She added a pair of sneakers to the stack, a tote bag, a toothbrush and things he'd always thought of as female survival gear.

Finally she headed for the register.

Liam hung back, observing her from behind a display that advertised a Blue Light Special on dinnerware. The clerk rang the items up, Jessie handed over a bill and got back only a couple of coins. Goodbye cheap motel room. He started forward as she scooped her packages from the cart, but she reversed direction so fast he almost stumbled as he scooted back behind the dinnerware.

When it was safe, he followed.

She led him straight to the rest rooms and disappeared into the ladies' lounge. He leaned against a counter a couple of aisles over, folded his arms, crossed his ankles, looked down at his feet like any other guy, bored as he waited for the missus. Obviously, she was going to change her clothes, but then what? Maybe Carrie was wrong, and she had more than fifty bucks.

The minutes dragged by. Jessie's followers wandered off. Liam shifted his weight, unfolded his arms, tucked his hands into the pockets of his jeans and planned his next move....

And then the door to the ladies' room opened, and all coherent thought flew away.

Bill Thornton's bride was gone. Proper, elegant Jessica had been replaced by Jessie, a woman ready to try anything, the quicksilver woman Liam had sensed was inside her from the beginning.

She'd stripped the roses from her hair and brushed it out so that it hung in honey-colored waves down her back. She was wearing the clothing he'd watched her buy, even the ugly lime-green jacket. But it didn't seem ugly now. As

Liam looked at her, at that face scrubbed clean of makeup and artifice, he knew, with gut-wrenching certainty, that everything he'd been telling himself was a lie.

He wanted Jessie still, wanted her in a way that frightened him. When she lifted her head and saw him, she suddenly stiffened. But what he read in her eyes in that single, unguarded moment told him that she wanted him in exactly the same way.

She turned and ran.

Liam went after her, let her keep her lead through the store, through the parking lot, picking up his pace only when she neared her car. Then he caught her by the elbow and swung her toward him.

She swatted at him with both hands. "Let me go," she panted. "Damn you, Liam—"

"Jessie." He clasped her wrists, gripped them tightly, held her hands captive against his chest. "Jessie, listen to me."

"What for? Haven't you done enough?"

He hadn't. He'd only kissed her once, held her once, but that wasn't why he was here. He'd come after her for Bill. She belonged to Bill.

"Forget what happened," he said gruffly. "It's history."

"History?" She laughed. "We were climbing all over each other five minutes before I was sup-

posed to say 'I do,' and you say that's history?''
Angrily she jerked against his hands. ''Maybe you
can forget what we did, but I can't.''

''Of course you can. Okay, we did something
neither of us is proud of, but—''

''I'd never be able to look at William again
without thinking of how I betrayed him.''

''Dammit, we all make mistakes.''

''Yes,'' she said coldly, ''but not all of us are
so callous that we can pretend they didn't happen.''

Liam let go of her. ''Bill wants you back.''

''Well, I'm not going back.''

''You have to! Otherwise—''

''Otherwise, what?'' She smiled thinly.
''You'll have to admit to your part in this mess?''

''This has nothing to do with me,'' Liam said
quickly.

''Oh, give me a break.'' Jessie's eyes narrowed. ''You're no better than I am. You decided
to find me and fast-talk me into going back to
William so you wouldn't have to live the rest of
your life dodging the sight of yourself in mir-
rors.'' Her mouth twisted. ''Spare me the lies,
Liam. This has everything to do with you.''

He stepped forward, his eyes hard and cold.
''Okay. I'm not proud of what I did, but I'm not

the one who decided to handle it by running away and leaving Bill at the altar.''

Jessie's face fell. ''Was he—was he very upset?''

''Was he…'' Liam laughed. ''Hell, no. The woman he loves leaves him a note and takes off just before she's supposed to become his wife. Why would he be upset?''

''I didn't want to hurt him,'' she whispered. ''I'd have done anything—''

''Anything but go through with the wedding.''

''How can you say that to me, damn you?'' Her face lifted, and there was the glitter of tears in her eyes. ''He's your friend. Do you really want him to marry a woman who—who was in another man's arms right before the ceremony?''

Not another man's, Liam thought. *My arms. Mine….*

''There's no point in ruining Bill's life because of a moment's stupidity,'' he said gruffly.

Jessie stared at him. Then she swung away and unlocked the door to her car. ''And what about my life?'' Her voice broke. ''Did you ever think of that?''

''Dammit!'' Liam grabbed her and turned her toward him. ''You love him. You said so. What am I supposed to say, huh? 'Bill, look, maybe it's better all around if the wedding's off?' ''

"Say whatever you like. Just—just don't break his heart by telling him the truth."

"Look, let's start again, okay? Bill asked me to find you, and to ask you to come back to him."

"Why didn't he come himself? Oh, don't bother answering. William knows you're a master at convincing women to do things they don't want to do."

"Fine. That's how you want to play it?" A muscle knotted in his jaw. "I'll take the responsibility. All of it, if that makes you feel better. What happened was my fault."

"It was! I certainly wouldn't have…" Jessie hesitated. "No. It wasn't. I wanted you to kiss me, Liam. I thought about what it would be like, all last night."

"Don't say that," Liam said quickly, trying not to think about the rush of pleasure he felt hearing her confession.

"Why shouldn't I? I can't tell William the truth, but I'm tired of lying to myself." Her voice wobbled again but her gaze was steady. "You're right. We made a mistake. Period. End of story— except that mistake made me face something I think I've known for weeks. I'm not right for William or maybe—maybe he's not right for me. Either way, I'm not going to marry him. Tell him I wish him all the best. Tell him…" Tears filled her eyes. "Oh, God," she whispered, "I'm so ashamed."

Liam didn't think. He reached out and Jessie went into his embrace as if she'd been born for no other reason.

He held her close, his face buried in her hair, his body warmed by hers. She wept softly, her face in the hollow of his throat, and he whispered to her, words he'd never even thought to use with another woman, words of comfort, of solace, and gradually her tears lessened.

"Liam," she said, and he felt as if a hand were reaching into his chest and closing around his heart.

She pulled back in his arms and looked up at him. Her eyes were tear dampened and swollen. He kept one arm around her, dug in his jeans' pocket, took out a folded white handkerchief, dabbed at her eyes, then held it to her nose.

"Blow," he said gently. She smiled a little and did as he'd asked, and he laid his hand against her cheek, threaded his fingers into her hair and tilted her face to his.

"I can't marry William."

Liam wanted to tell her that she could, but the words caught in his throat. A woman wasn't supposed to weep like this on her wedding day. He'd already made one wrong judgment, thinking she was after Bill's name and money, and he'd be damned if he wanted to make another.

"He's a wonderful man. And I love him, but not the way I should. I didn't realize that, Liam. I swear I didn't."

He nodded. He knew that, too.

Jessie gave a shuddering sigh. "Tell him I'll be fine. He mustn't worry about me. And tell him I'll get in touch with him, once I—once I get my head together."

"Come back with me. Tell him yourself."

She shook her head and moved out of his arms. "I can't. Not yet. If I did he might realize...he might see..." She opened the door of her car and got behind the wheel. "Goodbye, Liam."

"No," he said, "Jessie, wait—"

She moved quickly, heard his hands slap against the car as she put it in gear, and then she was moving and he was running across the lot. Seconds later, a shiny black Corvette was on her tail and she choked back a spurt of hysterical laughter. What else would Liam Malone drive, except for a car that was sexy and fast?

She drove recklessly, tossing aside her usual caution, but his car followed hers like a shadow. A horn blared. Jessie looked to her left, saw a white-faced driver shake a fist at her. Chagrined, she realized she was endangering everybody on the road, and she slowed her car. There was no reason to drive so fast. What was she running from? Liam? That was ridiculous. He couldn't make her do anything she didn't want to do.

Yes, he can, a sly little voice whispered inside her head. *All he has to do is kiss you, and you're lost.*

No, she wasn't. She'd never been the kind of woman whose head could be turned by a handsome man.

Well, then, the voice said, even more slyly, *maybe you're running from yourself.*

That was even crazier. Just because she'd turned to jelly in Liam's arms, just because he was all the dangerous things Bill wasn't, things she'd spent her life trying to avoid....

She had a plan. Maybe it wasn't great. Still, without money or credit, she had only one place to go where she could marshal her thoughts, and one way to get there.

Liam was right behind her as she took the exit ramp, but it didn't matter. She'd left her groom, her wedding and her carefully planned life. Now she'd leave the man who'd made her realize that she didn't want any of those things. If she had, she'd never have been unfaithful to William and yes, that was what she'd been, unfaithful, kissing a stranger, wanting him, still wanting him....

Jessie swiped at her eyes with the back of her hand, drove into the airport and pulled into the first parking spot she saw. Liam did the same thing. He was behind her as she locked her door and started briskly toward the AmericAir terminal.

"Jessie!" His footsteps pounded after her. "Jessie!"

He caught up to her, clasped her arm. She wrenched it free.

"Leave me alone, Liam."

"Do you think I'm just going to let you run away? We have to talk."

The terminal doors slid open. She stepped inside, walked to a departure board, checked it. If she remembered correctly, there'd been a morning flight to Miami as well as the one she and William had planned to take. Yes, there it was, Flight 937, leaving from gate twelve. With luck, she could swap her ticket and get on this plane. But there wasn't much time. She picked up her pace, almost stumbled when Liam did a quick two-step to get in front of her.

"You can't solve anything by running away from it."

She moved around him, dumped her tote bag on the conveyor belt at the security checkpoint and went through the gate with Liam right behind her. When she heard the buzzer go off, she heaved a sigh of relief.

Goodbye, Liam, she thought, and blinked back the tears that welled in her eyes again.

"Sir?" said a polite voice. "Would you empty your pockets, please?"

Liam bit back a groan, dumped his change into a receptacle and watched as Jessie merged with the crowd. By the time he started after her, she'd disappeared. He moved quickly from one gate to the next. She could be anywhere by now. If only he had some idea…

There she was, at the information desk at gate twelve. Liam looked at the sign behind the desk. Flight 937 to Miami, it said. Departing at 10:45. He looked at his watch. It was 10:15. Not that it mattered. Jessie wasn't going anywhere, not without a ticket. But she was. Everything clicked into place. No cash, no credit card needed, not if she'd made all her arrangements via the Internet. With luck, she could even switch to an earlier departure.

"Where are you guys going on your honeymoon?" he'd asked last night, as he'd tried to make conversation and get his mind off Bill's fiancée.

"Florida," Bill had replied with a quick smile at Jessie. "Hibiscus Key. Well—" he'd blushed

"—actually, it's a place called Couples' Cove."
He'd looped his arm lightly around Jessie's shoulders. "Jessica made the arrangements. She makes
all my travel plans on the computer, don't you,
dear?"

And Jessie had torn her eyes from Liam,
cleared her throat and said yes, yes, she did, and
they'd continued with some meaningless chitchat.

Liam swung away and ran through the terminal
to the AmericAir ticket counter while he dug his
cell phone from his pocket. There were two people ahead of him. "Emergency," he said, and
stepped quickly to the head of the line as he
punched in Bill's number.

"Hello?"

It was Carrie's voice. "Put Bill on," Liam said
curtly.

"He's resting. I hate to wake him, Mr. Malone.
He's had such a bad—"

"Give him a message. Tell him…" He looked
up. The ticket clerk was staring at him, eyebrows
raised. "Hang on," he said, and hit the mute button. "One seat, Flight 937 to Miami." He dug in
his pocket, took out his driver's license and his
credit card, handed them over. "Charge the ticket,
and there's my photo ID."

"Coach or first class?"

"First class. Look, pal, the flight's going to be boarding in—"

"It's already boarding, sir. If fact, I don't know if I can—"

"Just do it," Liam said tersely, and put the phone to his ear. "Carrie? Tell Bill… Tell him I…" Liam watched as the clerk began typing his ticket. Jessie was on that plane. She was leaving Seattle, putting three thousand miles between them. "Tell him that I've found Jessie. She's at the airport, and she's fine, and—" And what? "Tell him I'll be in touch," he said, and hit the disconnect button as the clerk handed him his ticket.

The attendant was just closing the door that led to the boarding ramp as Liam sprinted through the gate. "Wait," he yelled. "That's my flight."

The attendant opened the door and reached for the phone. "Talk about cutting it close—"

He thundered down the ramp to the plane. The flight attendant greeted him with a smile.

"Just about missed it," she said brightly.

He nodded, struggled to catch his breath. "Yeah," he said—and then he saw Jessie, sitting by the window, alone in the last row of the first-class cabin. She looked up and saw him, and for the first time in his life, Liam knew what people meant when they said they were terrified, because that was how he felt now, scared right through to the marrow of his bones.

His eyes never left hers as he walked down the aisle. ''I almost missed the flight,'' he said softly when he reached her. ''I probably could have bluffed my way into picking up Bill's ticket and using it, but I didn't want to.''

Jessie touched the tip of her tongue to her bottom lip. ''Why not?''

''Because I'm not standing in for Bill, or speaking for him. Not anymore. Do you understand that?''

Her mouth trembled as Liam sat down and took her hand. ''Yes,'' she whispered. ''Oh, yes, I understand.''

Liam took Jessie's face in his hands. This time, when their lips met, it was in a kiss so tender that it almost turned him inside out.

CHAPTER FOUR

THE SEAT BELT SIGN BLINKED OFF when the plane reached cruising altitude.

Liam looked at Jessie. The softness of her smile, the undisguised joy with which she'd greeted him, were gone. Instead, she stared straight ahead, features rigid, face pale, her hand turning to ice in his.

"Jessie," he said, and she looked at him, her eyes wide with a fear he could only guess at.

He wanted to gather her into his embrace. He'd always liked having a woman in his arms, in bed or on a dance floor, but women in need of soothing made him feel clumsy. That wasn't how he felt now. He wanted to hold her, not to kiss her but to comfort her, warm her, rock her against him as if she'd just awakened from a bad dream and only he could chase away the demons.

"It's a long flight," he said to ease the tension.

She gave him a strained smile. "I know. Almost five and a half hours."

Liam cleared his throat. "How about some wine? Or some coffee? I can ask the flight attendant to—"

"No, I'm fine."

She wasn't. The shadows under her eyes looked like bruises and he fought back the desire to press his mouth to that tender skin, to draw her close.

"Well," he said briskly, "I think I'm going to read for a while." He let go of her hand and fumbled in the pocket of the seat in front of him. "Sometimes these airline magazines are pretty interesting."

Airline magazines were interesting? He was running away with his best friend's fiancée, he ached with the need to make love to her, and now he was going to bury his nose in a magazine?

Damn right, he was. Otherwise, he was going to take her in his arms and say things he didn't believe in, things he'd never imagined ever saying to any woman, much less one who belonged to Bill.

"Let me know if you need anything," he said, as brightly as a waiter hoping for a big tip. Then he whipped open the magazine and pretended that the print wasn't one enormous gray blur.

JESSIE STARED OUT HER WINDOW.

Liam was reading. Reading, she thought, and

clamped her lips together so hard her jaw hurt. He'd turned her life inside out, made her run away from her wedding, followed her through half of Seattle and onto a plane headed for the other side of the continent, and now he was sitting next to her, engrossed in a stupid magazine.

It was hard to know who she despised more, herself for letting him ruin her life or him for doing it.

"Excuse me," she said coldly, and shot to her feet. Liam looked up, his brows lifted as if he'd never seen her before. "I have to go to the bathroom," she said, even more coldly, and he rose so she could march past him. It seemed like a good move, but it turned out that her timing was rotten. She was halfway up the aisle when a man in the first row stood up and went into the lavatory.

Jessie blew out a breath, folded her arms and leaned back against the bulkhead. Perfect. He was the only other passenger in first class, and he'd made it to the bathroom ahead of her. Well, why not? The entire morning had been perfect, starting with the moment she'd been stupid enough to think she didn't want to go through with the wedding, stupid enough to think the rush of lust Liam Malone had stirred in her blood was anywhere near as important as the love she felt for William.

As for what she'd felt when she saw Liam board the plane—what she'd thought she'd felt—that had been nothing but surprise.

She glanced at her watch, frowned and looked balefully at the Occupied sign on the lavatory door. What was taking so long? Airplane bathrooms were little more than high-tech closets, first class or not. She wanted to splash some cold water in her eyes, think about the best way to tell Liam that she'd changed her mind, thank you very much, but she wasn't going to Hibiscus Key with him.

Did he really think she'd let him take William's place in their honeymoon bed?

The door to the lavatory opened. The man who'd been inside stepped out. He smiled. Jessie glared and moved into the narrow space. The guy's cologne engulfed her. William wore cologne, too. She'd thought she'd liked the smell—it seemed masculine and fresh—until Liam had taken her in his arms. He didn't seem to wear any cologne at all. He smelled of things she couldn't quite put her finger on. Soap, maybe, and fresh air and leather. And of himself. Pure male, intriguing, sexy...

''Oh, stop it,'' she said through her teeth.

Scowling, she locked the door, then met her reflection in the mirror. It wasn't a happy moment. The lime-green jacket had been cheap, but it was ugly as sin. The rest of her wasn't much better. Brushing the gel from her hair had left it an unruly mess. Her face was as shiny as a polished apple. Her nose was pink, her eyelids swollen. How Liam could still want her was...

Not that it mattered.

Her scowl deepened as she turned on the water, scooped it onto her face, then dried off with a towel. Who cared what she looked like, or whether or not Liam wanted her? She'd been crazy to run, crazy to think she wanted him, crazy to—

There was a tap at the lavatory door. What was with people, anyway? Occupied meant exactly that.

The tap came again.

"Just a minute," she said irritably. She balled up the towel, dumped it, took a deep breath and undid the bolt.

Liam stepped inside the narrow little room. Jessie stumbled back as he shut and locked the door.

"Are you crazy? Liam, dammit, what are you doing? You can't—"

"Just shut up," he snapped, "just shut the hell—" His arms went around her and his mouth came down, hard, on hers.

He *was* crazy. And so was she, because the

instant she felt his lips on hers, she moaned, threw her arms around his neck and kissed him back. He groaned, spread his hands over her hips, pulled her against him and slid his tongue into her mouth. Jessie whimpered, arched against him and he whispered her name, slid his hands inside her jacket, under her T-shirt, and cupped her breasts. She fell back against the sink as he ran his thumbs over her nipples.

"Liam. Oh, Liam."

For one wild, wonderful moment, they were lost in passion. Then Liam tore his mouth from Jessie's, put his hands on her waist and leaned his forehead against hers.

No way was he going to take her like this. Not the first time. He wasn't even sure how he'd gotten into the lavatory. He certainly hadn't planned it. One minute he'd been sitting there, telling himself he really was interested in reading a review of a new Miami restaurant and the next, he'd looked up, asked himself why he was acting as if he was on an unimportant flight when he knew, dammit, knew, that this was the most important flight of his life. He'd shot to his feet and headed for the locked door and the woman behind it without really knowing why he was going after her or what he'd do when he got there. But when she opened the door, he knew he was there to hold her and taste her and remind them both that what had started in that garden was too powerful to deny.

She was looking at him now, a smile trembling on her mouth, and he sensed, without having to ask, that her anger had come from the same place as his fake disinterest. He sensed, too, that whatever was happening between them had never happened before, not to any man or woman on the planet.

"Jessie."

Her smile broadened. It lit her face, even her eyes, and he felt his lips curve in response.

"Liam?"

"I know what you're thinking."

She laughed. She blushed, too, and he realized he'd never seen a woman blush before, not quite like that, as if she really meant it.

"I know what you're thinking, too," she said.

Hell, she was really something. He wanted to kiss her again but he knew it would be a mistake. It was difficult enough to just stand here without taking her in his arms and finishing what they'd started.

"I didn't mean that." He grinned and stepped back the inch the cramped space permitted. "I mean, yeah, that's what I'm thinking, but—" he took a deep breath ''—you're thinking you did the wrong thing.''

Her smile faded. ''Yes.''

''That you shouldn't have run away.''

''Maybe,'' she said in a little whisper.

''You're thinking you know Bill and you don't know a damn thing about me, and that you've never done anything so crazy in your life.''

He saw her try to smile again, but she couldn't quite pull it off. ''Yes and yes,'' she said, her eyes lifting to his.

''Well, neither have I.'' He reached out, tucked her hair behind her ears, smoothed down the collar of her lime-green jacket. Then he looped his hands loosely behind her neck and leaned his forehead against hers again. ''I've never run away with a woman.''

''Never?''

Liam shook his head. ''I've done a lot of things on impulse, but nothing like this.''

''I thought—I mean…'' She licked her lips. ''William always talks about how—how successful you are with women. And I just figured—''

''That I swoop in, snatch one, and carry her off when the mood's on me?'' This time, she really did smile and he kissed her gently, capturing her only with the kiss. ''This is a first for me,'' he said softly. ''I wanted you to know that.''

She nodded. "Thank you for telling me."

Her tone was solemn. Liam took the edges of her jacket and drew her close. "You're welcome," he said, just as solemnly. "You should know another thing, too." He looked into her eyes. "We're not going to Hibiscus Key."

"We're not?"

He shook his head. "I know a place off the Florida coast. Flamingo Island. It's beautiful. White sand beaches, bright emerald water, soft blue sky, privacy so complete you'll think we've gone back to the Garden of Eden and that we're Adam and Eve."

"Ah," Jessie said with a smile she hoped didn't show what she was feeling. "A personal recommendation from Adam himself."

Liam had been there, all right. He thought of explaining how and why, decided this wasn't the time, and shook his head. "Only on business, sweetheart. Never with a woman."

"I didn't ask."

"You didn't have to." He framed her face in his hands, lifted it to him. "Everything about the next few days is going to be a first, Jess. For you, for me...for us."

The next few days. Well, he'd told her what he expected and she had to admire him for his honesty. William had offered forever, but that had been love. This was lust. She knew it, Liam knew it, and it was silly to pretend it was anything else.

"Jessie? Will you go there with me?"

She lifted her head and in that terrible, wonderful moment when their eyes met, she knew that she'd go anywhere with him, if he asked, that she would stay with him, if he asked.

"That sounds…" She smiled. "It sounds wonderful."

Liam kissed her. Then he unlocked the lavatory door and stepped into the cabin.

"The coast's clear," he whispered.

It was true. Nobody was watching them. The flight attendant wasn't in sight, and the man in the front row was sound asleep. Still, Jessie didn't take an easy breath until she was seated beside Liam again, safe in the protective curve of his arm. He drew a blanket over them, tucked it in and brought her head to his shoulder. It felt as if they were in a cocoon, with the rest of the world locked away.

"Close your eyes," he said. "See if you can get some rest."

She nodded and burrowed closer. She was exhausted, but she was too wired to sleep. So much had happened. She'd done things she'd never have believed herself capable of doing. Her life seemed to be spinning out of control and she still couldn't decide if that was terrifying or exhilarating. All she knew was that she'd never felt more alive than she did now. And she felt safe with Liam's arm around her, but how could that be? Nothing about him was safe. He was everything she'd avoided, everything she'd been afraid to want.

Maybe there were times it was best not to think too much about what you were doing.

Maybe this was one of those times.

NIGHT HAD FALLEN by the time they landed in Miami.

Liam told her he'd made some calls while she slept. Everything was ready for them, he said, holding her hand as he led her through the terminal.

She caught people looking at them. Why wouldn't they? Liam was so handsome. *Gorgeous* was the word. And she was probably glowing with excitement. It was hard to remember how frightened she'd been a few hours ago. She gave a soft laugh, and Liam looked at her and smiled.

"What?"

"Nothing. I just—I can't believe this is me. I mean, I never…" Jessie hesitated. "It's awful, isn't it? That this feels so right when William—"

"Don't think about Bill," Liam said quickly. "Not tonight."

He was right, Jessie told herself as she waited near the cash register in a brightly lit terminal gift shop. "I need some stuff," Liam had told her, and she'd nodded, knowing he meant things like a toothbrush, knowing he'd probably also meant condoms, but trying her best not to think about it. Not that she didn't want him to buy condoms. She was glad he saw that as his responsibility. The problem was, she could feel her nerves starting to take over again, feel the anticipation giving way to wariness.

Any second now, she half expected her conscience would demand to know if she had any idea at all of what she was doing.

She did. And she was going to do it anyway.

Liam caught her eye and smiled as he headed for the register. She smiled back, tried not to think about the condoms, looked down at the counter and the cheap souvenirs arrayed on it. She picked up a plastic alligator boasting a mouthful of teeth and an articulated tail, toyed with it, put it down, picked up a small plastic globe that held a bright green palm tree standing on white sand, set against a tropical cardboard sea. She tilted the globe and the sand turned the placid scene into a hurricane.

"Would you like that?" Liam said, and she looked up to find him standing close beside her.

"No." She gave a little laugh, put the globe down. "I mean, it's just silly, but..." Her voice trailed off. "Well," she said briskly, "did you get everything you needed?" Color flew into her cheeks. "I mean—"

"Everything I need, for now," he said easily. "There are shops at the place we're going to. We can take care of the rest tomorrow."

"Fine," she said, even more briskly. "I won't be able to pay you back until after I return to— until I can get to my bank again."

"Jess."

"Hmm?"

"What's the matter?"

"Nothing. Why would you think—"

Liam picked up the little plastic globe. "You were looking at this thing as if it were a crystal ball."

"Was I?" She tried to smile, didn't quite make it and shrugged her shoulders instead. "It's just weird, that's all. I mean, one minute, the scene inside is so peaceful. Then you just give it a little tilt and it's as if this storm comes along and sweeps everything away." To her horror, her voice suddenly quavered. "It's frightening. That the world can tilt and your whole life can change in the blink of an eye.''

''Let the world tilt,'' Liam said softly. He put his arm around her, drew her against his side. ''I promise, I'll keep you safe.''

THE PLANE THAT AWAITED THEM was small, and they were the only passengers. It lifted into a black sky hung with a huge ivory moon. Ivory, like the color of her wedding gown, Jessie thought, and shivered.

Liam shrugged off his leather jacket and draped it around her shoulders. He put his lips to her ear so she'd hear him over the roar of the engine. ''Cold?''

''A little.'' She hesitated, then put her mouth to his ear. ''How far is it to—what did you call this place?''

Her breath tickled his skin, her fragrance rose to his nostrils. Liam closed his eyes, told himself to take a couple of deep breaths when what he really wanted was to take a fistful of her hair and bury his face in it. But that would only make her more skittish than she already was. Jessie was vibrating like a tuning fork and only an idiot wouldn't have realized that she was having second and third and fourth thoughts. The last thing he wanted to do was rush her, or let her see how much trouble he was having hanging on to his self-control. He never lost control. Never. And that was all he'd done today, all he'd done since last night.

He sat up straight and cleared his throat.

"Flamingo Island," he said calmly. "I'll let you know when it comes into view."

When he did, Jessie looked out the window. All she could see was a glow in an otherwise inky sea. The plane circled, began its descent, touched down lightly. Liam thanked the pilot, climbed out, helped her down and led her to a canopied Jeep waiting in the short grass alongside the runway. The driver greeted him by name as they climbed into the back seat, and they set off.

"You won't be able to see much in the dark," Liam said, putting his arm around her shoulders. "I'll take you for a tour tomorrow. Okay?"

"Fine," she said, and she'd have laughed if she hadn't been afraid the laugh would turn into a sob. What was she doing here, in the middle of nowhere, with a man she didn't know? With her entire life, her oh-so-safe life, a million miles away?

The driver said something about the weather. Liam answered. Jessie just sat there, taking deep breaths and planning how and when to tell Liam she'd changed her mind again because she surely had. She wasn't going to stay on Flamingo Island and she certainly wasn't going to sleep with him.

Not that he'd said anything about sleeping.

Carefully, as if he might not notice, she eased free of his encircling arm.

They were traveling a road that skirted the water. She could hear the boom of the surf, smell the salt tang, but Liam had been right when he'd said she wouldn't be able to see much. Jessie bit her lip. Actually, all she wanted to see was the desk clerk, so she could find out how to arrange for a flight back to the mainland.

Finally the Jeep slowed. Several small buildings, and then a much larger one, blazing with lights, were just ahead.

Thank God, she thought—but the driver didn't stop. Jessie craned her neck and looked over her shoulder. "Wasn't that..." She licked her dry lips. "Wasn't that the hotel?"

"That was the main building, yes. But we have a private villa."

A private villa. She was still processing that when the Jeep bounced to a stop. Liam leaned forward, exchanged soft words with the driver. The man handed over a key; Liam handed over a tip and helped her from the Jeep. From the effusiveness of the driver's thanks, she knew it was a large tip. She'd been right, then, when she'd fig-

ured that his luck had been good lately. That was
the way it went for men like Liam Malone. Good
luck, followed by bad luck. One woman, followed
by another.

She spun toward the Jeep. "Wait," she started
to say, but she was too late. The vehicle was roar-
ing away.

"Jessie?"

Liam held out his hand. She hesitated, took it,
and he led her up a narrow path of crushed white
shells toward a villa that rose like a block of white
sugar in the moonlight. She hung back as he
opened the door and switched on the light.

Jessie caught her breath.

The villa was one enormous bedroom. White
tile floors. Soaring white walls. Wood ceiling
fans, blades turning lazily. A wall of glass looking
out on a white beach. And a bed. An enormous
four-poster bed mounted on a low platform like
something out of a stage set, and draped in yards
and yards of gauzy white lace.

Liam had brought her to a lover's paradise.
Long, hot days in the sun. Longer, hotter nights
in that bed. She felt as if a cold hand had wrapped
around her heart. They weren't lovers, she and
Liam Malone. They were a man and a woman
brought to this place by lust, and once they'd

sated their hunger, they'd go their separate ways. She'd understood that.

Except, she couldn't go through with it.

She took a quick step back. "I can't," she said. "I can't do this."

Liam shut the door, leaned back against it and folded his arms. "And just when, exactly, did you reach that decision?"

His tone was polite, his expression pleasant. But there was something just under his words, something flickering in his eyes, that made her shiver.

"Does it matter? I only know that—that—"

"That you can't do this." A muscle knotted in his jaw. "Is that how you ended up saying yes to Bill when he asked you to marry him?"

Her head came up. "What?"

"You heard me. Is that how it happened? Did you lie to yourself about your feelings, tell yourself you loved him when you knew that you didn't?"

Jessie stood straighter. She dropped the tote bag and put her hands on her hips. "I never lied to William."

A tight smile etched Liam's mouth. "I didn't accuse you of lying to him. I asked if you'd lied to yourself."

"That's ridiculous. Lie to myself? About my feelings?"

She tossed her head and the spill of her hair over her shoulders was like the swirl of a flamenco dancer's skirt. Liam unfolded his arms and dug his hands into his pockets. It didn't matter that she was beautiful, that he wanted her more than he'd ever wanted a woman in his life or that he could seduce her in a moment because, even if she wasn't ready to admit it, her need for him was as wild as his for her. What mattered was that she come to him on her own, that she put aside the lies and give herself to him fully. That was how he wanted her; it was the only way he wanted her. It was the way she wanted him, too, and he needed to hear her say it.

"Why would I lie? William's a wonderful man."

"You don't love him."

"He has so many wonderful qualities that I could never list them all."

"And you still don't love him."

"He's kind and good and decent, and he'd never, not in a thousand lifetimes, do what you've done."

"No, he wouldn't." Liam narrowed his eyes and stepped away from the door. "That's the dif-

ference between us, I guess. I see what I want and
I take it.''

Jessie's skin prickled. ''Charming. I bet that
goes over big with the ladies.''

''Maybe I should clarify that.'' He reached behind him, turned the lock, then came toward her
as lithely as a big cat, his green eyes locked to
hers. ''I only take what's offered to me. I'm honest in what I want, Jessie. I don't lie to a woman.''

''That's even better,'' she said, and hoped he
couldn't see the pulse leaping in the hollow of her
throat. ''Really a smooth come-on, Liam. You
telling a woman you know what she really wants,
even when she says you're wrong.''

He reached out, cupped her shoulders with his
hands. ''Don't do this. If you don't want to be
with me, say so. But, dammit, don't play games.
Not now.''

''I don't want to be with you. Okay? Is that
what you wanted to hear?''

''I want to hear the truth.'' His eyes were dark
and angry. She felt the press of his fingers, knew
the tension that was building inside him because
it was inside her, too. ''Say it. Say that you want
me.''

''You've no idea what I want, Liam. You—''

He kissed her. Not hard. She'd have fought

him, if he had. He kissed her gently, his mouth moving lightly over hers.

"Say it," he whispered. "Let the world tilt, sweetheart. Let it happen."

Jessie's heart thudded. How could he know her so well when he hardly knew her at all? He brought her hands to his chest. She could feel his heart racing under her fingers. A honeyed weakness was spreading through her bones. It would be so easy to do...

"Let go," she said sharply. "Damn you, let go of me!"

He did, so suddenly that she stumbled back. "To hell with it," he growled.

"Oh, that's nice." Her voice trembled. She grabbed her bag and stepped around him, heading for the door. "You can't get what you want so you say to hell with it?"

"*You're* the one who's not getting what you want, because I'm not about to deliver."

"What are you talking about?"

Liam grabbed her again and backed her against the wall. "You're a coward, Jessie. You're so afraid of behaving like a real woman that you want me to do it all. What did you have in mind, huh? Am I supposed to turn into a villain? Maybe you'd like me to play at being some kind of Don Juan, a guy who can talk a woman into bed even if she keeps saying she doesn't want to be there.'' He let go of her. ''Well, I won't do it. You cast the wrong guy in the part.''

Her hand whirred through the air and cracked across his cheek. His head snapped back; he cursed and grabbed her wrist before she could hit him again…and then she was in his arms, her mouth pressed hungrily to his, her fingers knotting in his sweatshirt as his fingers tangled in her hair.

''Jessie.'' He caught hold of her face and brushed her mouth with his. ''Sweetheart, I'm sorry. I didn't mean—''

''It was my fault. I was afraid, Liam. Not of you,'' she added quickly. ''Never of you. I was afraid of the way you make me feel.''

The look on his face made her breath catch. He swept his hand down her back, lifting her into him, watching her eyes darken as he pressed against her.

''Tell me how I make you feel,'' he said thickly.

''As if…'' Her jacket fell to the floor and his hands, his hard, exciting hands, slid under her T-shirt and over her skin. When he cupped her breasts, her voice broke. ''As if—Liam. Make love to me. Please, please, pl—''

Liam kissed her, swept her into his arms and carried her to the bed.

CHAPTER FIVE

WHAT HAD STARTED in the garden would end here. They'd known each other for little more than twenty-four hours. Still, as Liam drew Jessie to him, he felt as if he'd waited all his life to make love to her. He wanted to tell her that, but she reached her arms up to him and sighed his name, and words became meaningless.

All that mattered was touch. And taste. And scent.

He kissed her gently, moving his lips over hers, waiting for her mouth to soften and cling to his. When it did, he slipped his tongue between her lips, groaning with pleasure at the honeyed sweetness he found waiting for him. Her arms tightened around him, her body arched against his, and he rolled her beneath him, caught her bottom lip between his teeth and eased the small hurt with a kiss. Jessie moaned softly, and the need to take her pounded through his blood.

Slow down, he told himself, slow down. He'd

been a gambler most of his life and understood that when you bet on the toss of the dice, you put your money on today. Only a fool would bet on tomorrow, or think that far ahead. Right now the wheel of fortune had spun and the little red ball with his number on it had dropped into the slot. That was all he'd count on but, if he was very lucky, he could make the moment last.

He tunneled his hands into her hair and swept it back from her face. He kissed her temples, her eyelids, her throat as she arched against him again. Lord, she was beautiful, especially now, as the wildness he'd sensed in her from the beginning burst free. Little sounds were breaking from her throat; the musk of arousal rose from her skin. Such silky skin. Such hot, golden skin.

"Liam," she whispered, and kissed him, her mouth taking his mouth, her breath mingling with his breath. She slid her hands under his shirt, laid them against his chest. His body clenched like a fist. Slow down, he told himself again, slow down....

And then he stopped thinking.

He grasped the hem of her T-shirt and tried to pull it up, but the thin cotton tore apart in his hands, exposing her to him. She wore a sheer bra, the color of her skin. No lace, no silk, bows or ribbons, nothing but the lush roundness of her breasts and the tawny satin of her nipples.

The room swam out of focus. He bent to her, smoothed the tip of his finger over her breasts, kissed them, licked them. Jessie cried out, moaned his name as he kissed her and swallowed her cries.

He reached for the front clasp of her bra. Her hands, cold as ice, locked on his wrists.

"Wait," she said shakily. "Liam, please wait."

His body told him to ignore her plea. His mind, or maybe his heart, said something different. *I'm afraid of what you make me feel,* she'd said, and he'd reacted by ripping her clothes off.

He groaned, rolled over and threw his arm across his eyes. "Jessie," he said when he could trust himself to talk. "Sweetheart…"

He reached out to her but she moved quickly, clutched the blanket around her and stood up, facing away from him. "I'm sorry," she said stiffly. "I know you're disappointed."

Liam got to his feet. Gently he peeled the blanket from her hands and dropped it to the floor. "Jessie," he said again, and drew her back against him. Her body was rigid against his; he knew she wanted him to let go. Instead, he put his arms around her waist. "I'm the one who's sorry, Jessie. Can you forgive me?"

"There's nothing to—"

"There is." He turned her in his arms, stroked her back, pressed kisses into her hair. "I came at you with all the finesse of a sex-starved water buffalo."

She made a little sound, half sob, half laugh, against his shoulder. "How do you know how a sex-starved water buffalo would behave?"

Liam smiled. "It's something about males, I guess. Show us a beautiful female, we lose our cool." His voice roughened. "Especially if she touches some special place inside us."

Jessie lifted her head, leaned back in his arms. "Have I?" she whispered. "Touched something special inside you? Because—because that's how I feel about you, as if you've reached into me and—and…" She sighed and buried her face against him again. "And that's crazy. We don't even know each other."

"We will, though. I promise." Gently he scooped her into his arms. She looped her arms around his neck and sighed.

"You must think I'm an idiot."

"What I think," Liam replied as he made his way across the room, "is that we've damn near broken the how-long-can-a-human-being-stay-awake record." Jessie laughed. It was a real laugh this time, a wonderful sound, and Liam grinned at her. "You like that, huh?"

"You made it up. There is no such record."

"Well, if there isn't, there should be." He kissed her, then jabbed the light switch with his elbow. Velvet darkness swallowed the room. "Okay," he said briskly, "here's the plan."

"The plan?" Jessie swallowed. Liam was heading back toward the bed, washed in ivory moonlight. "Liam?" She hesitated. "I think you should know…I mean, if you think it's the light—if you think turning it off will—"

"I know that, sweetheart."

He laid her on the bed and stood over her. She caught her breath as he pulled off his sweatshirt. He was beautiful. The hard, masculine face. The broad shoulders. The wide chest and narrow waist.

"What I thought," he said huskily, "was that we'd get some sleep."

"I won't be able to sleep," she said quickly. "I'm too—too—"

"Let's try, anyway." She heard the thud of his sneakers as he kicked them off. His hands went to his waist and he opened his belt, undid his zipper. The denim rustled as he stepped out of his jeans and stood before her, clad only in a pair of dark boxer shorts slung low on his hips. "The thing is, I can't sleep with the light on." A smile curved his lips. "Or with most of my clothes on, either." The mattress dipped gently as he sat down beside her. Jessie could hear her blood beating in her ears.

"Liam," she whispered.

"Shh." He took her hands, brought them to his chest, and she caught her breath at the feel of hot skin, tight muscle, silky hair. "That's not so awful, is it?"

No. Oh, no, it wasn't. It was wonderful touching him. He was so alive, so real, so excitingly male.

His fingers were at the front clasp of her bra. This time she didn't stop him. A languid heat was moving through her body. She could almost feel herself turning to liquid. When the clasp gave way, he drew the bra off and tossed it aside.

"I want to feel your skin against mine," he said. "That's all, I promise. Is that all right, Jessie?"

She didn't answer. She couldn't, but Liam seemed to understand her silence. He put his arms around her and when her naked flesh touched his, she caught her breath. He lowered his head to hers and kissed her. Desire, sharp and hot, began to boil in her blood.

"Let's just get you out of some of this stuff."

She sighed her acquiescence, sat up so he could undress her. When she had nothing on but her panties, he eased her back against the pillows and kissed her mouth, her throat, her shoulders. She closed her eyes and waited, her skin tingling, for the feel of his lips on her breasts.

This was what she'd dreamed of last night. This slow, scalding seduction. Liam in her arms. A burning ache, low in her belly. When he finally stretched out beside her, she turned toward him, trembling, every breath searing her lungs.

"Liam," she whispered. "Liam—"

He put two fingers lightly over her lips, drew the blanket over them. Then he gathered her into the strength of his embrace.

She almost came apart at the first touch of his body against hers, the first awareness of his erection pressed against her belly. She waited for him to move against her, to strip away the last flimsy barriers that separated them, yearned for it to happen.

"Go to sleep, darling," he whispered.

He stroked her back, kissed her temple. After a while, his breathing slowed. So did hers, but she knew it was meaningless. He was pretending and so was she. Neither of them would get any sleep, not pressed together like this, with their hearts beating in unison, her breasts against his chest. Nevertheless, his heartbeat steadied. Hers did, too.

He really had fallen asleep, she thought in surprise.

Moments later, so did she.

LIAM CAME AWAKE SLOWLY.

It was just before dawn. A pale pewter light was seeping into the room, and Jessie was still in his arms. She was asleep, cradled against him, and he fought back the desire to dip his head and awaken her with a kiss.

Only when she was ready. Not until then.

He put out his hand and smoothed a silken tangle of honey-gold hair back from her cheek.

The amazing thing was, he'd made it through the night. A smile angled across his mouth. What he'd pretty much figured was that lying with a half-naked Jessie in his arms would kill him. The first touch of her skin against his had almost been his undoing. He'd told himself to lie still, slow his breathing, convince her he was asleep. It must have worked because, eventually, she'd sighed and relaxed against him.

Holding her, keeping her safe through the night, wasn't much of a price to pay for having her come to him without fear or hesitation.

The funny thing was that he'd never much liked

to spend the night with a woman. Not that he was a guy who was into wham, bam, thank you, ma'am. He always held a woman after sex, shared her bed for an hour or two before getting up and heading home. If a woman asked him to stay the night, and most did, he said he was a restless sleeper. It wasn't a lie. He almost always awakened sprawled across the bed, the blankets off and the pillows on the floor.

Liam drew Jessie closer.

This time, though, he'd awakened just the way he'd gone to sleep, lying in the center of the big bed, Jessie in his embrace, her head on his shoulder. Sometime during the night, she'd put her hand on his chest. It lay just over his heart. He'd moved a little, too. He'd thrown his leg over hers in what any shrink would surely have defined as a subconscious gesture meant to keep her with him.

Strange behavior for a man who preferred to sleep alone.

Maybe the simple truth was that sleeping alone wasn't as important as waking up alone. Maybe he just didn't want to greet the day with a stranger beside him, even if she wasn't actually a stranger. He'd never been into one-night stands. The thing was, no matter how hot the affair, a man and a woman were forever separate entities, and making love to a woman was less intimate than sleeping alongside her. It might sound crazy, but it had always seemed logical—until now. He'd just slept beside Jessie, they hadn't even made love, and he'd known her for all of—Liam lifted his arm, squinted at his watch. For all of thirty-something hours.

Thirty-something hours, and in all that time he'd phoned Bill exactly once and left a message that told him nothing. But then, how did you go about telling a man who was crazy with worry that he had nothing to worry about, because you'd not just found his bride, you'd run off with her?

Liam eased his arm from beneath Jessie's shoulders and sat up. He took one last look at her, then pulled on his jeans and made his way to a small alcove near the patio where a rattan cabinet hid a minifridge, a stocked wine rack and an electric coffeemaker, ready to go.

He turned the coffeemaker on. That was one of the first things he'd changed when he bought Flamingo Island Resort.

"We don't provide any food or drink in the villas," the manager had told him with an officious little smile. "Most of our guests are honeymooners. They don't want to be bothered with such things."

Liam knew the officious smile probably was

the result of the rumor that said he'd won the place in a game of poker. So he'd smiled pleasantly and pointed out that that was precisely the reason the resort would provide champagne, wine, coffee and tea, plus a basket of fresh-baked breads to be left on each porch in the morning.

"And by the way," he'd added with a smile that was more than a match for the manager's, "just so we understand each other, Mr. Edding, I didn't win this place playing cards."

Edding had paled. "No, sir. I never said—"

"Be sure you don't."

They'd gotten along just fine after that.

Liam took a bright red mug from the cabinet and filled it with hot coffee.

Two years had gone by since that day. Flamingo Island, always successful, had become a world-class resort. Liam had added two more properties to the string, and hadn't played so much as a hand of poker in all that time. It had taken a while, but he'd finally figured out that a man couldn't go through life gambling on everything.

Until he'd stood in the departure terminal at Sea-Tac Airport and decided to bet his honor against his need for a woman he knew he couldn't have.

The hot tropical sun was rising over the ocean,

turning the water to shimmering gold as he stepped out onto the patio. He sipped at his coffee, leaned his elbows on the sea wall and tried to figure out what to do next. A man of principle would call Bill and tell him everything. Good Lord, how could he do that? What was "everything," anyway? What would he say? "Bill, I don't know how to tell you this, but Jessie and I are together. We're in our own private world, and she won't be coming back to Seattle for a while."

"Liam?"

He turned around. Jessie was standing in the doorway. She'd pulled on his sweatshirt but not her jeans. Her hair was a confusion of honey-gold waves. Her eyes were bright as the ocean, her skin as flushed as the morning sky, and he knew, in that moment, that he was never going to let her leave him.

"I thought I smelled coffee," she said with a hesitant smile. "Liam? About last night—"

He was beside her before she'd finished the sentence. He swung her into his arms, kissed her, and she put her arms around his neck.

"I wasn't ready last night," she whispered. "But I am now."

Liam carried her inside, lay down with her in his arms. He rolled her onto her belly, drew her hair away from her neck and pressed his lips to her skin. The scent of her rose to his nostrils, a delicious blend of flowers, salt air, and woman. Gently he eased up the sweatshirt, eased down her panties. He heard her catch her breath as he kissed the long curve of her spine, the dimple at its base before turning her over.

"You're beautiful," he said huskily, his eyes locked to hers.

She smiled. "You are, too."

He laughed softly. "Men aren't beautiful, sweetheart. Handsome. Magnificent. Muscular and altogether fantastic, yes, but not—"

Jessie grabbed his hair and dragged his mouth to hers. "I'll give you all the compliments you want, later. But first..." She sat up, tugged the sweatshirt over her head and tossed it aside. "Look at me, Liam," she said, "and tell me you like what you see."

Like? There were no words to describe what he felt, looking at her. Her body was as beautiful as her face, her skin all flushed, her breasts high and rounded, the tips already beaded with excitement.

"I love what I see," he said softly.

"Touch me, then." She reached up, stroked her finger gently over his mouth. "Kiss me. Make love to me."

He was on fire for her. Liam stripped off his jeans and shorts, and went into Jessie's arms.

He'd dreamed of this, but the reality was better than any dream. The sweetness of her breasts, of her belly, the startled little sound she made when he opened her to him, found the secret flower that was the essence of her femininity and kissed it.

Her cry of shocked pleasure combined with her taste and rocketed through his blood. When she began to tremble, to convulse under the sweet torment of his mouth, he moved quickly up her body and, on one long, possessive stroke, sheathed himself in her satin heat.

"Jessie," he whispered, and when her lashes fluttered open, he bent to her, cupped her face and kissed her deeply. "Look at me, sweetheart, and say my name."

"Liam. My Liam." A long, keening cry burst from her throat.

"Jessie," he said, and then he let go of everything, the years of loneliness and of doubt, and exploded deep within the welcoming warmth of the woman he loved.

CHAPTER SIX

JESSIE SAT on the sun-drenched patio, wearing a white, fluffy robe provided by the hotel and drinking coffee while she waited for Liam to return from what he'd smugly referred to as a "secret mission."

She smiled over the rim of her cup. It didn't take much effort to figure out what that "secret mission" was. She'd made a face when she'd started to dress, teased him about only men not shuddering at the thought of putting on yesterday's clothes, and he'd gotten a glint in his eyes. Suddenly he'd wanted to know her favorite colors, whether she liked short summer skirts or long ones, if she preferred bikinis or what he'd referred to as "you know, those clingy, one-piece jobs."

She put down her cup, stretched her arms high overhead, then lay back on the chaise longue.

He'd gone to buy her something to wear, she was sure of it. Still, she'd act surprised when he turned up with a swimsuit and a T-shirt and shorts and, yes, she'd stop being silly about it and accept them as gifts because it was pointless to stand on ceremony with the man who was your lover.

Her lover. She rolled over on her stomach and closed her eyes. It was such a lovely word. The only bit of darkness came when she let herself think about the emptiness she'd face when their days here ended.

And the pain she'd caused William.

"No," she said aloud.

She wasn't going to think about that, not yet. It was too soon to think about what lay ahead. She was happy, happier than she'd ever imagined possible, and she wasn't going to spoil her joy for anything.

She sat up, stretched again and took her coffee cup into the villa and rinsed it in the sink. The serving cart, bearing the remnants of the gargantuan breakfast Liam had ordered earlier, sat waiting in the corner. She thought of the waiter's smile when he'd delivered it, all that food for only two people, and how she'd felt herself blushing, knowing what he must have been thinking, that only a man and woman who'd spent hours making love could possibly be hungry enough to tackle waffles and eggs and a hundred other things.

And she thought of how Liam had taken her in his arms after the door closed, how they'd laughed while she fed him strips of bacon and he'd licked her fingers clean until laughter turned to sighs and sighs to passion.

She thought about how much she loved him.

There wasn't any point in trying to pretend she didn't, not to herself. It was impossible to fall in love with a man you hardly knew, especially when that man wasn't the kind she'd ever imagined wanting, but there it was. She loved Liam the way she'd wanted to love William, and what good would it do her?

"None," she said softly as she sank down on the edge of the bed.

Liam loved making love with her. He loved holding her, and he even seemed to love being with her. But he didn't love her. He'd never love just one woman. That was just the way they were, the Liam Malones of this world. Her mother had told her once, probably in a moment of desperation, that she'd made a terrible mistake thinking she didn't have to hear her man say those simple words, and thinking she could be happy with one who preferred wandering the world to making a real home.

Not that she'd have to be concerned about any of that with Liam. Even if a miracle occurred, which it wouldn't, but even if it did, and Liam looked at her and said those magical words, "Jessie, I love you..."

Even if that happened, he could never be hers because the shadow of William, and what they'd done, would always be there, chilling their happiness.

Tears rolled down her cheeks, and wasn't that ridiculous? Here she sat, weeping because there wouldn't be a forever-after when that was exactly what she'd walked away from, choosing, instead, a few short, sweet days in Liam's arms.

Jessie sat up straight, scrubbed her knuckles over her eyes. Liam would be back soon and she didn't want him to see that she'd been crying, didn't want to waste whatever little time they had left on tears or recriminations or—

A knock sounded at the front door. He must have locked himself out. She dabbed at her eyes again, ran her hands through her hair and went to open the door. But it wasn't Liam on the steps, it was a bellman with a load of gaily wrapped boxes in his arms. There were more boxes in the Jeep he'd parked alongside the villa.

"Packages for you, Miss Warren."

"There must be some mistake. I didn't order—"

"No, ma'am. Mr. Malone did."

"But..." She stepped back as the bellman

started past her. It took two trips before he'd transferred everything from the Jeep. Jessie looked from the boxes to the bellman's smiling face. "I don't—I'm afraid I don't have anything to—"

The man's smile broadened. "Mr. Malone took care of that." He put his hand to his forehead, flipped her a brisk salute. "Enjoy the day, ma'am."

Jessie nodded. "You, too," she said, or thought she said, as the door swung shut. For a few minutes she just stared at the packages. Then, carefully, she unwrapped one, then another and another. Silk skirts, cotton tops, cashmere shawls and lace underwear spilled onto the bed.

"Liam," she said, laughing with delight, "oh, you crazy, wonderful man."

She took off her robe, let it slip to the floor, pulled on a cropped white top and a long, gauzy skirt and looked at herself in the mirror. Her eyes were bright with pleasure, her mouth was pink from Liam's kisses, her hair was a mass of curls and waves. She hardly recognized herself. What had become of Jessica Warren? Who was this woman in the mirror, wearing such beautiful things, her hair loose, her feet bare, all propriety and dignity forgotten?

Jessie's smile faded. And how could a heart soar, then break, all in the same moment?

"Liam," she whispered, "how can I let you go?"

Falling in love wasn't supposed to be like this. But, oh God, it was.

FALLING IN LOVE wasn't supposed to be like this.

Liam walked slowly along the shoreline, his hands tucked into the pockets of his jeans. He'd left Jessie on the patio, lying sleepily in the sun after they'd consumed a room service breakfast so huge even he'd laughed, and he'd been the one who ordered it. It was just that she'd smiled and said "you" each time he'd asked her what she wanted for breakfast and he'd felt honor-bound to take her up on the offer. When he finally reached for the phone, he hardly knew his own name so he'd ordered waffles and eggs, pancakes and bacon, biscuits and toast, strawberries, mangoes and coffee.

They'd eaten on the patio, and it was a good thing the villas were heavily screened by bougainvillea, because when Liam groaned and said he couldn't eat another mouthful, Jessie made a stern face and said he had to finish what he'd ordered. Laughing, she'd fed him a strip of crisp bacon. But when he reached the final bit and sucked her fingers into his mouth, her laughter had died, and they'd made love on the chaise longue, with the hot sun beating down.

Great. He was thinking what it was like to make love with Jessie and turning himself on.

"Malone," he said lightly, under his breath, "you're some piece of work."

Indeed, he was. He was a man in love, and the world had suddenly turned into a wonderful place, and never mind the gray smudge on the horizon, or the brisk breeze. It was a beautiful day, and it would be even more beautiful in—he looked at his watch—in just about five minutes, when the things he'd ordered were delivered to the villa.

After he and Jessie had finished breakfast and made love, they'd showered together. Liam gritted his teeth and told himself not to think about the way Jessie's skin felt wet, or how her hair streamed down over her breasts, or how he'd soaped her body, all of it, all of her....

He cleared his throat.

They'd put on the robes the hotel provided. Jessie had scooped up her clothing and wrinkled her nose.

"What?" Liam had asked, and she'd laughed and said that only a man would look so perplexed when a woman shuddered at the thought of taking a shower and then putting on the same stuff she'd worn the previous day. He'd clapped his hand to his heart, as if she'd wounded him deeply, accused her of being the female equivalent of a chauvinist pig, admitted she was probably right before dropping a kiss on her smiling lips. Then he'd put on his jeans and sweatshirt. "Stay just the way you are," he'd warned, "while I undertake a dark and dangerous secret mission."

And, he thought with smug assurance, he had.

He'd walked to the main building. First, he'd seen to his own things. He kept simple clothing— jeans, T-shirts, chinos and a blazer—in the owner's suite. He'd packed some of it and arranged for delivery to the villa. Then he'd gone to the gift shop and, well, maybe he'd gone just a little bit overboard.

"I need some things for a lady," he'd told the clerk. "She's…" He'd held his hand up, just about at mid-chest. "She's, uh, maybe so tall. And…" He'd started making curves in the air while the clerk watched politely and he felt his face turning red. "And she's, I don't know, a size six or maybe an eight. Her hips are…well, her waist is…"

The clerk had finally shown him some pity. "Lisa," she'd called, and a girl had come out of what he figured was the stockroom, a pretty girl about Jessie's height and weight. "Is the lady similar to Lisa, Mr. Malone?"

"Yes," Liam had answered, because he knew better than to think anybody wanted to hear him babble that Jessie wasn't similar to any other woman in the world.

The clerk had dismissed Lisa with an imperious wave of the hand. "What kinds of 'things' did you have in mind, sir?"

Shorts, he'd told her, and T-shirts. Oh, and a swimsuit. And how about a couple of those long filmy skirts? Those little cotton tops? Those silk things, with the lace?

"Camisoles," the clerk had said with a quick smile.

"Camisoles, right. And sandals. And that dress, the one with the little flowers." He'd paused at a counter, picked up a little vial, opened it, sniffed it, smelled lilacs. "This, too," he'd said, "and that. And this—"

In the end, he'd ordered too much to carry, so he'd arranged for it to be delivered.

"Your lady is a lucky woman," the clerk had said, and Liam had replied that he was the lucky one....

It wasn't true.

His smile fled. He bent down, plucked a small white stone from the sand and threw it far out into the surf. He wasn't lucky, because this couldn't last. Jessie had made love with him, but she still belonged to another man. Not just any other man, either. She belonged to William.

Liam stared blindly over the water. Hell, no. Falling in love was not supposed to be like this.

He sighed and began walking again. Not that he was any kind of expert. Until now he'd figured love was a concept dreamed up by salesmen trying to sell soap. One man, one woman, bells ringing, fireworks going off—how could any of that be real?

But it was. You saw a woman, a special woman, and all that stuff happened. And if you were lucky, it was that way for her, too, so that both of you knew it could be like this for the rest of your lives. He knew, anyway, and even if Jessie hadn't said so, she knew it, too. It was there, in her eyes, in the way she kissed him, in everything she said and did.

She loved him, he loved her, and what could possibly come of it? Nothing but grief, all around.

"Dammit," Liam said. What else was there to say without putting back his head and howling his anguish to the gods who had to be looking down and laughing until their sides split? Fate sure had a hell of a sense of humor. Liam Malone, who'd figured love was about parts of the body that hadn't a damn thing to do with the heart, who'd thought that even talking about settling down marked a man as a sucker extraordinaire—that very same Liam Malone was in love.

"Find my Jessica," Bill had said, "and do the right thing."

Liam mouthed an oath, kicked at the sand and watched the shiny particles rise into the air. Maybe the day wasn't as beautiful as he'd thought. Little whitecaps danced on the restless sea and that dark smudge in the distance was growing. The woman at the gift shop had mentioned that a storm might be blowing in.

"It won't last," she'd promised. "Trouble in paradise never does."

She had it wrong. What never lasted was paradise. How come he hadn't remembered that? Life had a way of holding out happiness, waiting until you reached for it and then snatching it back. He should have told that to the clerk—although it was probably just as well he hadn't. She'd only have looked at him as if he was nuts. Not a good thing, he thought with a little smile, for the staff to label the owner. Not that it seemed so great that he owned Flamingo Island or that he'd turned his life around.

It would only mean something if he could share it with Jessie.

He'd kept it a secret from Bill because he'd wanted to tell him in person, how he'd awakened one morning with a fortune in his wallet and a French movie star in his bed. He'd been on a hot streak that month, winning hand after hand at high-stakes poker tables, dazzling the oil barons and investment bankers he'd outplayed, and he'd opened his eyes that particular day, looked at the famous face on the pillow beside his, then at the opulent gold-leaf ceiling in his posh hotel suite, and said, "Malone, just what the hell are you doing?"

So he'd kissed the movie star goodbye, dumped his money into the startup stock of an Internet company he'd heard about over a hand of poker. Two weeks later, he cashed out, rich. Rich beyond his wildest dreams. But it became boring, reading the financial news and watching his money make more money. He took a chunk of it, looked around for opportunities, bought this place for no better reason than that he found it peaceful and beautiful. The next thing he knew, he'd turned himself into a man he'd thought he'd never want to be. To his amazement, he liked the transformation—but he'd never planned on falling in love. Love hadn't worked for his parents, who'd probably died screaming at each other as their car hit the overpass abutment, or for the rich and famous he'd known over the last decade.

Except it had happened. With Jessie, the only woman he'd ever love. He'd tell her that, slowly. Work up to it, because as much as he loved her, it scared him.

The villa door swung open. Jessie smiled at him. She had on one of the outfits he'd bought, a little white top with a long, filmy skirt, and she'd left her hair loose, the way he liked it.

"Jessie," he blurted. "Sweetheart, I'm crazy in love with you."

She didn't say anything. Then, just when he thought he'd made the worst mistake a man could ever make, she threw herself into his arms.

"Liam," she said. "Oh, Liam, I was so afraid it was only me."

He swept her up, kicked the door shut and, for a little while, nothing mattered but showing each other exactly what being in love meant.

THEY LAY IN EACH OTHER'S ARMS in the center of the bed, safe and secure in the aftermath of their lovemaking.

Liam inhaled the fragrance of Jessie's hair. "You smell delicious. Is that the perfume I gave you?"

"Mmm-hmm. It's lovely."

"And what you were wearing. I loved you in that. You know, the long skirt and that top, the one that looks like somebody shrank it."

She laughed softly and snuggled closer. "You must have emptied out that gift shop."

Liam took her hand from his chest and brought it to his lips. "Did I buy the right size? If there's anything you don't like—"

"Everything was perfect, but I can't let you spend so much money on me."

"I'd give you the world, if you'd let me."

Jessie lifted her head from his shoulder and kissed his mouth. "Thank you," she said softly. "But even if the cards have been good to you lately—"

"Aha." Liam grinned. "So, Bill told, and the deep, dark secret's out, huh? That I used to be a gambler?"

"Uh-huh. Give you a deck of cards and you're…used to be?"

"That's right, sweetheart." He rolled over, gently eased her onto her back. "I've reformed."

"A reformed rogue." Jessie touched the tip of her finger to his mouth. "William will be pleased to…I mean, that's nice to hear." She smiled, though the smile was wobbly. "But I can't see you working nine to five."

"People change." A muscle knotted in his jaw.

"You think you know exactly who you are and what you want out of life. Then, I don't know, you walk down a street or read a book..." He cleared his throat. "Or you agree to be the best man at an old friend's wedding, and—"

"Don't." Jessie put her hand over Liam's mouth. "Please," she whispered, "not yet."

"We have to talk about it. You know that."

"Yes. But—"

"I love you with all my heart, Jess." His voice was deep, his words a whisper. "I want you to know I've never said those words to another woman, and I never will."

"Liam. Oh, God, Liam—" Her voice broke. "What are we going to do? I thought—I thought this was just a—a.... I don't know what I thought. When I first saw you—"

"I know. It was the same for me."

"It terrified me but I told myself it was only— that it was only—"

"Sex," Liam said softly. "Yeah, so did I. A couple of hours in bed." He pulled Jessie into his arms and held her close. "Then I got on that plane and saw the way you looked at me. Or maybe it was when I undressed you and you went into my arms so trustingly. I only know that I love you, that I'll always love—"

Jessie pressed her mouth to his. He could taste her tears in her kiss.

"I'll always love you, too," she whispered. "But—but you know that this is all we can ever have."

"No! Don't say that." He sat up. "I want to marry you, Jessie. I want to do all those things I never believed in. Buy a house. Have kids. Live happily ever after. Sweetheart, don't you understand? Without you—"

"My life will be empty, too." The words shuddered from her lips. "I tried to tell myself we could make a life together, Liam. But we can't. William will always be between us." She began to weep. "You know what we have to do."

He did know. Each beat of his heart reminded him of his promise to Bill. "I'll do the right thing," he'd said. But the right thing had changed. The world had changed. Right was wrong, and promises were pain.

"I'm not giving you up," Liam said fiercely.

"You love William as much as I do, and he adores you." She took an unsteady breath. "You're his hero."

"God." He let go of her, sat up and raked his fingers through his hair. "Some hero I turned out to be."

"He told me once that you and I are the two

most important people in his life." Jessie knelt beside Liam and took his hand. "It would be bad enough if one of us let him down, but if—if we betray him—"

Liam couldn't listen to any more. She was right but he wouldn't admit it, not to her, not to himself. Instead, he sprang to his feet.

"There's got to be a way!" He grabbed his jeans and stepped into them. "My mind's going in circles. I have to take a walk." He stopped and took Jessie's hands. "I'll come up with something. I'm not going to lose you, Jess. Not after I spent my life looking for you."

Jessie laughed, but by the time she rose from the bed and put her arms around him, her laughter had turned to tears.

"I know," she sobbed. "I'll never forget you, or this time we spent together. I'll always adore you, Liam, always."

He kissed her as if the world were going to end at any moment. And, in a way, it did, because when he returned to the villa less than an hour later, Jessie was gone.

CHAPTER SEVEN

RAIN BEAT DOWN on the island, and a driving wind rattled the fronds of the palm trees that towered over the villa.

Inside, a grim-faced Liam faced three hapless hotel employees.

"It's a simple question," he said coldly. "Surely one of you can answer it."

The desk clerk who'd arranged for Jessie's flight to Miami, the driver who'd taken her to the airstrip, even the chambermaid who'd gone to the villa hours ago to make the bed and had ended up, instead, directing Jessie to the office, looked at him, then at each other. No one spoke. Finally the desk clerk shifted his feet.

"I've explained, sir. The young lady phoned the desk. She said she wanted to leave the island. She asked—"

"I know what she asked," Liam snapped. "What I'm having difficulty with is that you didn't think to inform me."

"I'm sorry, sir. There didn't seem to be any…"
The clerk licked his lips. "We—we didn't know
that you'd object." He looked to his companions
for support. Both of them were nodding their
heads vigorously. "We were only doing what
your guest asked us to do, sir."

"I see." Liam folded his arms and glared at
the man. "Do you always do what guests ask you
to do?"

The clerk swallowed dryly. "We—we try to
accommodate all requests, Mr. Malone."

"Suppose a guest wanted to jump off the roof?
Would you let her do that?"

"No, sir. Certainly not. But—"

You're acting like an idiot, Liam said to himself, while the clerk stumbled for words. Just what
was it he expected these people to have done?
Tell Jessie she couldn't fly out without permission? Wait for him to give his okay? Guests of
the hotel were supposed to be treated with courtesy, and they'd done that. As for Jessie—she'd
done what had to be done, what he hadn't had the
courage to do despite his promise to Bill, and now
he was venting his anger on these poor people
rather than dealing with the truth.

He and Jessie could never have a life together.
One of them, at least, understood the meaning of
the word *honor.*

"—did the best we could, sir, by accommo-dating the lady's wishes, and—"

"That's okay," Liam said, interrupting the clerk's stumbling explanation. "You're right. I'm wrong." He dredged up a smile. "In fact, I was way out of line."

Color began seeping back into the man's face. "If we'd known you wanted us to speak with you first, Mr. Malone—"

"Forget it. It's a free country. The lady wanted to leave and that's that." Liam clasped the man's shoulder, then shook hands with all three employ-ees. "There'll be something extra in your pay-checks this week," he said briskly, and herded them to the door. "How's that sound?"

"Thank you," they said, "thank you very much, Mr.—"

Liam shut the door, let the smile slip from his mouth and sank down on the edge of the bed. After a moment, he buried his face in his hands. Jessie was gone and he couldn't go after her even if he wanted to. The smudge on the horizon had turned into a charcoal bank of clouds, spewing rain and wind. Until the weather cleared, there was no way off the island.

Besides, what was the sense in going after her? Their affair had been doomed from the beginning.

Jessie had said it all in the last few minutes they'd been together.

"You're his hero, Liam."

Liam groaned and fell back against the pillows. Oh, yeah. He was Bill's hero, all right.

If only he'd met Jessie a year ago. Six months ago. Hell, a day before Bill put that ring on her finger would have been enough. What a difference that little bit of time would have made. He and Jessie would have met, there'd have been that same wild, lightning-hot attraction….

No. He wasn't going to do that, play a game of "if only" that would do nothing but make the pain worse. Liam sat up and scrubbed his hands over his face. He'd lost Jessie, lost her forever….

To hell with that. Bill was his oldest friend, yes, but Jessie—Jessie was everything.

He sprang from the bed, grabbed his leather jacket, reached for the phone. No way was he going to lose her. He loved her. He adored her. He…

He had no right to her.

The jacket fell from his hand. There was no way around the truth. He'd betrayed Bill, made a promise he hadn't kept. Now he had to go back, face Bill as Jessie was going to do, admit his guilt and ask his forgiveness before fading out of the picture. Anything else—like loving Jessie—he'd relegate to the past.

Liam lifted his head. He could hear the faint sound of an airplane engine in the distance. He went to the door, opened it, looked up into a clear, rain-washed night sky. The small plane that ferried guests to and from the island, that had taken Jessie from him, forever, was coming in for a landing. He could tell the pilot to gas it up, turn it around.

Not yet.

Tomorrow was soon enough to fly west. Once he did, it would all be over. Could it really be only a couple of days since he'd first seen Jessie, days that had changed his life, forever?

Liam sank down on the bed again, lay back and put his arm over his eyes. *Jessie,* he thought, *Jessie, my love.*

Early the next morning, he was on a flight headed for Seattle.

IN MOST PARTS OF THE COUNTRY spring meant flowers, sunshine and birdsong. In Seattle, tucked between the rainforests of the Olympic Peninsula and the towering Cascade Mountains, spring meant rain.

Jessie had never minded that. She'd heard some people say the gray skies were depressing, but she loved the misty feel of the air, and those moments when the clouds parted and Mount Rainier was visible on the horizon always made her spirits lift.

Nothing could make that happen, not this spring.

Except for a stop at her bank, where she'd picked up a new ATM card and used it to take some money from her account, and then an hour spent buying a few things to wear, she'd been huddled in her hotel room ever since she'd arrived in the city. She'd intended to face William immediately but once she stepped into the hotel, she'd realized she had to get herself in hand first. She felt as if her life had stopped when the plane carrying her away from Liam lifted into the air. She'd watched their villa recede and then the hotel until, finally, the island had been only a small dot in the vast ocean.

"Liam," she'd whispered, and she'd wept for what could never be, the lifetime of love they might have shared. If only they'd met some other time, some other place.

Jessie sighed.

Perhaps not.

What she'd shared with Liam couldn't possibly last. She'd always known that. Such fire, such heat, would only burn out over time. For all she knew, it had already turned to cold ashes, otherwise why wouldn't Liam have come after her?

No. No, she didn't want him to do that. She wanted to set things right. If William was willing to take her back, she'd—she'd...

She'd never let it happen.

Yes, she'd beg his forgiveness, tell him he was a wonderful man and that he deserved to find a woman who'd make him happy, but she wasn't that woman. She loved Liam. She always would, for the rest of her life, even though she'd never see him again.

A sob caught in her throat.

"God," Jessie whispered, "help me, please."

She reached for the phone, punched in the number for the big house on the lake before she had too much time to think about what she was doing. Her heart was thumping; her hand was so wet her fingers slipped on the plastic handpiece. Who would answer? The maid? The cook? Or William, himself. What would she say to him? What—

"Thornton residence."

Jessie blinked. "Carrie?"

"Jessica?"

"Yes. It's...did I dial the wrong number? I'm sorry. I've been so—so upset that—"

"*You've* been upset?" Carrie gave a cold

laugh. "I hardly think so. William's the one who's upset."

Jessie closed her eyes. "I know."

"You don't know. How could you, when you and that man have been—have been…"

"William—William knows about—about Liam?"

"Certainly he knows. That man called from the airport. We know you and he flew to Florida. Together."

Each word was a brand and an accusation. "Carrie." Jessie took a breath, expelled it and rose to her feet. "Put William on the phone, please."

"I don't know that he'll want to talk with you."

"Maybe not. But ask him, will you?"

"He's busy. If he has time later, maybe he'll call you back."

The line went dead. Slowly, Jessie hung up the phone. William couldn't call, not without her phone number, and Carrie hadn't requested it.

Something had changed while she'd been gone, some delicate shift of power and loyalty. Jessie thought about it for a minute. Not that it mattered. William might, in fact, despise her, refuse to see her. He certainly had the right.

Still, she had to face him.

Jessie put on her jacket, picked up her car keys and locked the door to her room behind her.

LIAM PULLED TO THE CURB just before Bill's driveway and sat staring straight ahead as the car idled.

"Come on, Malone," he muttered, "get it together."

He had to before he faced Bill. It had all seemed so clear back on Flamingo Island. Confront Bill, explain that what had happened was nobody's fault but his, that he'd never intended to betray their friendship, wish him well and walk away. He'd worked it all out during a couple of endless hours spent pacing the first-class lounge at the Miami airport, refined it during almost six hours of flying time.

So how come he still didn't know what he'd say when Bill opened the door?

Liam smiled grimly. All things considered, he might not have to worry about it. He'd ring the bell, Bill would open the door and their conversation would begin and end with Bill delivering a hard right to Liam's jaw.

That was what he'd do, if a man stole Jessie from him. Not that one punch would do it. He'd want to kill the bastard. Jessie was his. She'd always be his. Nobody could ever take her from...

Liam crossed his hands on the steering wheel and pressed his forehead to his wrists.

She wasn't his. That was the point of this whole infuriating exercise. He'd come back to acknowledge the truth, that he had no claim on Jessie, even though he'd never stop loving her, that he was the worst friend a man had ever had, a lying, cheating, double-dealing, no-good bastard.

"Just admit you're a rat," he muttered, "and then get the hell out."

He straightened in his seat, put the car in gear, shot up the driveway—and looked up just in time to see a small white car come hurtling up behind him.

"Son of a—"

He jammed his foot on the brake pedal, felt the jolt and heard the glass breaking as the white car's headlights shattered. He threw open the door and jumped out.

"Damned idiot," he snarled, as he strode toward the other car. "Where'd you learn to drive?" This jerk needed driving lessons. That was fine. Better than fine, considering his mood. If Bill slugged him, he couldn't slug back, but if this idiot so much as made a sound—

"Get out of there," Liam said. He yanked open the door, reached in…and saw Jessie. Her face was pale, her eyes were red rimmed. From tears, he knew, because he'd cried, too, in his heart, and he knew, too, that the person he'd really been lying to was himself.

No matter what happened, he would never let her leave him again.

"Jessie," he said, and she was in his arms before her name had left his lips.

"Liam," she sobbed. "Oh, Liam, my love."

"Why did you leave me?"

"Why didn't you come after me?"

"I didn't want to leave you, but—"

"I wanted to go after you, but—"

They spoke together, words, voices, crossing in a hurried blur. Then they fell silent. Liam's arms tightened around her, Jessie raised her face and they kissed.

"I love you," Liam said fiercely against her mouth. "And I'm not letting you go."

"Don't." She sighed. "Oh, don't. Not ever. I need you, Liam, I need you and love you and—"

The door to the house swung open. Liam and Jessie turned and saw Bill and Carrie standing in the entrance. Jessie started to pull away, but Liam kept an arm around her waist, anchoring her to him.

"Well," Carrie said, "isn't this a pretty sight?"

Liam ignored her. "Bill," he said steadily.

Bill Thornton's expression was unreadable. "Liam."

"William," Jessie said, "William, I'm so sorry."

"It's my fault," Liam said. "Not hers." He dropped his arm from Jessie's waist and took her hand. Her fingers were icy, and he squeezed them reassuringly. "Jessie had nothing to do with what happened."

Bill's mouth thinned. "How noble."

"Bill, look. Neither of us planned this. I mean, we didn't expect…"

"And that's supposed to make it okay?" He took a step forward. "My best friend. And my fiancée. What a fine pair you make."

"William." Jessie's voice broke. "We never meant to hurt you. You have to believe that."

"The only thing I have to believe is that I never knew either one of you. I'd have trusted you with my life, Liam. And Jessica…I thought you were the most wonderful woman in the world, but now—"

"Watch what you say to her," Liam said, his voice hardening. "I'm the one who made a mess of things, understand? You want to take a shot at me, go ahead."

Bill stared at the two of them, then shrugged his shoulders. "What would be the point? It wouldn't change anything.'' A tired smile lifted one corner of his mouth. ''Besides, the last time I tried that, Malone, I ended up almost needing to have my jaw wired shut, remember?''

Some of the tension eased from Liam's stance. ''Yeah, but that was ten years ago, and you were dumb enough to think you could tackle me five yards from the goalpost.''

''It was just a game of pickup football,'' Bill said. His eyes went to Jessie, then back to Liam. ''You weren't defending something as basic as your right to fall in love with Jessica.'' He cleared his throat. ''That's what this is all about, isn't it? You're in love with her.''

Liam's jaw knotted. ''Yes.''

''And you, Jessica? Do you love him, too?''

''Yes,'' Jessie whispered. ''I love him with all my heart.'' Tears rose in her eyes. ''But you'll always be special to me, William. I want you to know that.''

''Special,'' Bill said, and gave a bitter laugh. ''And I'm supposed to take comfort in that?''

''I promised you I'd do the right thing,'' Liam said, his eyes steady on Bill's. ''It's true, I made some detours along the way, but in the end, I know that what I'm doing now *is* the right thing.'' He paused, twined his fingers through Jessie's. ''I love Jessie. And she loves me. She can't marry you because it would be a travesty. Everyone would end up cheated—you, me, and her—and not one of us would be able to live down the shame for the rest of our lives."

After a long moment, Bill sighed. "I guess that's one of life's toughest lessons, that the right thing isn't always easy to figure out."

"No," Liam agreed, "it isn't."

"Anyway, I'm not blameless. Part of this mess is my fault, too."

"That's not true," Carrie said, with indignation. "You didn't do anything!"

"But I did." Bill took Carrie's hand and held it tightly. "I didn't give Jessica any options. One night she agreed to have dinner with me and the next thing she knew, I was making her part of my life. Isn't that right, Jessica?"

"If you mean that you were wonderful…" Jessie smiled shakily. "You sent me flowers every day. You phoned all the time."

"Sure. I figured if you were right for me, all I had to do was convince you that I was right for you. I guess I thought, well, if we were a great team in the office, we'd be terrific as husband and wife." He cleared his throat. "Obviously, I was wrong."

"Bill." Liam cleared his throat, too. "I don't expect you to forgive us—"

"Good." Bill stood straight and tall, and looked directly into Liam's eyes. "Because I haven't. You want the truth, Malone? I don't know if I'll ever forgive you. Accepting what's happened is one thing. Forgiving it is another."

Liam nodded. "I understand. Let's—let's give it some time, okay?"

"Yeah," Bill said, "let's do that."

He stepped back, still clasping Carrie's hand, and the door swung shut. Liam stood motionless for a long moment. Then he swallowed hard, turned to Jessie and took her in his arms. She was weeping, and he drew her close and kissed away her tears.

"Don't cry," he said softly. "It's going to be okay."

"Poor William. He's so hurt." She sniffled, and Liam dug out his handkerchief and handed it to her. "He was right, you know." She smiled through her tears. "We were a great team in the office. We should have left it at that."

Liam smiled, too, as he took her in his arms again. "You liked being assistant to the CEO, huh?"

"Yes." Despite her tears, she tilted her chin in defiance. "Don't tell me you're one of those male chauvinists, Malone, who doesn't like the idea of his woman having a job."

"To begin with," Liam said gently, "you're not going to be my woman, you're going to be my wife."

Jessie sighed. "I like the sound of that."

"And you're right, I don't like the idea of you working for some guy."

"Now, wait a minute, Liam—"

Liam kissed her. "Working *with* some guy," he said, smiling into her eyes, "an equal partnership kind of thing, well, that's different."

"What are you talking about? Do you mean you're thinking of starting some sort of business?" She snuggled against him. "Oh, that would be lovely. But you don't have to do it for me. I know you like to bounce from place to place, and if that's what you want, it's what we'll do."

Liam wrapped his hand around the back of her neck and tilted her face to his. "I have a lot to tell you, sweetheart. About me, about my life…" He could feel his heart lift. "Let's just say I've got some irons in the fire that can use your skills and, no, we're not going to bounce from place to place, unless that's what you really want."

"I just want you," Jessie whispered. "Only you, my love."

"Always," Liam said softly. "For all the rest of our lives."

EPILOGUE

THEY WERE MARRIED less than a month later, in the solarium of the handsome house they'd bought on one of the beautiful San Juan Islands in Puget Sound.

Jessie had wanted to be wed in the garden, because a garden was where they'd met, but Liam convinced her to take pity on their guests and have the ceremony inside the solarium. The northwest was still in the grip of a chilly spring, but that day the sun shone. The first of the spring crocuses had pushed their heads through the snow and Jessie had decorated both the house and the solarium in the same soft lilac color.

She wore white silk; Liam wore a black tux. A guitarist played softly in the background. There was champagne and caviar, oysters and Dungeness crab, and on top of the five-tiered wedding cake, in place of the figures of a bride and groom, there stood a small globe that Liam had given Jessie at breakfast.

It was made of crystal and, inside it, a tiny porcelain bride who looked suspiciously like her, and a porcelain groom who more than resembled Liam, embraced before a bright green palm tree standing on white sand, set against a tropical cardboard sea.

Jessie had wept with happiness.

"Turn it over," Liam had said gently. She did, and as the sand turned the placid scene into a hurricane, she saw the inscription engraved on the bottom of the globe.

Let The World Tilt, it said.

Now, the ceremony that would join them forever was moments away. Their future stretched ahead, brightly shining. There had been some difficult moments as Jessie's friends made peace with the fact that she'd fallen in love with another man on what was to have been her wedding day, but she and Liam were so much in love that no one could fault her, or him, for following the dictates of their hearts. And they were filled with plans, plans that Liam had already put into motion. He was CEO of Flamingo Resorts; she was Chief Financial Officer. They worked together, played together, loved together.

Their lives had taken the shape fate had meant them to take all along.

And it would all be perfect, Jessie thought, as

she stood in the encircling curve of her husband's arm—they'd both agreed that they didn't want to be separated, not even for the hours prior to their wedding. It would be perfect, but for one thing.

"You're thinking about Bill," she said softly.

Liam nodded. It was the first time she'd referred to William by his nickname. Liam knew that, in some subtle way, it marked a passage in their lives.

"Yeah," he said. "I am. I didn't really expect him to come." He ran an index finger under his collar. "I just thought—"

"Liam?"

"I thought, well, maybe he'd realize that our friendship—"

"Liam." Jessie looked up at Liam and smiled. "He's here, darling."

Liam stiffened, then looked across the room. Bill and Carrie were coming toward them. A huge smile broke over his face.

"Bill." He stepped forward. "Man, I'm so happy you—"

"Me, too."

The men stared at each other. Then Liam held out his hand and Bill clasped it.

"Good to see you," Bill said.

"Yeah." Liam grinned. "Same here."

Bill let go of Liam's hand and drew a smiling Carrie forward. "We're engaged, Carrie and I." He looped his arm around her shoulders. "Crazy, isn't it? That so much good came out of this whole thing?"

"I think it's wonderful." Jessie touched her cheek to Carrie's. Then she took Liam's arm and smiled at the others. "Just wonderful."

"So," Bill said briskly, after a moment had gone by, "what's the deal here, huh? Did you manage to bribe some poor slob into standing up for you?"

Liam laughed, though Jessie noticed his green eyes were suspiciously bright.

"Actually, I figured, why go to all that trouble when the best man of my choice was going to show up any minute?"

Bill grinned. "You really sure you want to do this, Malone? Sign your freedom away to one woman?"

"Absolutely." Liam turned to Jessie and took her in his arms. "For all of my life."

Jessie smiled. "Forever," she said, and kissed the only man she had ever, would ever, love.

ASSIGNMENT: SEDUCTION
by
Cathy Williams

Cathy Williams is Trinidadian and was brought up on the twin islands of Trinidad and Tobago. She was awarded a scholarship to study in Britain, and came to Exeter University in 1975 to continue her studies into the great loves of her life: languages and literature. It was there that Cathy met her husband, Richard. Since they married Cathy has lived in England, originally in the Thames Valley but now in the Midlands. Cathy and Richard have three small daughters.

Look out for
THE BOSS'S PROPOSAL by Cathy Williams
in Modern Romance™, April 2001

CHAPTER ONE

IT WAS nine-thirty at night. This was dark, unfamiliar territory and even inside the taxi it was freezing cold. Outside, with the wind rustling wrappers and paper along the street, the detritus of people who couldn't be bothered to find the nearest bin in which they could deposit their rubbish, it would be an icebox. A menacing, littered icebox. All that was needed now were a couple of howling, rabid dogs and some dustballs to complete the happy scene.

This had better be good.

'You sure you got the address right, lady?' The taxi-driver's eyes met hers in the rear-view mirror. 'Somebody meeting you at the other end? 'Cos this ain't the most savoury part of London.'

'Oh, somebody's meeting me all right,' Melissa muttered grimly under her breath. She crossed her slender legs and stared with mounting exasperation out of the window.

Even for him, this was too much. To give her forty minutes' notice, to *drag* her from the cosy warmth of her little flat not to mention the tantalising prospect of a ready-made meal curled up in front of the television, on the pretext that he *needed* to have a meeting with her *urgently,* didn't bear thinking about.

In the three years that she had been working for him, Robert Downe's utter disregard for convention had seen her working until three in the morning, taking notes at meetings conducted in the most unlikely places, being whisked off on his private jet an hour after she had stepped foot through the office door, but when she was home, her time had always been her own.

He demanded total commitment from everyone who worked for him, and from her he expected not only that, but a ready, obliging and preferably thrilled smile on her face to accompany his occasionally outrageous demands. But, as he had airily informed her at her interview, fair was fair. The minute she left the office, she would be absolutely free to shed her working clothes and indulge in whatever took her fancy, without fear that he would invade her privacy with unwanted work requests.

What he had omitted to mention was quite how thoroughly her well-paid, invigorating job would eat into so many hours of the day that the notion of having any sort of coherent, stable, routine private life was almost out of the question.

Her brilliant, temperamental, utterly dedicated boss didn't possess a nine-to-five mind and he was frankly bewildered by anyone who didn't share his lack of respect for clocks, watches and anything else that attempted to impose restrictions on the working day.

'Here we go, lady. Big Al's. Been in there a couple of times myself.' There was wistful nostalgia in the cab driver's voice as he harked back to what was undoubtedly his bad old days, judging from the unappealing sight that greeted her eyes. 'Looks worse on the outside than it is on the inside. And don't mind them blokes on the bikes. Gentle as lambs, they are.'

The herd of gentle lambs, some ten of them, began revving their motorbikes. One of them spat forcefully into the gutter, said something in a loud voice and there was a wave of raucous laughter.

I'll kill him, she thought to herself, *even if it means saying goodbye to the best job I'm ever likely to have. How could he have brought me here?*

'Want me to wait for you, just in case your mate ain't inside?'

'No.' Melissa sighed and handed over the fare, including

a generous tip just in case she needed him sooner than she thought.

'Like hanging out with the rough sort, do you?' The taxi-driver caught her eye in the mirror and winked knowingly, a seedy gesture to which Melissa could find no response that came anywhere near the realms of politeness. Instead of answering, she opened the car door and swung her body outside.

The freezing cold attacked her like a vengeful lover that has been kept waiting for too long, and she pulled her coat tightly around her, shoving her hands into the pockets and walking quickly towards the bar, head down to protect herself from the biting wind. Outside the bar, a couple of loiterers were arguing over something. Out of the corner of her eye, she saw them pause in mid-flow to look at her and although her face registered no fear whatsoever, a thread of clammy apprehension uncurled inside her in sickening waves.

She pushed open the door and was greeted by a blast of wailing country music, a fog of smoke and the deafening babble of voices. In the middle of the room, a circular bar held sway, and around it was draped a collection of abnormally hairy men, largely dressed in faded denim. Sprinkled in between these flowers of shy beauty was a selection of blondes, mostly drinking out of bottles. Melissa had to steel herself against making an involuntary moue of distaste.

Towards the far end of the room, which was much bigger inside than it appeared on the outside, were three pool tables. In the background, Tammy Wynette continued to lament the passing of love.

It took a matter of seconds to locate the object of her irritation and she strode towards him, head held high, heels clicking purposefully on the wooden floor, hands still thrust into the pockets of her coat, tan-and-navy bag firmly secured under her arm.

A number of curious eyes followed her path across the

room until she stopped, glaring, in front of her boss, legend in financial circles, talented, eccentric creator of vast wealth from little more than a background selling fish at Billingsgate Market with his father at the age of twelve, breaker of women's hearts, many of which she personally had had to deal with when love's first passion had grown bored and restless.

He was holding court at the far end of the room. He had pushed his chair away from the table, the better to accommodate his long legs and appeared to have his audience enraptured with whatever he was saying.

Somewhere very deep inside her, she could feel the full force of his overwhelming personality and his devilish good looks register on her consciousness. As it always did. In all the time she had worked for Robert Downe, he still had the power to unsettle her simply by the way he looked.

He was shockingly, no *scandalously,* good-looking. His hair was black and very short and his eyes were deep midnight blue, the blue of the sky when daylight has all but left and darkness is beginning to spread its wings. Sexy eyes. She might be immune to him but she had always reluctantly conceded the appeal he had over the female sex. Whatever their marital status, whatever their age, height, weight, class, profession or personality, his mere presence had always been enough to turn heads.

'You're late,' were his opening words, while three pairs of eyes settled on the petite, olive-skinned brunette with interest. Melissa ignored them all and focused her slanting brown eyes on her boss.

'Would you mind telling me *what* was so important that you had to *drag* me out of my warm flat, halfway across London at this time of the night? An urgent meeting, I recall you saying?' She tilted her small head meaningfully, and her thick, straight brown hair which she had left untied in her haste to meet her boss, swung against one shoulder. 'Strange, but the music is so loud here that I can't see how we could *possibly* have a conversation, never mind *conduct a business meeting*.'

It was one of her boss's occasional grumbles that no one, *but no one,* spoke to him as irreverently as she did, but it was, she knew from experience, the only way to deal with some of his more flamboyant moods. She worked too closely with him to be daunted by his forcefulness and anyway, it would have been out of character for her to tiptoe around him. In her own self-contained way, she was every bit as forceful as her boss.

'Whoa!' There were cries of delight all round and Robert flashed her a pained expression which she knew meant nothing at all. Had he forgotten that she had seen him in action over the years and knew that he was as humble and vulnerable as a barracuda on the prowl?

'See what I have to put up with?' he addressed no one in particular, and Melissa folded her arms and looked at him, gimlet-eyed.

'Yeah. Well, it beats Allie at the office,' one of the bearded men commented morosely. 'Sixty if a day and a shrew with it. Surprised I ever get any work done.'

'You don't work, mate. You draw.'

'You're an artist?' Melissa asked, side-tracked.

'Architect. For my sins.'

'With a face like that,' Robert said gravely, 'he had to go in for a job that kept him away from the public eye.'

Melissa felt a wicked urge to smile and had to remind herself that there was nothing to smile about because she had been rudely yanked from her privacy for what was fast appearing to be no reason at all. That was the problem with Robert Downe. He could move from infuriating to funny in the space of seconds with no recovery period in between.

'At least yours truly here doesn't have to rely on pretty-boy looks to get places,' he replied, grinning at Robert and winking at Melissa.

'Oh, my loyal secretary doesn't find me in the slightest bit good-looking, do you, Mellie?' He gave her one of those scorching stares from under his lashes. It was a look she had seen him direct at his leggy beauties from time to time, and she raised one eyebrow cynically.

'Which,' she said to her small audience, 'is why I'm still working for him.'

'You wouldn't swap me for all the tea in China. You know that,' he said huskily and she clicked her tongue impatiently.

'Work?' she reminded him. 'The reason I'm here?'

'Oh, if you must. Don't you want to relax for a few minutes?' He flashed her a winning smile which she returned with a warning frown. 'It's Harry's birthday today,' he said, tilting his head in the direction of a bearded hulk at the bar, and drinking straight out of the bottle. 'The big forty. The daddy of the lot. We've got a bit of a surprise for him.' Robert leaned over confidentially.

Melissa felt a twinge of unease at his closeness. Without consciously realising it, the lines between them were important to her. She needed the sanctuary of her home life, the untouchability of her privacy to keep his forceful personality at bay. She could handle him in a work capacity, where she was sure of herself and of her role but here, in a darkened bar, surrounded by his cronies, in an environment that stripped them of the invisible labels that defined them both, she realised that she was exposed and vulnerable in a way she didn't care for.

'Birthday cake,' Robert confided. 'Of the surprise variety. You know, one of those large affairs that house an attractive semi-clad woman who's a dab hand at a song-and-dance routine.'

'Oh, so nothing very chauvinistic then,' she said tartly. 'Is that why I'm here, Robert?'

'No, no, no!' He waved his hand vaguely at her. 'You're worse than a minder,' he muttered ungallantly under his breath, while his friends watched them, avidly curious. 'Face of an angel, heart of a born dictator.'

Melissa flushed. Only because you don't know me, she wanted to retort, but instead she drew in a deep, steadying breath.

'Okay, we'll use Al's office. Half an hour and you can be on your way, back home so that you can tuck yourself neatly into bed and settle down for the night.' He stood up, towering over her, six foot one of sheer, unbridled masculinity.

Wealth had given him access to whatever he wanted. He could afford to liberally adorn his house with the most expensive paintings and rugs and he frequently indulged a taste for opera which seemed so out of keeping in someone who had probably never been to the theatre until he was a man, let alone an opera. But however much money and power he wielded, neither could subdue that hard restless edge which could be as intimidating to adversaries as it could be sexually arousing to women.

He had fought every inch of his way up and it showed in the aggressive, uncompromising angles of his face. He looked like a man who was afraid of nothing. In fact, the opposite—a man who was accustomed to instilling fear whenever it suited his purposes.

Happily, Melissa was thoroughly unimpressed by this particular quality. She looked up at him, one eyebrow expressively raised as he manoeuvred his way around the table and the clutter of chairs.

'When's the wedding, Robbo?' one of his friends asked and there was a round of bawdy laughter.

Melissa watched as dark color surged into her boss's face and for a few seconds, she witnessed one of those rare occasions when he appeared to be rendered temporarily speechless. It didn't last long.

'Ah, I wouldn't want to end up like you lot for all the money in the world. Henpecked, the lot of you!' He grinned cheerfully at them.

'That's only because you haven't found the right woman to henpeck you into blissful submission. Yet. Although, the little lady next to you does show…'

'Right. Think I'll leave you bunch on that high note. Back out in an hour.' He reached down to the bottle on the table and then straightened with it loosely in his hand.

From a couple of feet away, Melissa watched him with peculiar intensity. Over the years, she had seen a fair amount of him outside work, but never totally relaxed as he was here. She had seen him in his capacity as her boss, entertaining clients, had even accidentally met him at the theatre once in the company of one of his glamour women. Always, he had been immaculately and expensively dressed in one of his many hand-tailored suits, only that primitive sensuality giving away his unpolished background.

Here, he was in faded jeans and a checked shirt which hung over the waistband and was rolled to the elbows, exposing his sinewy forearms. She looked away, idiotically ruffled by his blatant masculinity.

Al's office turned out to be a smart little affair, at odds with the rough-and-ready atmosphere outside. There was a small wooden desk, on which a computer terminal lay at rest and on another thin desk which protruded at right angles from this, were a fax machine, two telephones and several files, neatly stacked. The carpet was thick and cream and the walls were painted an unusual shade of green that gave the room a pleasant, leafy atmosphere. Robert took the chair behind the desk and gestured for Melissa to take a seat on one of the two facing him.

She had already removed her coat and draped it over the back of the spare chair. Now, she waited in silence, hands folded on her lap, legs crossed, for her boss to fill her in on whatever he had summoned her to say.

At least the slightly wild look had vanished from his face. At this moment in time, an unpredictable boss was something she could do without. In some of her more introspective moments, it occurred to her that there was something sad about her inability to cope with any shows of excessive behaviour. Hysterics, drunkenness, passion, intensity, they all fell into the same uncomfortable category, one that she was not equipped to handle. Restraint had been her mother's guiding principle and while a part of Melissa resented the limitations that placed on her behaviour, she was incapable of changing it.

'So,' he drawled, leaning back into the chair, which obligingly tilted back, affording him ample room to stretch his denim-covered legs onto the side of the desk. He linked his fingers together behind his head and proceeded to stare at her. 'What do you think of my schoolyard friends?'

Melissa looked steadily at him. 'They seemed very likeable.'

'My perfect model of restraint,' he said lazily, his eyes half closed as he continued to survey her. 'Do you ever shed your secretarial garb?' he enquired.

Melissa stared blankly at the wall behind him. This amused, frankly insolent line of enquiry was something she thought he had left behind a long time ago. When she had first started working for him, he had been intrigued by her personality. Intrigued that someone who was only twenty-two could be so self-contained, so cool, so collected.

He had seen nothing amiss in probing into her private life, asking questions about her likes and dislikes, her past, her background, even her sex life. It hadn't taken her long to inform him that her personal life had nothing to do with him, after which he had ceased peppering his polite see-you-in-the-morning chit-chat with seemingly innocuous but bitingly curious questions about what she would be getting up to later on.

'Okay, okay!' He raised both his hands in a mock gesture of defeat. 'I forgot. Remarks like that are strictly off limits! I can tell from that frozen look on your face!' But he was grinning, unperturbed by the fact that her face had remained rigidly unyielding. 'Work,' he carried on. 'I would have saved this for tomorrow, but as you know I'm off to New York in the morning and won't be back for a week, and this can't keep.'

'You could have telephoned me with your instructions,' Melissa pointed out.

'True. But it would have spoilt the surprise.'

A little thread of alarm shot down her spine. She didn't like his use of the word *surprise* nor did she like the expression on his face when he said it. He looked *quietly satisfied*.

'What surprise?' she volunteered tentatively. Surprises were something else she didn't much care for. How much her mother had to answer for! Without a husband, Melissa had always known that life couldn't have been easy for her mother, not least because the past had made her bitter and suspicious of other people and their motives.

Having watched her marriage finally crack under the weight of her second husband's rampant womanising, she had seen it as her divine mission to instil in her daughter a healthy disrespect for anything roughly resembling impulsive behaviour. Impulse, she was fond of saying, had been the downfall of your stepfather. Impulse, she would preach, shaking her head and pursing her lips into a thin line, had been the devil in disguise.

In fact, recklessness, in Melissa's mind, had come to rank as a grievous sin, punishable by something vague, unformed but definitely awful. By the time adulthood had arrived and with it an ability to put things into perspective, her mother had died and was beyond the reach of questions, and her daily homilies had turned into ingrained truths, stronger than reason and more frustratingly powerful than logic.

'There's a little job in the offing,' he said, watching her. 'Have you got a current passport?'

'You know I have,' Melissa answered, at a loss to know why she had to be called halfway across London to be told this.

'A good friend who can look after your flat for a while? You know, feed the goldfish, water the plants, et cetera.'

'I don't have any goldfish.' She gave him a perplexed frown. 'Just like I don't have a clue where this is leading. I'm sure the plants can survive for a couple of days anyway.'

Ominously, he sat forward and rested his chin on the tips of his joined fingers. 'The time scale is a little broader than that,' he informed her. 'A couple of months rather than a couple of days. And guess what, here's the really big surprise, *you're going home. Back home to Trinidad. A chance to relive all those great childhood memories.*' He sat back with an expression of triumph on his face. 'Now how's that for a surprise!'

CHAPTER TWO

MELISSA had ten days in which to arrange the technicalities of putting her life in England on hold for two months, and in which to contemplate the essential difference between *surprise* and *shock.*

Surprise, she could have pointed out, is when you open the door to your flat, thinking that the world has forgotten your birthday, only to be welcomed by all your friends and the sound of popping champagne corks.

Shock, on the other hand, is when your boss tells you that a gem of an idea which he's been nurturing from seed for months, little expecting it to ever really go ahead, has taken root, that his little gem of an idea involves an island you barely remember and rather wouldn't in any case and that you'll be going there with him on business.

'You never mentioned this to me,' was all Melissa could find to say after he had made his announcement.

'Excuse me while I reach for my hankie so that you can mop up your tears of delight at my little bombshell.'

Bombshell, she had thought, was the operative word, even though she had kept a steady smile on her face while she tried to formulate a few reasons why she couldn't possibly go with him.

Trinidad, sun-soaked, slow-moving, lush paradise, belonged to her past. When she thought of it, she could barely conjure up memories of all those years she had spent there between the ages of five and eleven, when her stepfather had been posted on the island with the oil company for which he had worked. All she could remember were the rows between her parents. Long, bitter arguments that seemed to rage from one day into the other, with small breaks in between. As she had got older, the reason for the rows had become clear and with understanding came a new, deeper reason to run and hide from the shouting and the angry accusations and counter accusations.

She always felt that her aversion to confrontations stemmed from those childhood experiences when the raised voices of her mother and her stepfather had been enough to reduce her to a curled ball taking refuge in the corner of a room somewhere.

Of course, those memories were a secret, private place she shared with no one, least of all her boss.

'I couldn't possibly leave the country for months on end,' she had objected.

'It's eight weeks, not *months on end*.'

'What would happen to my flat?' She had only been a few seconds into her objections and she could see that already his temper was beginning to fray at the edges. 'I wouldn't feel happy about leaving it unoccupied for months.'

'Why not?'

'Because it might be broken into.'

'It might be broken into even when you're in it.'

'My plants…'

'Can be watered by a friend. You *have* got a couple of those lurking around, haven't you?'

'Of course, but…'

'No buts, Mel.' He had sat back in the chair and regarded her with fatalistic calm. 'Truth is, I never expected to get hold of this land, but I have and I'm going to need you there with me. You know the way I work and you can handle all the faxes and communications from London and New York without me having to hold your hand and explain things. You're single, unattached…' His voice had drifted speculatively into silence. 'Aren't you? No boyfriends hovering somewhere in the background, clamouring for tea at seven-thirty and sex every other night?' There had been a thread of insulting amusement in his voice when he said that.

'Why not *every night?*' she had snapped, instantly regretting her outburst when she saw the glitter of interested curiosity that lit up the deep blue eyes at her unexpected response to his needling. 'You can't leave the office for months, anyway.'

'I can do precisely as I like. I *own* the whole damn show or had you forgotten?'

And so every twist and turn she had tried had resulted in a dead end and she had found herself grudgingly and resentfully agreeing to his request.

Ten days to buy as much light clothing as she could find in shops that were fully stocked with coats, jackets and woolly jumpers, to arrange with her neighbour for her plants to be watered and the flat to be checked every so often, to sort out the distribution of work between the two girls who reported to her who seemed panic-stricken at the prospect of working on their own, until she reminded them that she would be calling twice a day to make sure that there were no problems.

The arrangements, she thought now, staring absent-mindedly through the airplane window to a bank of grey nothing outside, had been remarkably smooth. Robert had been right. She could shed her life for weeks on end without any difficulty whatsoever. There was no one who would miss her, no children to consider, parents to consult, lover to soothe. Not even a cat to fret over.

It gave her ample time to worry about the whole traumatic exercise of returning to her past. It also provided a wonderful springboard for a new and equally disturbing line of thought which involved being in the presence of Robert Downe twenty-four hours a day without the respite of her private time away. True, the hotel would afford her a certain amount of protection but the thought of eating lunch and dinner with him made her feel a little ill.

He hadn't given her a schedule of his work timetable while out there, but she quickly decided that whatever it was, she would subtly alter it to ensure that business meetings with his lawyers and contractors and designers and architects and all the other people who would be turning his land into a hotel, took place over lunch and dinner. During which time she would either be present, taking notes whenever necessary but basically sliding happily into the background, or else in her hotel room, away from him completely.

By the time the plane landed at a little after six-thirty in the evening at Piarco airport, nerves had been joined by a healthy curiosity about the place she and her mother had left behind fourteen years previously, stripped of all their possessions, fleeing like a couple of thieves in the night while her stepfather remained on the island with the latest in his line of outside women.

There was growing familiarity as she made her way through passport control, lining up behind all the other non-Nationals. She collected her luggage and made her way through customs, to find a sea of people crowding the barriers outside.

The heat was thick and furnace-like. The navy-blue slacks and blouse she had worn for the journey adhered themselves to her body like cling film while she anxiously cast her eyes around for her lift to the hotel.

Robert Downe was nowhere to be seen.

A short, black man asked her if she wanted a taxi and she abstractedly refused, still holding out some hope that her wretched boss would appear even though she knew him well enough to realise that if he had become involved in a phone call five minutes before he was due to leave for her, it was more than possible that he wouldn't show up for a good while yet. She had dragged her cases to the side and resignedly sat down for an indefinite wait on one of the benches, when a skinny, middle-aged man with coffee-brown skin approached and asked her if she was Melissa James.

'Yes!'

'Mr. Downe sent me for you. The car's over there.'

'How did you know who I was?'

'He said that if I arrived late, I would find you waiting somewhere at the side with a long-suffering look on your face, Miss James.'

Remind me, she thought sourly, to murder my boss as soon as I see him and scatter his body parts to the four corners.

'And where…is…Mr. Downe?'

'Back at the Kiskidee. He was hard at work when I left.'

They had reached a dusty saloon car parked at an angle in the No Parking zone. He slung her cases in the trunk, opened the back door for her, and as soon as he had settled into the driver's seat, they sauntered slowly off. It was a relief that the driver was uninterested in making conversation. It gave her time to settle back and watch with a mixture of nostalgia and unease as the landmarks of her past unfolded before her eyes.

Lots seemed to have changed, yet nothing much. The roads were better, at least so far, and as they entered Port of Spain, she could see all the old familiar buildings still there, rubbing shoulders with a few new office blocks. Dim memories of childhood friends stirred at the back of her mind and she wondered what they were up to now. All ties had been severed when they had returned to England and now she could only vaguely recall names and faces.

The drive, stopping and starting and finally moving smoothly as the city was cleared, then the outskirts, then the mountainous winding road along the rocky, lush northern coastline, took over an hour and a half. By the time they hit the first beach along the route, one she remembered very clearly, it was too dark to see anything and she was too tired to be disappointed.

She just wanted to get to the hotel now, have a shower and put her feet up in the privacy of her room.

She must have nodded off because when the car shuddered to a stop, her eyes flew open to see the indistinct outline of her boss peering through the window at her.

'Here in one piece!' he said, pulling open the door so that she nearly fell out of the car and had to regain her balance. 'Sorry I didn't make it to the airport to collect you myself.' He held her by her shoulders at arm's length and stared down at her. 'I've missed you! There's a pile of work waiting inside.'

'Thanks,' Melissa answered drily, shrugging out of his grasp. 'Nice to feel wanted.'

She fell into step alongside him, while ahead of them, their driver carried her suitcases as though they weighed nothing. All around them the noises of the night, crickets and frogs and the rustle of small animals in the undergrowth, were like a background symphony. She could hear the night breeze sift through the trees and bushes and the sound of the ocean like steady, even breathing, rising and falling and forming a soothing lullaby with the other sounds of the night.

'Where's the hotel?' she asked, perspiring profusely as they made their way along a narrow path bordered with foliage and flowers. They had stopped outside a house and before answering he pushed the door, which had been slightly ajar and turned to her.

'House, actually.'

She stepped through the door into a tiled, airy room, and rounded on him, aghast.

'What do you mean *house*?'

'Just dump the bags by the table, Raymond. I'll take them to her room in a little while. See you tomorrow. Tell your wife there's no need for her to show up before nine.'

'You told me we'd be staying in a hotel!' Melissa said shrilly, as soon as they were alone.

'How does it feel to be back home?'

'Now you inform me that we're sharing a house?'

'You look as though you could do with a shower. You're perspiring. It's those clothes you're wearing.'

'This is a ridiculous situation! I can't stay in a house with you for the next two months!'

'Why not?'

'Because *I just can't.*'

'Even if I promise not to touch you? However tempted I might be by your sizzling sex appeal and that wicked little way you have of looking at me out of the corner of those big, brown eyes?' He grinned and she glared at him. 'Okay! I reserved two rooms at the nearest hotel but even the nearest was too far away from the land, so in the end I had to rent this house. It's more convenient. Now why don't you go and freshen up and then join me outside on the porch. I'll fill you in on what the general schedule's going to be over the next week or so.'

'Robert…' She sighed and folded her arms. The thoughts in her head were too big to explain rationally and her most disturbing thought was the one that was the least possible to elaborate. How could she tell him that she could cope with all his moods, keep up with the frenetic pace he set himself, remain as cool as a cucumber when he stormed through the office because something was bugging him, but the thought of being in his company when work no longer comprised the four walls around them, sent her into a state of mild panic? How could she ever explain that his deliberate teasing threw her into a tizzy, even though she didn't know why?

'Yes?'

'Where's my bedroom?'

'Along the corridor to the right. Last on the end. See you in a minute.'

He was whistling as he walked away.

This had not kicked off to a good start. This had all the promise of being one of her bigger life mistakes. No safe hotel with lots of people around, no sanitised conference rooms booked for work and meetings. Just the two of them and without the trappings of an office, who knew what mischief he might feel inclined to indulge in. His warm, sexual teasing could be as intrusive as fingers along her body and although she had always made sure to keep the lines between them very clear, she hadn't cared for a couple of his insinuations earlier on. She would have to be as business-like as possible, even if she risked seeming a bore in the process.

She showered quickly and hurried outside, where the night air felt cool against her and the sound of the sea was steady and rhythmic, like an African drumbeat. From the open patio, she could look down the small slope and glimpse beach through the coconut trees and bush that fringed the little inlet.

'I'm on the beach!' His voice floated up to her mingled with the sound of the surf and when she squinted into the darkness, she could make out a shape standing ankle-deep in the water. 'Stairs down to the left!'

Melissa licked her dry lips and tentatively made her way down the concrete steps to the beach, holding on to the iron railings on the side with one hand, clutching her notepad and pen with the other.

The dark shape on the beach was waiting patiently for her, looking at her slow progress down, his arms folded, his feet planted solidly on the sand, slightly spread apart. It was too dark to see the expression on his face, but his silhouette was reminiscent of something powerful and indestructible.

'I thought we were going to do some work,' she said, when she finally hit sand. The inlet was small, with a thick fringe of bush and trees spreading densely back from the sand, climbing up the small incline that led to the house. The sand felt firm and compacted under her feet and the sea was a black swell beating against the sand.

'I changed my mind,' he freely admitted, walking towards her, then past her to what she now saw was a towel spread on the sand, and upon which he flung himself, linking his hands beneath his head and staring up at the starless sky. 'Actually, I thought you could tell me a bit about the country. After all, you lived here for…how long…? Five years? Six?'

'I don't remember much about it,' Melissa said warily, watching his prone shape on the sand, the way his short, baggy T-shirt rode up to expose the firm skin of his torso, the length of his muscular legs. 'We left when I was eleven.'

'Why was that? Daddy got a transfer back to England?'

'No,' she said flatly. 'What are your plans for tomorrow? Will I be staying put here and working or do you need me to come with you to meetings?'

'Sit down. My neck's beginning to hurt looking up at you. Besides, I can't see your face when you're standing so far away. It's too dark.' He shifted a bit and patted a little free patch of towel next to his hip. 'It's very disconcerting addressing a faceless disapproving voice. Come and sit by me and tell me all about what you *do* remember of the place. Come on,' he said persuasively, 'I don't bite, you know.' He laughed throatily. 'So you can relax. Look at where we are, for heaven's sake! Warm night air, sea, sand, stars in the sky…no place for frosty disapproval!'

'I'm here to work, Robert,' Melissa reminded him. 'If you wanted someone to enjoy a romantic, tropical setting with you, then you should have considered bringing your… your…' Her voice, firmly assured when she had started her little speech, petered out into awkward silence.

'My…my…*lover?* Was that the word you were searching for, Melissa? Haven't got one at the moment, actually. Besides, the last thing I need out here is a lover. I just need *you* to relax a bit. This isn't an office now. We're both going to have to adjust to that fact.'

'We only came as far as this beach a few times,' she said eventually, yielding to his request for information simply because she knew that if she didn't, he would pester her until he got what he wanted. She made no move to sit next to him, though. That was taking relaxation a little too far for her liking. A sudden, graphic image of her thigh bumping against his made her brain temporarily cease functioning, then it recommenced, sending messages to her mouth that it should continue speaking, whatever the content.

'Most people tend to stop at Maracas Bay which is further back. This is just a little too far for a day trip. I…it's a lot more developed than I remember. Are there any shops around here? There weren't fourteen years ago. Just vegetable and fruit stalls by the side of the road. Any shopping entailed a trip to the city.'

In between her babbling, her mind toyed with the delicious and illicit image of his body brushing against hers, the feel of his hard, muscular flesh pressing against her, the touch of his fingers along her stomach and thighs and breasts. She gulped and felt faint. Rather than perch on his towel and send her already fevered mind into further overdrive, she slid down onto the sand and pulled her knees up to her chin, hugging them with her arms.

'No shops,' he confirmed, sitting up and looking at her. 'You'll get your shorts dirty sitting on the sand. In case I haven't mentioned it Raymond's wife will be coming in daily to clean and cook, and yes, you'll have to come to some of my meetings with me to take notes but a lot of the time you'll spend here. I've managed to get hold of everything you'll need to work. Fax machine, computer, printer, stationery, the usual.

'Tomorrow we'll be going to the city centre. I have a meeting with the lawyer and in case you're worried that I'm going to take advantage of your presence here to turn you into a workhorse, you're wrong. You'll work the same hours you work in England and you can do what you like with your free time. Did you keep in touch with any friends over here…?'

'No.'

'Why not? Or is that question off limits as well?' He had a knack of making her reticence sound like a sinister cover-up.

'*As well?* As well as *what?*'

'Really want me to tell you?' he asked softly. 'Put it this way, Mel. You've worked for me now for over three years. You probably know me a damn sight better than any of my women ever have, yet I don't know a thing about you. I haven't got a clue what makes you tick.'

'That doesn't make any difference to how I do my job.' Her heart was thumping. In the darkness his face was all shadows and angles and impending threat.

'I never said it did. I do find it a bit odd, though. What have you got to hide?'

'Nothing. I'm reticent by nature.' She stood up and brushed herself down with trembling hands. The silence between them took on a sound of its own, as definite as the sound of the sea or the fluttering of a bird's wings inside a cage.

'So tomorrow…' she said, clearing her throat.

'Meetings. I'll want you with me. After that…we'll see how things progress…no point planning too far ahead…is there? Life tends to short-change people who are stupid enough to do that…'

CHAPTER THREE

MORNING came earlier than Melissa expected. There was no alarm clock to drag her out of bed at seven-thirty, but nevertheless she was wide awake by quarter to six. The curtains at the windows were light, airy voile and were not designed to prolong sleep, whatever the constitution of the bedroom's occupant. Not a room for nursing a hangover.

She luxuriated in the king-size bed for a few minutes, drowsily taking in her surroundings which she hadn't really paid much attention to the night before. The wooden flooring, with a few bright rugs strewn here and there, the light wicker furniture, the pale walls with indifferent seascape scenes set in wooden frames adorned with sea shells.

It was tempting to fling on some shorts and a T-shirt and amble down to enjoy the scenery, but that posed the small problem of bumping into her boss, who might be similarly prowling around at this ungodly hour. She had spent an unreasonable amount of time lying in bed the previous night, trying to work out what it was about Robert that had unnerved her from the minute she stepped foot in the house the evening before. When she tried to analyse what he had said, her memory failed her and really, he had acted no differently than he always did, treating her with the outspoken, occasionally exasperating openness that came from familiarity.

So why had she suddenly found his presence so disturbing? She had scurried back to the house from the beach, grateful for the cover of darkness, like a scared rabbit that has only just managed to escape a predator.

It wasn't as though she didn't know him and wasn't all too familiar with his moods.

She took her time getting dressed, and then gazed at her reflection in the mirror. Her face was smooth and olive-hued, her features pleasant but unremarkable, her hair shiny and well kept but certainly no exotic mane of blonde curls. She lacked the voluptuous curves of the sort of women her boss was wont to court. It was ridiculous to imagine that he would see her in a different light simply because the normal constraints of work had superficially been removed, and vice versa. Clothes, she reminded herself, do not make the man.

By six-fifteen she was warily tip-toeing her way out of her bedroom, ears pricked for the first hint of noise coming from his, and hearing nothing, she scampered out of the house with a sigh of relief and headed down towards the beach.

In the greyish, early morning light she could appreciate what the blackness of the night before had successfully concealed. The lush foliage interspersed with leaning coconut trees, pressing against the sides of the railings, desperate to break the slender iron barriers and clamber over the concrete steps.

As she skirted down the twisting concrete steps, she caught different glimpses of the sea. The beach itself was small, a tiny cove which, she recalled, became virtually sandless when the tide was high. Now, the tide was low and the sand was scattered with the dregs that had been washed up from the ocean overnight. Twigs, seaweed, bits of wood, shells, broken chunks of coral.

As soon as her feet touched the beach, she removed her sandals and felt the sand between her toes, not white and grainy but pale brown and compacted.

'I didn't expect you up so early.' The booming voice came from somewhere to the left of her, out of sight but too close for comfort, and she momentarily froze.

He emerged from behind a bank of bushy undergrowth clad only in swimming trunks with a towel slung over his shoulders. His short hair was still slightly damp, which made it stand up in spikes. His body was powerful and sinewy and shamefully brown. How was this situation ever going to work out? Secretaries shouldn't have to confront their bosses when said bosses were virtually naked. Pin-striped suits protected both parties from that sort of ridiculous familiarity.

'You didn't wear your swimsuit,' he accused, eyeing her tidy shorts and polo shirt outfit up and down. 'This is the best time for a swim, you know,' he continued conversationally, either unaware of her embarrassment or else choosing to ignore it. 'Cool, peaceful.' He massaged his neck with the towel and then gazed upwards at the sky with what she thought was an undue amount of dramatic appreciation. 'The perfect time to be at one with Nature.'

'I had no idea you were so spiritual,' Melissa said, snapping out of her nervous reverie. She walked briskly away from him, towards the sea and then stood at the edge of the water, her sandals still in one hand, aware that he had followed and was standing a little behind her.

'Didn't I say that there were lots of things you didn't know about me?'

'No. You said that I knew everything about *you* and you knew nothing about *me*.'

'So you *do* listen to what I say, even when it has nothing to do with work,' he breathed against the nape of her neck. 'Sometimes I wonder. You look as though I'm speaking a foreign language whenever I make a personal remark.'

'Do I?' Melissa asked innocently, not daring to move an inch because she would probably bump into him and the thought of that brought her out in a cold sweat.

'You know you do. But heck, you're a shy private person…you might not believe this, but I'm a very shy private person as well…'

That made her swing round with a laugh of sheer disbelief. 'Oh, please!'

'I am,' he protested meekly.

'Since when?' She looked at him with frank amazement, unconsciously registering the fact that he hadn't yet shaved and the dark shadows around his chin lent him the rakish air of a pirate.

'What makes you think that I'm not?' he countered neatly, folding his arms and looking down at her with interest.

'The fact that you shamelessly intimidate people when you want to? And don't try to deny that, I've sat in enough meetings with you to know the methods you employ and the adjective shy doesn't spring to mind here. And what about your women? How many of them have trooped into your office over the years? Distraught and wailing because you've decided that their expiry date has arrived? You don't seem to mind that most people know all about your private life!'

'They only think they do,' he replied smugly. 'When I want, I can be as secret as the grave.'

Melissa gave him a wry look of scepticism and tilted her head to one side, 'Well, that's as may be.' She kicked her feet in the sand.

'Sure, the odd blonde has occasionally put in an appearance in my office…but that just means that I don't mind a bit of speculation on the part of my loyal staff when it comes to that…it'd be quite a different matter if I were serious about a woman. There's no way I wouldn't respect her privacy.'

'Uh-huh?' she grinned, turned her face to the rising sun and closed her eyes, loving the smell of the salty air and the feel of the breeze blowing warmly against her face.

'You'd be very surprised,' he said gruffly. 'Look, why don't you come in for a swim? There's no need for us to start work yet.'

'A swim?' Melissa's eyes snapped open.

'Why not?'

'Because…well because…'

'You *did* come equipped with a few swimsuits, didn't you?'

'Yes, of course, but…'

'But what? I'm not asking you to perform a striptease! Can't you take off your working hat just for a minute and loosen up? I'm not going to bite you!'

'I never said that you were!' Her face reddened at the accuracy of his shot. 'A short swim *would* be nice, as a matter of fact.'

Fifteen minutes later, she was back on the beach, this time wearing a black bikini with a big T-shirt over it. She had brought one of the beach towels with her and she rested it neatly on the sand, along with the divested T-shirt, and peered out towards the horizon. The sun was edging up quickly and bringing with it the promise of fierce heat.

She tentatively strolled down to the edge until the water was lapping against her ankles. When she looked up, she could see his head far out in the distance, past the breakers.

'Coming?' he shouted, 'it's all perfectly safe! I've vetted it personally for sharks!'

In which case, she thought cynically, what are *you* still doing in the water?

She took a deep breath as the cold water slapped against her body, then she dived under a wave and began swimming out. She was fairly out of breath by the time she reached Robert, who was waiting for her on his back, arms behind his head.

'You have to admit that this is refreshing,' he told her, staring up at the sky while she looked at his averted profile and paddled inelegantly in the undulating water. 'Lie on your back. Like me. Or you'll get out of breath.'

'What time is the meeting?'

'Eleven. Just imagine what England would be like now…cold, wet, grey… I think I could retire to a place like this.' He paused for a fraction of a second. 'Did you miss it when you left?'

Melissa flipped onto her back and considered his question, or at least considered whether or not to answer it.

'Not for long. Things were hectic when we came back. I was busy with a new school, new house, new life...'

She sighed involuntarily and he said, without hesitation, 'Why do you say *new life?* Surely it was just a change of environment? Everything else was the same?'

'Not quite.' She closed her eyes and allowed herself to relax and enjoy the effortless bobbing of her body on the surface of the sea. 'Stop probing,' she added for good measure, and smiled when he chuckled next to her.

'Now why would I do that?' he asked equably. 'We're not in England now. You can't threaten to walk out...' He was referring to the threat she had made a long time ago when his curiosity had gone a little too far. 'You're my prey here,' he murmured in an amused, husky drawl. 'Nowhere to run...just you, me...the opportunities to get to know one another better are limitless...' He laughed throatily, then loudly as she spluttered down into the water in alarm.

'Sorry,' he said, when she surfaced for air, her face red with confusion at his words. 'I didn't mean that. It's always so tempting to get behind that prim and proper air you carry about with you like a suit of armour.' He was looking at her, his eyes squinting against the sun. 'You should be careful, you know,' he murmured, warming to his subject, as her skin went a couple of shades deeper and her brown eyes interlocked with his blue ones, 'some men are turned on by that look of Victorian modesty. Knocks the socks off the usual tarty blondes who leave nothing to the imagination...'

'What are you trying to say?' she whispered foolishly, and he grinned at her. 'Oh, shut up,' she sputtered indignantly, looking away. 'I'm going inside. I'm getting a little water-logged here.' She ducked under the water and began swimming back to shore. She heard a smooth sound alongside her and glanced across to find him cutting an easy path through the water at her side, overtaking her. She deliberately slowed down to give him time to get well clear of her and then she watched covertly as he left the calmer waters of the deep behind and effortlessly dived beneath the bigger breakers near the shoreline, rising up beyond them until he was standing, calf-deep and watching her.

Distracted, she felt herself ambushed by an enormous wave that seemed to come from nowhere, and as she tried to push herself under, it lifted her off her feet. Fifteen seconds in a washing machine and then she was spat out, dazed and standing inches away from him. She glared up and thought that if his grin got any wider he would have to have his face surgically stitched back together.

'Quite a tumble,' he said gravely, mouth still twitching as he looked down. 'And bits of you are showing the after-effect.'

Melissa followed the direction of his eyes. In the underwater chaos, part of her bikini top had ceased to do its job and one breast was half out with more than a glimmer of brown nipple exposed. She gave a shriek of horror and adjusted her swimsuit but she could feel the colour rush into her face.

She couldn't look at him. She just couldn't meet those wickedly amused dark blue eyes. She remained where she was in frozen silence for what seemed like decades, although she knew that it could only have been for a few short seconds.

If she had had more experience with men, she might have found the right words to laugh the whole thing off, but she hadn't.

'No need to feel embarrassed, Mel,' he pointed out. 'I've seen women's bodies before.'

'That's not the point. You've never seen...you've never seen...'

'*Your* body before?'

'This is a ridiculous conversation!' Her face was bright red and she had never felt further from the serenely efficient secretary who could survive her boss at his most demanding without turning a hair. She had always thought that she knew how to handle him, but she was fast discovering that her skills in that area were in urgent need of polishing. Those snippets of charm and wit which were second nature to him were diluted when in England. Now, without anyone else around, she could feel them bombarding her and her reaction was one of confusion rather than indifference.

'You're absolutely right,' he agreed amicably, and she silently released a sigh of relief that he had decided to drop the conversation. 'I may have seen lots of women naked, but I've never seen *you*. Not that I haven't done my fair share of wild imagining.' He laughed as she fell into his trap, mouth half open with a retort, and she gritted her teeth together and made a stifled, frustrated sound under her breath.

'*You*, if you don't mind me saying, are the most…the most…'

'I know,' he answered placidly, 'that's why you love me.' He grinned at her and nodded in the direction of the house. 'Shall we go up for breakfast? Before you burst a couple of blood vessels?' He stepped aside with a gallant bow, allowing her to precede him, which put her in the unnerving position of knowing that his eyes were firmly focused on her as she manoeuvred the steps back up to the house.

She decided that she would very rapidly have to re-establish the status quo between them. Things were slipping and he was getting under her skin in a way he never had before, or perhaps had never had the opportunity to before. Ringing telephones, people bursting into the office unannounced, meetings and trips abroad, they all tended to reduce conversations to the pertinent, and when she accompanied him in her capacity as secretary to his thousand-and-one business engagements, it had always been simplicity itself to make sure that dangerous atmospheres of intimacy were not established.

She could kick herself for not being a bit more thorough in her line of questioning about this particular trip. She had happily assumed a number of things, most importantly that they would be staying in a hotel rather than in a house miles away from civilisation.

As soon as she reached the top of the steps, she paused to allow him time to fall in beside her and remove his vantage point of five paces behind.

'I'll just have a shower before we eat and get down to work,' she told him briskly.

'I'll make sure that the files are ready and waiting,' he told her, with equal briskness. 'And you'll be pleased to hear that Raymond's wife, Denise, will be in the house. Cook, cleaner and unwitting chaperone.'

'I don't need a chaperone,' Melissa answered smartly, not looking at him, 'I'm here as your secretary and that's as far as it goes.' Just in case he started getting any ideas, she thought. The Devil works on idle hands and hands that are housebound can get very idle indeed, especially when they're accustomed to being kept busy. It was as good a time as any to establish one or two boundaries before she found herself with a situation for which she was not prepared.

'Of course,' he said a little too quickly.

'Good.' They had reached the house and through the open patio doors, she could make out the shape of a dark-skinned rotund woman, who was sweeping the tiled floor with single-minded zeal.

'Besides,' he whispered wickedly into her ear at about the same time as Denise looked up at their approaching figures with a smile of recognition, 'I'd hate to shock poor Denise. Wouldn't you?' At which he drew away and entered the house with a carefree, merry whistle on his lips.

CHAPTER FOUR

MELISSA thought that the drive to Port of Spain would be an hour and a half of acute, badly concealed embarrassment sitting in close quarters with a man whose presence was growing on her like a burr under her skin, but in fact the drive sped past.

They both sat in the back seat with Robert's Louis Vuitton briefcase open between them, and together they went through the daunting stack of files concerning the property, using the particular shorthand which they had developed unconsciously over time.

Her eyes barely left the papers in front of her, her questions were succinct, as were his replies and by the time they had cleared the winding, rugged coastline with its confusing baggage of ill-formed memories, she had managed to absorb all the relevant facts about the purchase.

'I still don't understand why you chose this particular island,' she said, allowing her eyes to drift thoughtfully over the scale drawings of the hotel in front of her. 'Tourism isn't big over here. In fact, most people haven't heard of the place.'

She crossed her legs, primly clad in her knee-length flowered skirt and absent-mindedly pushed a loose strand of hair away from her face. She had tied her hair back and as usual, her technique was already letting her down.

'I know. Clever, wouldn't you agree?' he said with satisfaction, stretching his arm along the back of the car seat so that his hand was disturbingly close to the back of her head.

Melissa wondered whether she would have been as hypersensitive to that one week ago. How many times had they shared a taxi? Hundreds, she was sure. Or quite a few at any rate. He *must* have sat exactly as he was sitting now, with his arm extended behind her, his legs crossed so that his knee wasn't a million miles away from her own. Why was she now finding it difficult to concentrate on anything except the tantalising possibility that he might accidentally brush the back of her neck with his fingers?

'Would I?' she asked, conscious that she was leaning forward by a couple of crucial inches in an attempt to avoid the possibility of her head crashing into his hand.

As if reading her mind, he removed his arm, but only to shift the briefcase off the seat onto the floor, so that he could adjust himself into a more comfortable position, then back went the arm and forwards went her head.

'Think about it, Mel, the usual Caribbean haunts are becoming saturated. It won't be long before they're overstocked with hotels and the discerning tourist begins to cast his curious eyes around for somewhere a little less developed.'

'At which point, those curious eyes fall on this underdeveloped island and lo and behold, what should be waiting but your hotel?'

'Very good!' he said approvingly, settling a bit more comfortably in the seat and spreading his long legs wide to accommodate the lack of appropriate space in the back of the car. His khaki-clad knee inevitably rubbed against her leg and now, with her body straining away from his leg and his hand, she could uncomfortably feel her muscles begin to ache. She sighed and relaxed, determined to ignore his proximity.

'I got the land at a very good price and I've done my homework on the place, checked out all the attractions. It's just going to be a question of targeting the right market.'

The car bumped over a giant-sized pothole in the road and she found herself crashing inelegantly into the man next to her.

'The roads don't seem to have improved from when I was last here,' she muttered, shuffling away from him. 'I don't think your flood of potential tourists are going to warm to the bumpy roads.'

'Nonsense. They'll find it charming. Don't you know *anything* about human nature?'

Melissa turned to him, eyebrows raised. Robert, she had realised over the years, rarely professed ignorance on any subject, including those on which he was totally ignorant. She had known him to deliver lectures to some of the most important financial gurus in the city, having prepared nothing on the subject and with only cursory preparation of the details he needed. He would simply charm his way through an hour of speech, relying on his wit and his ability to think on his feet, to get him through. And get through he invariably did. He was the sort of man who would stick in the throat of the conventionally educated academic.

His education had been erratic and conducted as much in school as in the street, his university had been the proverbial university of life but his brain was unsurpassable. She doubted that there were many subjects he would not have been able to grasp in the minimum amount of time and tales of his exploits in the world of finance were legendary throughout the company. Everyone knew how he had risen from street trader to a man whose reputation for financial wizardry was beyond compare. He seemed to have been born with an innate ability to judge the movement of the money markets and by the age of twenty-seven he had already made a fortune.

All the more fascinating to his legion of admirers, was the fact that he seemed to have remained unchanged by his position. He dressed without respect for convention, paid no lip service to politeness unless it was deserved and had almost no tolerance for idlers.

Human nature, though, was quite a big subject for Robert to declare himself an expert on.

'Don't tell me you've been keeping a degree on psychology hidden up your sleeve,' she said, turning to look at him. She wished she had brought her sunglasses with her instead of leaving them on her dressing table, because the sun pouring out of the bright blue sky was blinding. Robert, naturally, had had a bit more foresight, and he slipped on his dark Oakley shades so that his eyes were conveniently obliterated while she had to content herself with shading hers with one hand.

'You *know* I'm little more than an uneducated lout,' he said grinning. 'I never came close to a university to get a degree on *anything,* never mind psychology! No, I just understand what makes people *tick,* if you know what I mean. People don't go abroad so that they can experience exactly what they left behind at home. Think about it, if *you* went abroad somewhere, would you want everything to be the same as in England? Same roads, same food, same shopping, same scenery? You might as well just stay put!'

'Some people like the creature comforts,' she pointed out stubbornly. 'They might find bumpy roads a little annoying, and then have you considered the fact that this hotel is going to be miles away from civilisation? No shops, no night-life, no clubs, no chemist, a couple of restaurants but nothing fancy?'

'Of course I've considered it!'

'And…?'

'Another plus, of course. *You* might call it boring, but others would find the solitude and isolation quite an attraction.'

'*I* wouldn't call it boring at all, actually,' Melissa couldn't resist pointing out at the last minute. 'I happen to *enjoy* peace and tranquillity.'

'So you wouldn't be bothered by the lack of night-life?'

'No.'

'Or entertainment?'

'No.'

'And what about those missing shops and chemists?'

'I was trying to point out potential drawbacks,' Melissa told him patiently.

'I know,' he replied humbly, 'and I'm grateful to you for doing that. I have no idea where I'd be if it weren't for you, bringing me down to earth whenever my wild schemes threaten to get out of hand.'

Melissa looked at him narrowly to ascertain if he was poking fun at her, but it was impossible to tell because of the sunglasses which, offputtingly, reflected her face back at her.

'So if *you* wouldn't find any of those things drawbacks, why shouldn't there be other people who think like you do?'

'Would *you* enjoy being so far out of the mainstream traffic?' she said, throwing the question back at him. 'I wish you'd remove those shades,' she said irritably.

'Sure.' He slid the shades down his nose so that he was peering at her over the top of them and with a click of her tongue, she reached out and removed them altogether.

'*You,*' he said lazily, 'can be a very masterful woman when you want. I like that.'

'You haven't answered my question.' His tendency to digress away from the serious business of work to the dangerous matter of her personal life, was threatening to get out of hand. At first, she had thought that it might have been her imagination, but she was beginning to clue in to his technique, which seemed to be based on lulling her into a sensible conversation, only to hijack it somewhere along the line.

Scarily, she was beginning to discover that his unsubtle intrusions might be unwelcome, uninvited and downright aggravating, but they were also fiercely thrilling.

'So I haven't,' he agreed, resting his head back against the seat and closing his eyes in the manner of someone giving something a great deal of thought. 'Let me put it this way,' he said eventually. 'I may not be able to spend the rest of my days cut adrift from the human race, or at least cut adrift from all the mod cons that make up day-to-day living, but I would happily spend a couple of weeks in total isolation. Just the roar of the sea, the shrieking of the gulls, the sound of the breeze blowing through coconut trees at night. What better than a walk on the beach under a sky as black and soft as velvet?'

What better indeed?

Melissa's eyes became unfocused and she gazed dreamily past Robert's shoulder.

'With the sea lapping against your ankles?'

Melissa nodded in appreciation.

'And the sand indenting under your feet? Hand in hand with your loved one...have you ever done that?'

'God, no.' She laughed as she swam out of her pleasant reverie about black skies and lapping water and holding hands with loved ones. 'Maybe I'll consider it, though, when the loved one appears on the horizon.'

'And then,' he continued crisply, 'aside from the benefits of solitude, there's the wildlife. Did you know that one of the most important bird sanctuaries is only a short drive away?'

'Yes. I did, as a matter of fact,' she answered, surprised as yet another memory dislodged itself from its burial place. Under the force of her mother's bitterness and her vivid memories of leaving under a black cloud of unhappiness and parental despair, she had totally forgotten that not all of her past deserved to be wiped out. There *had* been good moments and the bird sanctuary in question had been one of them. She had gone with her class on a school trip and she could remember the excitement, at the age of nine, of the long drive to Asa Wright, the thrill of seeing all those birds, a profusion of colours, the tour through the reserve, the bathing in the small, freezing waterfall, the denseness of the rainforest around them.

She turned to Robert, her eyes alive, and for no other reason than the sudden need to share her memory with the man next to her, she told him about the trip, the fun she had had. She could even remember some of the weird names of the birds. Honey-creepers, white-bearded manakins, and of course the hummingbirds.

That memory seemed to open a door to other, less painful memories, and she found herself telling him all about other places she had visited as a child. He was a good listener. Attentive, asking just the right questions, and they arrived in Port of Spain, the capital, without her even realising that their long drive was at an end.

'Sorry to have been so boring,' she apologised with a grimace, as Raymond opened the back door for her and waited for her to get out. The heat was blistering after the air-conditioned coolness of the car.

'You were anything but,' he said seriously, turning to give Raymond a few instructions, then looking down at her. 'You keep your past so well hidden, that I always assumed that there *was* something to hide.' He took her elbow and ushered her through the small garden that led to a black-and-white Colonial-style house, with its intricate woodwork and veranda that skirted the circumference of the dwelling.

'It's not quite as straightforward as that,' Melissa told him, with a shadow in her eyes. For once, she had no inclination to retreat from confidences. She had nothing shameful to hide but she had been *made* to feel as though she had by her mother, who had never recovered from her husband's infidelity and had dragged her daughter down with her.

'We'll pick this conversation up later,' he promised, but her eyes were shuttered and she stared straight ahead as they climbed the six steps up to the front door of the renovated house. Next to the door was a discreet brass plaque with the name of the lawyers on it.

'There's nothing *to* pick up,' Melissa said truthfully. 'Most people have untidy childhoods and I'm no exception.'

He pressed the doorbell then leaned against the wall and stared down at her.

'On the contrary. I find you quite exceptional. Are you aware that you…'

What he had planned to say was lost as the door was opened by a neatly dressed girl with a broad smile. They were shown through an open-planned office, where the sound of hands flicking quickly over computer keyboards was nicely accompanied by the intermittent ringing of the telephones.

Chris Ali's office was off the main area and after the initial rounds of introductions, during which he expressed polite interest in the time she had spent in Trinidad, they settled down to business.

After all this time, Melissa still admired the way her boss could control the ebb and flow of meetings with effortless ease. Every point put forward by the lawyer was probed, laid bare and only put to rest if Robert was completely satisfied with the conclusion.

They meticulously went through page upon page of detail, ranging from the location of the land to the land boundaries, to intricate tax questions which she faithfully transcribed but barely understood.

Coffee was brought in, and after an hour, some sandwiches on a plate and glasses of freshly pressed, ice-cold orange juice.

Watching how Robert operated was an object lesson in brilliance. His body language was perfectly relaxed, utterly at ease, but his eyes were watchful and his questions were polite but cleverly leading. He plied the young lawyer for opinions on the economic market, the trends in tourism, the financial climate, long-range forecasts for the American dollar, and Melissa could see his brain ticking away as he compiled the information and processed it all for further use.

Hotels were something of a pet hobby for him. With the advent of his first million had come the birth of his fascination for hotels, mostly in weird and wonderful places catering for an adventurous minority, travellers as opposed to tourists.

He expanded on the various styles of architecture of his various hotels and how dependent it all was on the culture, not to mention the weather, of the country. He picked his lawyer's brain mercilessly about advantages and disadvantages of the style of hotel he had chosen, nodding when an idea was mulled over, taken on board and stored as a possibility.

Melissa couldn't transcribe expressions, but she knew him well enough to absorb when something of particular importance was being said so that she could incorporate it in the private report she would write up for him.

Sometimes he would quiz her afterwards on what sort of *feeling* she had had about someone or something that had been said. Meetings with him were not places to relax, and by the end of their session, she felt suitably drained and eager to get back to the house.

'I could fall asleep,' she yawned, as the car picked up a pace and Port of Spain was gradually left behind.

'Don't tell me you've got jet lag.'

Melissa didn't answer. She closed her eyes and let her body slump in the car seat, not caring whether she was jostled into him or not. He obligingly settled comfortably into the back seat as well. One unfortunate jolt and they would collide like two rag dolls.

'I hope not,' he continued, turning his head to look at her from under his thick, black lashes. Melissa reluctantly opened her eyes to find his face rather closer to hers than she expected. 'Because we have one more stop to make before we get back to the house.'

She stifled an inward groan and tried to perk up at the prospect of another gruelling meeting. Her wrist was still killing her from the last one!

'What's that?'

'The land. The all important piece of land that's going to enable me to build the most stupendously unique hotel this island has ever seen. It's a five-minute drive past the house and I thought you'd be interested in having a look.'

'Oh, yes. Great.'

'You're already beginning to go brown, do you know that?' he murmured, and she straightened herself and shook off the remnants of exhaustion.

'I tan quickly,' she said, adjusting her skirt and her legs at the same time.

'Your skin is like satin.' He stretched out one finger, trailed it softly against her cheek and by the time her body had reacted with a start, the offending finger had been removed and his hands were decorously linked on his lap.

'What was that for?' she demanded in a shaky voice.

'Nothing. I just wanted to see if it felt as soft as it looked.'

'Well, don't.'

'And it does.'

She didn't answer. Instead, she stared straight out of the window at the trees and houses that comprised the scenery. Where his finger had touched, burnt as though electric volts had been put through her skin and in the enclosed space of the car, she could feel his eyes on her, doing as much damage as his single finger had done, turning her blood to glue and her pulses to mush.

'Did you manage to get everything Chris said?' he asked, changing the subject with such ease that she realised, with a mixture of relief and disappointment, that he was unaware of the effect he had on her. She nodded with her head still averted and only relaxed when he began chatting about work and plans for the hotel. By the time they bypassed their house and reached the plot of land, it was still hot but the sun was beginning to turn the deep, mellow colour that precedes nightfall.

'If you remember the plans,' he said, once they were standing outside the car and gazing at the land from various angles, 'the front will be on the very edge of the drop and the rooms will be stepped so that every balcony overlooks the sea. The pool will be over there.'

Melissa did her best to obligingly follow the direction of his finger, but he had unbuttoned his shirt and her eyes, with a stubborn will of their own, kept slipping to that slither of bronzed torso peeking out from between the open shirt. His body was hard and muscled and toned to perfection.

While he enthused on the subject of eight huge rooms, four above four, positions of bathrooms and laundry rooms and kitchens, the intricacies of the health and safety regulation laws that required exits at appropriate distances, she fought a losing battle not to stare as a light breeze whipped his shirt further apart and exposed yet more tantalising skin.

His waist and hips were narrow enough for his khaki trousers to dip sexily down as he walked. The gap between waistband and skin was just big enough for a finger to be inserted.

She closed her eyes, perspiring slightly, stepped backwards and hurtled into an uneven patch of rocky ground.

CHAPTER FIVE

THE pain in her ankle was the equivalent to a mosquito bite in comparison to the pain in the curve of her back, where she had unluckily crashed into mud and rock. The ground had clearly been brushed and probably flattened, as well, but it was still uneven enough to make the wearing of sensible shoes an absolute must. Melissa's shoes were sensible in the carpeted environment of an office but utterly useless in this sort of terrain. From her inelegant position sprawled on the ground, she could see that one of the offending articles of footwear was lying several inches away from her foot and the other was half off.

Why? Why, why, why? When she was trying so hard to claw back some of her well-controlled, efficient, unflappable secretarial sang-froid, did she have to trip and fall flat on her back because she had been too busy trying not to look at her boss's body? He had always *had* the same body and she had always been in full possession of twenty-twenty vision, so why was she suddenly so stupidly transfixed by the sight of his bronzed torso, however well muscled it was? Or had she *always* stared at him, but safely, from behind her well-tailored suits and well-tailored, bland expressions? That was a thought she decided quickly not to pursue.

She tried to stand and weakly fell back to the ground with a moan of pain and self-disgust.

Robert was covering the distance between them and before he could say anything, she looked up at him, squinting against the fading sun, and blurted out, 'I'm all right.'

She propped the palms of her hands behind her and made

a determined attempt to support her words with some action. Unfortunately, her body refused to cooperate.

He knelt down, instantly invading her body space.

'No, you're not.'

'Robert, please. I'm fine. Or at least, I will be in a minute.' He had shifted his attention from her face and was now contemplating her foot, then, to her intense discomfort, he gently touched her ankle, his hands soft and exploratory, sending little waves of startled awareness up and down her spine.

'It's not broken at any rate.'

'Oh, good!' Melissa answered in an unnaturally high-pitched voice.

'Now, I'm going to ask you to support yourself as much as you can.' He had swivelled back around and was peering at her from his disconcerting squatting position. She knew, without a shadow of a doubt, that this was the most embarrassing situation she had ever found herself in. Aside, she thought, from the beach scenario of the evening before.

One embarrassing situation could be termed an unfortunate mistake but what, she wondered, would one call two? Especially in the space of as many days? Was there any psychobabble jargon for someone's body deliberately ambushing their intellect?

'I have a bruise, Robert. I haven't cracked my spine in five places.'

'How do you know?'

'How would *you?* You're not a doctor!'

'Just do as I say, Mel.'

She grudgingly inched her body up slightly and rubbed the tender spot at the base of her spine.

'Right. I'm going to carry you back to the house.'

'Don't be ridiculous! You can't *carry me back to the house!* You'll collapse!'

As soon as the words left her mouth, she knew that she had waved a red flag to a bull. Now, if the house happened to be ten miles away and situated up a ninety-degree incline, he would rise to the challenge of getting her there, caveman style. She could read as much from his raised eyebrow and the glint of his teeth as he smiled wryly and indulgently at her. With a sigh of defeat, she let her body go limp as he lifted her off the ground in one sweep, swiftly and gently enough for her to feel no sharp twinges.

Although sharp twinges might have taken her mind off the hardness of his chest pressed against her like a branding iron and his masculine aroma that filled her nostrils like a mind-distorting drug.

'This really isn't necessary,' she muttered feebly, closing her eyes in a damage limitation gesture because *feeling* his body was enough to contend with, without having to see it, as well, in all its annoying glory.

'Yes, it is. Haven't you read your manual?'

'What manual?' She risked opening one eye to see that the house, thankfully, was now within range of sight.

'The updated Employee Manual, Code 256.'

'I've never heard of it.'

'In that case, let me summarise Section 12, Employer/Employee Responsibility, as defined by the government under the 1982 Act.'

'What are you talking about?' she asked, distracted enough to forget the aroma and the muscled torso.

'To paraphrase, "the employer," namely myself...'

'I'm aware of your status in the firm!' she snapped, sinking back into her state of mortification.

'"...is responsible for the safety and health of his employees and should any misadventure arise due to negligence on his part, then he is legally bound to compensate said employee for aforementioned."'

Melissa wondered whether he could possibly be seen to hold himself responsible for her inability to drag her eyes away from his body. Perhaps if he had seen fit to be several stone overweight…

'I mean,' he added softly, looking down at her and addling her further, 'what if you decide to sue me? It's my duty to do my utmost to ensure that you receive prompt attention.'

It was getting quite dark now. She couldn't clearly make out his expression, but to her ears, what he was saying was beginning to sound a little ridiculous. Was he making fun of her? Was there really some manual that she had failed to read during her term of employment with him? She couldn't believe that there was. She had always been so assiduous when it came to details like that.

'Naturally, I shall call a doctor out as soon as we reach the house…although, I have to warn you, he might be a while. It's dark, we're far enough away from civilisation for us to be on another planet, and as I'm finding out very quickly, things and people don't tend to move at the speed of light over here.'

'There's no need for a doctor,' Melissa nearly begged. She had visions of her mortification being dragged out over a period of hours when in fact she knew that all she needed was to swallow a couple of painkillers, put her feet up and probably take it easy on the walking for a day or two.

'I know you're just saying that because you don't want to make a fuss, Mel. I haven't worked with you all these years for nothing.'

'I'm saying that because there's nothing wrong with me that a good night's sleep won't cure!'

'Sleep doesn't cure a sprained ankle,' he pointed out. They had finally made it to the house and he pushed open the kitchen door which had been left ajar for them. 'At least, not to my knowledge.'

'No, but two aspirin and some basic dressing should do the trick and I am more than capable of attending to both.' With that firm statement, she could almost *feel* her business-like efficiency creeping back into her bones. 'I did that first-aid course a couple of years ago, and I passed with flying colours.'

He had walked over to the sofa and he now gently deposited her on it, then vanished to have a word with Raymond, which was slightly deflating since she could feel herself gathering pace in her figurative secretarial garb and she would have appreciated making him aware of the fact.

When he returned, it was with a glass of water and two painkillers.

'Raymond is going to go back to the land to get your shoes. Here are some aspirin.' He handed her the water and she picked the tablets out of the palm of his hand, then he dragged the solid coffee table a few inches toward the sofa and perched on it.

'Now, your ankle and your back…'

'Yes,' Melissa said eagerly. 'painkillers for the back and I was telling you about my first-aid skills. If I tell you what to bring, then perhaps…'

'No can do.' He was shaking his head ruefully.

'What do you mean *no can do?*'

'If you don't want me to call a doctor, and I think we could get away without one, then it's my sole responsibility to tend to you. Need I refer you to the previously mentioned "Employer/Employee Act?"'

He bent down and a flare of unreasonable panic rushed through her as she felt his arms circle her prone body.

'*What* are you *doing?*'

'Taking you to your bedroom. I've turned your air-conditioning on so it's nice and cool in there.' He strode purposefully in the direction of her bedroom while she clamped her teeth together in frustrated impotence.

'There's no need for all this,' she virtually wept, as he laid her on her bed. 'Those painkillers are kicking in. All I need now is a good night's sleep and…'

' ''Employer/Employee Act?'' '

'Will you *stop going on about that!* I've never even *heard* of such a thing.'

'I knew there had to be something my incomparable secretary had missed! Now. The ankle's a little swollen but looks fine. I'll have a look at your back first. On your stomach.'

Could things get worse?

She eased herself over and felt alarm and dismay flood her body as he eased her shirt up to the level of her bra strap and gently pulled the skirt and knickers down together to the firm swell of her buttocks. 'Ahhh.' Fingers against flesh, light, feathery touches that made her shiver and did unfathomable things to her pulse rate. 'Superficial bruising. Not very pleasant to look at but no swelling, which is a relief.'

Such a relief that he nevertheless continued to skim his fingers along her back and make knowledgeable noises under his breath while she did her valiant best to control her accelerated heartbeat and appear composed. As though this was all in a day's work.

Eventually, he neatly pulled her shirt down and informed her that he would rub some cream on the bruise but a diet of painkillers might well be necessary over the next couple of days. She omitted to point out that he was merely echoing what she had said herself only minutes before.

'Now, ankle.' He disappeared for a while, allowing her some privacy to arrange herself on her back with her clothes respectably tucked around her prone body, and returned with a larger than average first-aid kit. 'You'll need a bath before I can get to work on seeing to these cuts and bruises. I'll run one for you.'

Melissa eyed him balefully as he headed into the en suite bathroom and began running water, testing it occasionally until the temperature was right.

'Now don't move a muscle' he called, meeting her eyes

in the large mirror above the double basins in the bathroom. 'I'll have to bathe you.'

It took a few seconds for that to sink in, then her mouth dropped open in unconcealed horror.

'Absolutely not!' His hands? On her naked body? His eyes scouring the curve of her small breasts, possibly even brushing against them? She didn't care how many naked women he had clapped eyes on in his lifetime, or touched intimately for that matter. There was no way under the sun that she would allow him to get near her even if that meant remaining in a state of mud-encrusted shabbiness until all her bruises had vanished.

'Employer duties?' He strolled out of the bathroom and each step was a threat that had her sliding back into the mattress as though hoping for an unexpected escape route through it.

'Can take a running leap!'

'But, Mel.' He shook his head in an unconvincing display of paternalistic concern. 'We've known each other for years! You can't possibly feel uncomfortable in my presence!'

He paused at the side of the bed to stare down at her and she glowered up at him from her disadvantaged position.

'*Robert*…' she said warningly, and he cocked his head to one side, listening mode.

'Do I understand from that tone of voice that you don't want me to bathe you?'

'Very perceptive.'

'But…' He frowned. If she weren't busily engaged in trying to squash an uncharacteristic state of panic, she would have openly guffawed at his ludicrous changes of expression. Did he think for a minute that she was going to fall for that *Trust me, I know what's best* look? 'How are you going to get yourself to the bathroom, never mind manipulate yourself into the bath, soap, get out of the bath, towel yourself dry and get into some fresh clothes?'

'Which particular manoeuvre is posing a problem for you, Robert?'

'All of them.'

'In that case you'll just have to take my word for it that I can manage. Now, if you don't mind…' She looked meaningfully in the direction of the bedroom door while he continued to survey her with the expression of someone having difficulty in absorbing a certain train of thought.

But, thankfully, he left. And to ensure that his absence did not come to an untimely end in the middle of her laborious ablutions, she hobbled painfully to the door, locked it and then set about the time-consuming business of trying to get clean.

As he had shrewdly predicted, every move awakened new and hitherto undiscovered areas of pain. Having made it to the bathroom, she felt in need of several hours' rest. Exhausted, she sat on the lid of the toilet and contemplated the business of now removing all her dirty clothes, getting into the bath, and then repeating the whole thing backwards.

It took approximately forty-five minutes. She knew because she timed it on the clock propped up on the dressing table in the bathroom. Ten minutes to remove her clothes, a few torturous minutes climbing into the bath, a wonderfully long and enjoyable soak, which she could have remained blissfully lapping up if her ears hadn't picked up the distant but persistent sound of knocking on her bedroom door, accompanied by Robert's distinct though undefined voice. It didn't take the IQ of Einstein to figure out that he was probably yelling to find out whether she had drowned in the bath.

With a gleeful giggle, Melissa held her nose and submerged herself under water so that she couldn't hear a thing. When she reemerged, it was to find that his voice had miraculously disappeared.

By the time she had killed a few more minutes, taking her time in the bath, *just to prove to herself that she wasn't going to be intimidated into getting out before schedule,* then slowly dried and shoved on the easiest things she could grab hold of, her stomach was beginning to rumble with hunger.

'I know I look awful,' was the first thing she said to him when she finally left the comforting four walls of her bedroom and ventured out into the living area. He had showered and looked annoyingly refreshed and sinfully handsome in a pair of dark green shorts and an old cream jersey which did a great deal for his body and not much for her struggling self-composure.

'It was the least cumbersome thing I could manage.' She made her way to the chair, sat down and winced.

'Time for a few bandages? Cream for the back might have to wait until tomorrow. I'm afraid the first-aid kit wasn't quite as comprehensive as I expected. Remind me to put that on my list of *musts* for the hotel. Every possible nonprescription medication under the sun.'

'For the difficult guests?'

He walked over to her, knelt at her feet, which made her feel wickedly in control of him, and held her foot in his big hands, then he pulled out a long strip of bandage, like a magician pulling a rabbit out of a hat, and he began to wrap her ankle with professional speed.

'*Difficult*'s not quite the word,' he said drily, his hand moving quickly over her foot. 'Some might say that in the absence of a readily available doctor, something or someone must be available on site for anything that might happen. What do you think of hiring a medic full-time to stay in the hotel?'

He stood up, surveyed his handiwork with smug satisfaction although she could see that his mind was already running away with other thoughts. It was amazing how thoroughly you could get to know someone when you worked closely with them. She had never realised it before, but she knew far, far more about him than she would ever have imagined.

It was only now, and here, confined as they were in an unnaturally close situation, that she became aware of how easily
they communicated without going down the usual avenues
of speech. She could read his moods, understand what he
wanted to say almost before he verbalised it himself.

'Food?' he looked at her enquiringly, and she in turn
looked at her neatly wrapped foot, and nodded absent-
mindedly at him, head down-turned. When she next looked
up it was to find him standing by the kitchen doorway, staring
at her with a plate of sandwiches in his hand.

'Something light all right with you? Denise made some
sandwiches. Wasn't sure when we'd be back, you know how
meetings have a tendency to drag on.' He pushed himself
away from the door frame towards her.

'I'm impressed,' Melissa said, as he sat down opposite her
and deposited the plate on the table between them. 'I never
knew you were that much of an expert in wrapping feet.'

Something else that was odd, and even more disconcerting
was the fact that neither of them had noticed, certainly, *she*
hadn't until now: the lines of demarcation, such as they were,
between them, had vanished. Here he was, bringing food to
her, when normally she would be attending to him, bringing
the cups of coffee, ordering food to be brought to the office
on the odd occasion when they had had to work late. Yet,
worryingly, it felt natural and comfortable.

'That's because you've never been the damsel in distress.'
He stretched out his long legs, leaned forward to take one of
the sandwiches and bit lustily into it. 'And I've been waiting
long enough to show you my potential as a knight in shining
armour.' He looked at her for such a long time that she could
feel the colour slowly invade her face, like a fever. 'You
don't believe me, do you?' he asked softly.

'Of course I don't.' Her voice was shaky, as was her laugh.
'You were asking my opinion about employing someone at
the hotel full-time as a doctor,' she reminded him, looking

away. Thank goodness he couldn't read minds. What murky things he would find in hers, she shuddered to think. Things she herself barely knew how to address. Disturbing things best left unspoken.

'So I was,' he said eventually, after a silence long enough to make her aware of the fact that he knew she was changing the subject and he was willing for the moment to oblige her diffidence. 'What do you think about that idea?'

CHAPTER SIX

'YOU can't come into Port of Spain with me,' Robert told Melissa the following morning when she had hobbled out of the bedroom and into the sun-drenched living room. There was a slight morning breeze blowing, bringing the smell of the sea with it, and an overhead fan made it blissfully cool.

'I've *got* to!' Melissa protested, sinking into the chair and feeling grateful yet ridiculously pampered as Denise fussed around her with a breakfast of warm coconut bake, butter, guava jelly and fresh fruit juice. 'I'm here as your secretary! I know my ankle's going to make things a bit slow, but if you can bear with me, I can more than manage to do my job!'

'Out of the question.'

'Why? *Why* is it *out of the question?*' Her voice was thick with dismay. She was being paid an astronomical bonus for this trip and the thought of having to abandon her duties because of her own stupidity was enough to bring a flush of guilty colour to her face.

'"Employer/Employee Act,"' he reminded her gently. He had finished eating his breakfast and now sat back to enjoy his coffee, shifting his long body until he found the most comfortable position. He was already dressed for going out—long cream-coloured trousers, subdued cream shirt with fine, navy lines running down it, brown loafers worn without socks so that she could glimpse brief flashes of brown ankle whenever he adjusted his legs.

She was staring. Again. She did it unconsciously. Frightening. Even more frightening was the notion that he might have noticed, that he might have spent the last three years

150

noticing something she had never even been aware of herself before.

'Oh, not *that* again,' she groaned, and he shook his head ruefully.

'Afraid so,' he murmured, looking at her over the rim of his coffee cup with a *That's life, what can a poor man do?* expression on his face. 'As your employer, I can't do anything to compromise your health and dragging you around town from meeting to meeting from dawn till dusk isn't exactly going to do you and your bruised body parts a world of good.' He lifted his shoulders, helplessly.

'And don't I have a say in all of this?'

'Absolutely none. But don't worry, you'll have more than enough to deal with here at the house. The fax phone's been going every three seconds since I got here. Lord knows, you'd think my people couldn't manage a day without me.' He smiled smugly at her and this time it was her turn to look mildly amused at his arrogance.

'Hopeless, isn't it,' she agreed with a straight face, 'being needed so much. Mind it doesn't go to your head and give you an outsized ego. Sir.'

He grinned at her. 'Well at least your sense of humour's intact, even if it *is* at my expense.'

'I wasn't making fun of you,' Melissa informed him with wide-eyed innocence, looking down when he raised his eyebrows with outright incredulity at her statement.

''Course you were. I think you see it as one of your missions in life. To make sure that I keep my feet rooted firmly on the ground. My mother would have approved of you.' He stood up and stretched, then stuck his hands in his pockets and looked down at her. 'Now are you sure you can get from A to B without too much difficulty? I won't be gone long, just until after lunch.'

'I'll be fine. And I thought I couldn't possibly go with you because you were going to be trekking from meeting to meeting.'

'Slight exaggeration. I want you to make some enquiries into what we talked about yesterday.'

'On-site medic for the hotel?'

'Yup. There must be other hotels in the same situation as we are. Out in the middle of nowhere land. Maybe you could call a few and ask them how they handle the problem. There are maps of the island in the office so you should be able to pinpoint the relevant places. Anything else I need to tell you?' he asked absent-mindedly.

'Yes. Have you brought your electronic organiser over? I need to start filling in your diary.'

'Haven't actually.' He grinned winningly at her, like a little boy seeking approval before he confesses to some misdemeanour. 'I've been using scraps of paper.'

'Very naughty,' Melissa said, unable to resist grinning back at him because it was so *very like what he would do*. For someone who was known as a mover and shaker in the dangerous financial world of the city, he had a few stupidly endearing idiosyncrasies that would wrong foot the most cold-blooded of the opposite sex. He was the ultimate in power, wealthy and razor-sharp intelligence, a man who could and did, build castles in his head and then proceed to fearlessly transform them into reality, yet he still managed, at will, to project an elusive air of vulnerability. Naturally, he was capable of ruthlessly using those very traits to get what he wanted and from whom. She decided that she must, at all costs, remember that.

'I know. That's why I need you so badly to manage me.' He glanced at his watch, then back at her. 'Right. I'm off now. Raymond's going to drive me to town but Denise'll be here until I get back. She's going to prepare some lunch for you so you don't have to worry about food, and I'll stock up on the way back. You just need to concentrate your pretty lil' head on your work and I'll be back before you know it.'

'Absolutely no need to rush.'

'What makes you think I don't want to?' he asked, tilting his head to one side.

A remark to which she responded by tilting *her* head to one side in a manner identical to him, and saying, sweetly, 'What makes you think I *want* you to?' Before he could see that as anything in the least flirtatious, she carried on, in the same breath, 'I shall work a lot quicker if I'm left to my own devices, unless, of course, you have things to dictate to me…?'

'One or two letters. I'll need you to set appointments for me to meet with the architect and the interior designer, as well as the tourism guy.'

'On individual scraps of paper?'

'I'll get a desk diary from somewhere and bring it back with me this afternoon, although,' he added en route to the door, 'I happen to find the scraps of paper a lot more individual…'

'…But a lot less practical!' she called after him, mentally plotting the day ahead, relieved that he wouldn't be around. She heard the bang of the front door and actually gave a sigh of sheer bliss at the sudden sense of peace.

She could hear Denise in the kitchen. She would pop her head in briefly to let the older woman know where she was, then she would devote the morning to working solidly. She had never been one of those people who could contemplate a day of complete inactivity with an easy mind. She was happiest when occupied and the sea breeze combined with the daytime noises of the birds and the rustle of the coconut trees and leafy foliage was enough to bring on a deep sense of contentment.

She tried to remember whether, as a child, these surroundings had ever had the same effect on her, but if they had, then the memory eluded her. She remembered the heat vividly enough, but contentment was something she had only fleetingly glimpsed in her life, usually, now that she thought about it, at the end of a long but satisfying day at work, when she and Robert had accomplished everything on the agenda and had celebrated in quiet camaraderie with a take-out meal at the office before pushing off to their respective houses.

Except, she thought now, Robert wouldn't have been *pushing off to his house,* would he? Replete after a take-away Indian or Chinese, happy at the prospect of curling up into bed, just managing to catch the last of the ten o'clock news? For him, the night would have been just beginning. He would have been pushing off, all right, but pushing off into the arms of some blonde bimbo somewhere for a light supper followed by something far more interesting than an empty double bed and a cup of decaffeinated coffee.

Her mouth tightened and she walked slowly, like a very old woman, towards the kitchen, where she informed Denise of her whereabouts.

'Just in case you think I've dropped off the side of the cliff,' she said, smiling.

'Mr Robert says that you know this place.' Denise flashed crooked, white teeth in her direction. 'He say you lived here when you was a chil'. That true?'

Melissa nodded. 'Only for a few years when I was very young. I barely remember it.'

'Must be nice coming back, eh?'

'Strange, if anything.'

The other woman resumed wiping the kitchen counters. 'Different coming back here with a nice young man, though, eh?'

'Well, he's nice enough and young enough, I guess, but he's certainly not mine.'

Denise stopped and gave her a beady look. 'He might be

by the time you'se ready to leave.' She gave a cackle of laughter and shook her head, shaking with mirth.

No wonder her stepfather had found infidelity so easy under the hot, unforgiving sun, she thought, making her way to the improvised office. Sex was always available, always on offer, and the heat and the sun and the lazy atmosphere were all ingredients that went into the hot pot of adultery.

He couldn't keep his hands off the women, her mother had railed until the day she died, unforgiving to the bitter end. *Men! Never think about the wife they're two-timing.*

Was that why she, Melissa, had never gone out of her way to cultivate long-lasting relationships with men? Because deep down she was guided by still more pearls of wisdom gleaned from her mother? She had never thought about marriage as something particularly desirable and whenever she heard of someone who had become the victim of her partner's infidelity, she hardly ever registered surprise. After all, her stepfather had been very meek and mild to look at.

Her mind, released on this train of thought, continued to worry away at it throughout the morning, while the rest of her functioned happily on automatic, replying to all the faxes that had accumulated over the past twenty-four hours, making phone calls to England, sorting out problems long distance, and laboriously checking up with every known out-of-the-way hotel on the island to find out what they did about on-site medical services.

She had switched off the air conditioner in the room, preferring to open the windows and turn on the overhead fan, and the balmy breeze had her yawning every half an hour, even though she didn't feel in the least bit sleepy.

She was only aware of the passing of time when she heard the click of the office door and looked up, expecting to see Denise, only to clap eyes on Robert instead.

'What time is it?' she gasped in surprise, swivelling on her chair so that she was facing him instead of the computer terminal.

'A little after three.'

'A little after three!'

'I know, I know. Time flies when you're having fun, doesn't it?' He strolled across the room to her desk and perched on the edge, then he picked up a stack of typed letters and began flicking through them absent-mindedly.

'How did your meetings go?'

'Meeting. Just the one.' He pushed himself off the desk, went to the generously sized two-seater sofa and sprawled languorously on it, his long legs extending over the arm, his hands folded beneath his head as he yawned and stared lazily in her direction. The action of raising his hands to his head had yanked his shirt out from the waistband of his trousers so that bare skin peeped out at her. Her small, pointed breasts began to ache treacherously.

'And how did it go?' *Just the one meeting? Did one meeting going over fairly routine stuff with a surveyor take over four hours?* 'If you let me have the reports I can sift through them and get out any letters you want to send by tonight.' *Maybe he had decided to do a little island exploring on his own? And why not. There was a hell of a lot to see and there was no need for him to rush back to the house, not while she was competently holding the fort.*

'Sure. Everything was pretty straightforward, though. No unforeseen problems. I'll just need a letter confirming the meeting and the outcome. Report's on the dining room table.'

And of course, the chartered surveyor would have recommended somewhere lively for a spot of lunch and Robert Downe being Robert Downe, lively was an atmosphere he took to like a duck to water. Not a man made to sit for long on his ownsome when there would doubtless have been lots of pretty girls around, if only in the form of waitresses.

'How about you? Any problems?'

'Huh?' She dragged her wayward mind back to the matter at hand, namely her boss, indolently reclining on the sofa and staring at her with smoky-blue eyes.

'Work? Gone to plan? Found everything you needed? No hitches?'

'Good, yes. Fine. Letters typed. One or two issues back home. I've jotted down the problems for you and said that you'd send them an e-mail when you get back.'

He was undoing his belt, much to her consternation. He whipped it off and then tucked his hand a fraction under his waistband. Her aching breasts, exasperating enough to deal with, had now summoned various other zones of unwanted arousal, including between her thighs, which was growing damper by the minute.

She shifted uncomfortably in the swivel chair, aware of his eyes on her.

'I've also done a bit of checking around on the subject of the on-site medic,' Melissa carried on hastily. Small, cheese-cloth-flowered dresses and bare legs were no way to assert a sense of authority in front of one's boss.

'You're fidgeting. You shouldn't sit in the one place for too long. Your back will start playing up. Have you been stretching your legs regularly?'

'What?' she asked, caught off guard.

'Your legs. Have you been putting weight on them? One of the people I had lunch with happens to be a doctor and she told me that you should make sure not to shy away from exercising that ankle of yours or else when you do finally put weight on it, it'll be agony.'

'There was a doctor at the meeting?' was all she could find to say in response to this.

'No, don't be ridiculous, Mel. What would a doctor be doing at a business meeting between me and my chartered surveyor? I suppose it's conceivable that he might have been suffering from some bizarre illness that required twenty-four hour medical supervision, but then that wouldn't have been likely, would it? No, we met up with one or two people at lunch. Lizzie has a thriving practice in Maraval and her friends Gail and Monique do something or other in an advertising company. Interesting girls.'

'So interesting that you can't remember what they do exactly…' She grabbed the stack of typed letters and briskly tapped them against her thighs, straightening the papers, then she stared down at them with an efficient frown.

The black-printed words were a blur. She wasn't seeing them at all. In fact, she wasn't really seeing anything at all. She was too busy thinking, miserably, that for someone whose middle name had always been *Restraint,* her emotions appeared to have veered wildly out of control.

Lizzie? Gail? Monique? Probably three perfectly ordinary women, nothing much to look at, but she still felt racked with unreasonable jealousy at the thought of them talking to Robert, amusing him, capturing his imagination.

'The girls over here are quite something to look at, don't you think?' he mused, staring upwards at the ceiling and leaving her to the privacy of her raging thoughts. He shifted his eyes slyly across to her. 'And so *friendly,*' he murmured. 'Would you believe I've been invited to two parties already?'

'Good!' Melissa said brightly, focusing with glassy-eyed intensity on the indecipherable print in front of her. 'It's a brilliant idea to sample some of what the island has to offer.' She flicked through the letters, then did a bit more brisk tapping of them on her knees.

'Of course, you're invited, as well…'

'I'm not much of one for parties myself.' She looked up at him. 'I'm a dreadful bore as you well know.'

'I hate it when you put words into my mouth. Besides,' he added airily, 'one of these parties happened to be tonight and I had to explain to them that I have my little invalid to look after.'

'I am *not* your invalid!' Melissa snapped. She slammed the letters down on the desk and folded her arms belligerently across her chest. 'I wouldn't *dream* of standing in your way of a good time, tonight or any other night for that matter. I'm *perfectly capable* of looking after myself and if you *dare* tell me once more about your responsibilities as my employer, I'll *throw* the heaviest object I can find straight at you!'

Tears of frustration and anger were gathering in the corners of her eyes and she blindly looked away, even though the computer terminal was now nothing but a blur.

With one surreptitious hand, she rubbed her eyes vigorously and tried to stifle the emergence of any giveaway sobbing, choking sounds.

'What's the matter? What's wrong?'

His urgent, concerned voice was close enough to her ear for her to draw back in horror. An unappealing snuffle threatened to surface and she sniffed it back, accepting the handkerchief that was thrust into her hands without looking at him.

'Tell me, Mel. What the hell is wrong? What's upset you?' He caressed the nape of her neck, under her sweep of dark hair, massaging and kneading it gently. His voice was thick and husky with worry, which only made her gulp and feel worse. She didn't want to be his responsibility or anyone else's for that matter.

'Nothing,' she muttered thickly, and he carefully tilted her chin until she was facing him, though her eyes remained stubbornly downcast.

'What did I say to upset you?' he whispered. He was still stroking her hair away from her face. 'If I wanted to go to some damned party, then I would, believe me. You know me well enough to know that I'm perfectly capable of going my own way if I want to, hang the rest of the world. Is that

what's upset you? The fact that you think you're forcing me
to be somewhere I would rather not be? Is that it? Tell me.'

'I've been a nuisance, with this ankle, hobbling around like
an invalid. Hardly much of an asset, am I? Less than a week
into my stint and I can't function!'

'You're feeling sorry for yourself, Mel…'

'And why not!' Her head shot up. 'Why shouldn't I?' She
glared at him balefully. 'Who else do I have to feel sorry for
me?'

May tomorrow never come, she thought as soon as the
words were out of her mouth.

'Is it being here?' he asked quietly. 'Has this place brought
back too many memories for you? Somehow I imagined that
you might have relished returning to some old stamping
ground.'

His voice was very soothing. Lulling even. Or maybe she
was just going into some strange hypnotic trance induced by
the mild breeze, the sound of the overhead fan, and too little
food in her stomach.

'Why? If I had ever wanted to return to my *old stamping
ground* as you put it, then I would have. I never returned
here because I have quite a few unpleasant memories of it.
You see,' she paused and her voice trembled when she spoke,
'this was where my mother's marriage to my stepfather all
fell apart. The marriage fell apart and so, coincidentally, did
my mother. In that order. Most of my years here were spent
with their arguing voices ringing in my ears.

Leaving was a relief, even though the bitterness never
ended for my mother. Oh, no, sir, she carried that all the way
to her grave and she made sure that I was fully aware of
every moment of her suffering. Men were all scoundrels and
my stepfather had been the ringleader of them all. You would
have thought that no one had ever experienced the same or-
deal that she had. Although,' Melissa sighed wearily, 'I suppose putting up with all of that when you're not even in your

own territory must have been terrifying. Such a small island. The whole world knew about what my stepfather was up to and with whom and by the time I hit eleven, so did I, courtesy of the other kids in the school.'

'That must have been horrendous,' he murmured in a low voice, and she closed her eyes, reliving the moment. 'I'm sorry I dragged you here. You can book the next flight out if you want and I'll see what I can do about rustling up a replacement out here.'

For the merest second of a heartbeat, she toyed with the idea of running back to England, away from the uncomfortable flux of emotions which had been stirred into life under the tropical sun. She knew that without him around, in these odd circumstances, her wildly out-of-sync heart would once again return to normal and when she did face him again, their relationship would have returned to its old familiar footing.

Temptation lasted no more than the length of time it took to blink your eye.

'Don't be silly,' she said, opening her eyes to look directly into his. 'I'm here to do a job and here is where I shall stay. If you can overlook the unsightly limping for the next day or two.' She gave him a shaky smile.

'Good girl.' A fraction too long. His eyes held hers for just a fraction too long. 'Because I do believe I couldn't do this thing without you…'

'What thing?' He stood up and she raised her face to look at him.

'This hotel thing…sorting out business thing…living thing…take your pick…'

There was the sound of rushing in her ears, which she quickly smothered. 'And I don't think I could do *this* thing without *you*,' she quipped lightly. 'You know…this *eating* thing. I haven't had a bite since breakfast so would you mind…?'

'It would be my deepest pleasure.'

CHAPTER SEVEN

'YOU'RE fussing.'

'I'm trying to make sure that you don't go hurtling down and crack your ankle again.'

'That was *three weeks ago!* I think it's safe to say that I'm steady on my feet now and am perfectly capable of manipulating a few rocks and uneven ground.'

'Don't forget that this was the site of the disaster.'

'I twisted my ankle! Hardly what I would call a *disaster!*' But she didn't pull her arm away. Over the past three weeks, which had seen her variously working like a slave and pampered like the invalid she certainly not after the first few days, she had become accustomed to his casual touches. A helping hand here, an arm strategically placed there, the brush of his fingers as he placed a tray on her lap.

'Why are you being so solicitous?' she had asked suspiciously the first day he had insisted on bringing her a morning cup of tea in bed.

Robert Downe was brilliant, irascible, intolerant of stupidity, notoriously generous with his staff, sexy, witty, charming. Solicitous, he was not. Or at least not that Melissa had ever seen. In fact, he was the last man on the face of the earth she could ever imagine fretting around a woman. Women, his attitude had always indicated, were there to be wined and dined, courtesy of expensive restaurants. He freely admitted that entertaining them in his own space was something he preferred to steer clear from, just in case they *got ideas.*

'Because you can't move.'

'My ankle feels a bit stiff and my back's sore but I'm not *bedridden*.'

'No, but you might well be if you insist on taking things too quickly and leaping around the kitchen when you don't have to…'

Which had effectively shut her up because the thought of launching into a debate on whether she really intended to *leap around the kitchen* for the sake of a cup of tea, was enough to make her head spin.

And he had not stopped with the first cup of tea. He insisted that she put her feet up every three seconds and, bewilderingly, insisted on cooking the food for them both himself, even though Denise was more than happy to oblige.

He was, much to her amusement, an enthusiastic, adventurous and absolutely useless chef.

As soon as she regained her freedom of movement, she began to edit some of his creations, watching from a stool in the kitchen and tactfully restraining some of his more inappropriate combinations.

'I'm amazed,' Melissa said, looking around the plot of land, which was now furiously being worked on by a small army of labourers. She had not ventured out to see the plot of land since the accident and progress was being made in leaps and bounds.

'By the time we leave, the shell should more or less be finished, barring unforeseeable delays.' He was standing just behind her and she could feel the steady rise and fall of his chest as he inhaled and exhaled. The past few weeks in the sun had turned him a deep brown, just as it had turned her a similar colour. Conversely her hair seemed to have become a shade lighter. Now, the ends of her two stumpy plaits were burnished gold.

'Look over there.' He casually curled his long fingers along her soft upper arm and pointed to a completed section of the hotel. 'You can see what the eventual layout of the rooms will be like. Each room overlooking the sea. Huge windows so that the sea breeze can blow through.' His voice throbbed with enthusiasm, and she found herself smiling. 'Mosquito nets. I've always found mosquito nets disproportionately romantic.'

'So have I,' Melissa echoed softly, her eyes dreamily conjuring up the image he was painting. 'I would love to…' She stopped and flushed.

'…make love under one?' he finished for her.

'I didn't say that,' she replied promptly.

His voice was soothing, as though he was kindly trying to calm a ruffled child. 'No, of course you didn't. Now, shall I take you somewhere for lunch after I've had a quick word with the contractor? You've been stuck indoors for too long.'

'I've enjoyed it, actually. And I haven't been *stuck indoors*. I go for a swim every day around lunch-time and I do all my reviewing outside in the sun.'

'You didn't tell me you've been bathing in the sea.'

'I'm sure I mentioned it to you.'

'You didn't.'

'Well, I guess it didn't seem very important.' With day drawing to a close, the sun was far less fierce than it had been earlier on. The sound of the surf, as usual, was a steady pounding and her mind began to drift away down the road of mosquito nets and romantic evenings spent under them.

Her thoughts had never been as sensual as they were out here. Whilst before she might have contemplated the usefulness of a mosquito net, now she found herself deliberating on how much fun could be had under one. With the right person.

'Of course it's important!'

His explosion surprised her enough into looking up at him, squinting against the dull glare, and not quite sure whether she had confused the ferocity of his response with the sound of building work.

'What if something happened to you? That beach is deserted! For God's sake, woman, don't you use your head!'

Melissa stiffened. 'I'm a strong swimmer, Robert. And more to the point, I'm not a child. There's no need for you to supervise me!'

'There is if you indulge in such recklessness as bathing there when there's no one else around to help if you happen to get into trouble. And what about your injuries?' he demanded, as an afterthought. 'What about your back and your ankle? You might be able to swim across the channel in optimum conditions but even you would have to admit that you'd be a fool to risk your life swimming when you're disabled.'

Melissa's mouth dropped open at the thunderous expression on his face.

Was the man deranged? Had the heat scrambled his brains? And if not, couldn't he see how insulting it was to be accused of crass stupidity? Was he quaking at the thought of what obscure rules she had been contravening in the wretched Employer/Employee code book by actually doing something off her own bat, without him around to say yea or nay?

'I didn't realise that I had to ask your permission before I drew breath,' she said coolly, and he groaned in frustration and ran his fingers through his hair, which was longer now in the absence of any nearby hairdresser to keep it regularly cropped short.

'That's not what I'm saying.'

'Well, it certainly sounds that way to me.' She walked off towards the edge of the land and looked down at the rolling sea beneath. The incline down to it was gentle, a bank of bush and trees that swayed in the breeze, a mass of sharp greens and yellows and browns that formed a continuous carpet until the fine grainy sand took over.

She felt him next to her but didn't look around.

She was fiercely independent. So, she imagined, was he.

So why then was it that he couldn't see how loathsome it was for her to feel like a supplicant, someone in need of someone else's shoulder to lean on. The fact that she had actually *enjoyed* leaning on him, even when she really no longer needed to, was something she uneasily chose to overlook.

'I think I'll head back now,' she said, addressing the panoramic view in front of her and ignoring the rather more menacing one next to her.

'Why?' he demanded bluntly. 'There are still some things I want to point out to you so that we can tally it all with the drawings later.'

Melissa looked at him and sighed. She knew she had no choice but that any such prolonged tour was hardly necessary.

'Fine.'

'The pool will be over there. We had to alter the original plan to accommodate *that* crop of coconut trees that I wanted left untouched. I was concerned about you. All right? There was no need to react as though I'd maliciously committed a crime.' His profile was hard and unyielding and stubborn. With a sudden burst of clarity, she glimpsed the boy of ten, a miniature version of the man standing mutinously next to her, his arm almost but not quite touching hers. A young, dark-haired, reckless daredevil who would dig his heels in should anyone try and stand in his way. Lord, but he must have been a handful! She almost smiled at the thought of it

'Thank you for your concern,' she compromised in a polite voice and he turned to glare at her.

'Politeness is the most effective way of squashing someone else's foul mood, but it won't work, Mel. You act as though I'd insulted you by voicing my concern and I want to know why.'

'And *I* want to know why you're getting so hot under the collar about something as trivial as my taking a dip in the sea when you're not around. I paddle, Robert! My feet never stop touching the bottom! I know how unpredictable the water here can be!' She began walking away and he fell into step with her. 'Women,' she said, flashing him a sidelong, withering look, 'no longer need to consult a man every time they want to do something. In case you haven't noticed, we now make informed choices and use our own heads in the process!'

'How could I fail to notice?' he fired back, 'you've been working for me for the past three years, haven't you?'

'Is there an implied insult there somewhere?' Melissa stopped, put her hands on her hips and looked at him narrowly.

'Not that I'm aware of, although since I clearly have no idea what goes on in women's heads, I'm probably wrong.'

Storm waves were gathering in Melissa's head and what made matters worse was the fact that she knew full well *why*. If nothing else the past three weeks were a lesson in how susceptible the average person is to someone else's attention. She had always stood on her own two feet, even as a young girl. Her mother's muttered complaints, instead of eroding her self-confidence, had forged a kind of closed resilience in her that had gradually, over the years, turned into an inability to open up to other people. Any vulnerabilities had always been neatly hidden under her hard-working efficiency. She had worked hard at school, hard at college, hard at work and if men had been turned off by that, then she had never really thought about it.

Robert, intensely masculine as he was, had managed to worm his way under her skin with his sudden gentle consideration for her. The fact that he had succeeded in convincing her that he was enjoying every minute of his new-fangled personality had only made him more appealing. Now it hurt to admit that she had confused his easy compliance with his inborn sense of responsibility towards an employee.

'Yes,' she snapped, worked up, 'you probably are.' She headed forcefully in the direction of the house, arms folded across her chest, chin jutting out, and when he continued to meet her pace, she said, without looking at him, 'I thought you wanted to have a word with your contractor. *Please* don't let me stand in your way.'

'I wouldn't dream of letting you stand in my way. After all, we men *do* occasionally make informed choices, as well, you know. I can call Bob in the morning.'

Her skin was prickling with anger by the time they arrived back at the house and she could feel her whole body rigid and tightly strung like a piece of elastic pulled to its full stretching point. If she so much as looked at him, she would probably snap and snapping was out of the question. Raging, hurt, insulted and mortified by the ferocity of her own response she might well be. She was also still his secretary and secretaries, however well they worked with their bosses, were not indispensable.

If she didn't control her wayward temper, she might well find herself out of a job and the thought of leaving Robert, never seeing him again…

She pushed a trembling hand through her hair and feverishly contemplated what her brain had obligingly locked away for longer than she cared to think. She could feel the perspiration glistening on her skin like droplets of water and her body was engulfed in a fierce, burning heat as she blindly made her way to the kitchen and poured herself something to drink.

'Look. I apologise for…well, for losing it back there,' Melissa said, speaking to but not looking in the direction of the man glowering by the entrance to the kitchen. She took a long, shaky breath and a deep gulp of cold juice. 'I guess the heat got to me.' So this was what Love felt like. Wonderful, marvellous Love that put foolish grins on people's faces and made them think that they could do anything.

She never anticipated that it could also make you feel as though a knife was being turned very slowly somewhere deep in your gut. She had always imagined that that sort of thing happened when everything had turned sour.

'Losing it is nothing to be ashamed of. We all do it from time to time.'

'Perhaps you're right.' She finished the juice, made a production out of washing, and then when she had no option but to turn around and face him, she said, eyes still lowered, 'I think I'll go and have a shower now.'

He stepped aside to let her pass and she knew that the hairs on her arm were standing on end as she brushed past him. She *knew* now, knew that her forbidden love for him had inalterably changed everything between them. She would never be able to look at him again, hear his voice, watch the way he moved, without desire clawing through her body like burning iron spikes, ripping her to shreds. A few seconds of revelation had destroyed everything.

Her mind was churning as she stepped under the shower, turning it to *cold* in a vain attempt to wash away her gut-wrenching panic.

A little under three weeks left to go. She would have to endure it the best she could, but the minute she returned to England, she would hand in her notice.

She dried, then peered into the huge bathroom mirror to see if she could glimpse any noticeable changes in her face. A woman in love should *glow,* shouldn't she? Even if love had wreaked havoc with her sanity? There was, she noted sadly, no glow. Her skin was flushed, true enough, but there was nothing radiant about the woman staring back at her.

She had a small hand towel wrapped turban style around her hair and the bath towel barely skimming her body when she pushed open the bathroom door into the bedroom.

There he was, leaning against the door, hands thrust into his pockets, casually relaxed. The air-conditioning, which she had turned on as soon as she entered the bedroom, to combat the raging heat coursing through her, had obviously drowned out the sound of the door opening and closing.

'What are you doing here!' Melissa said, when her vocal cords had finally caught up with her brain. She clutched the towel tightly at the top and at the same time lowered the other hand to the bottom of the thigh-skirting piece of cloth.

'I came to finish our conversation.'

'Well you can get out because my bedroom is no place for continuing a conversation! And you should have knocked!'

'I did,' he protested meekly, 'but no one answered and I just came in when I found it was unlocked.'

Melissa's feet appeared to be tacked to the floor with invisible nails, as did the hand gripping the towel for dear life.

'It's time we sorted this thing out once and for all.' He pushed himself away from the door and strolled lazily towards her while she, unable to flee, struggled with a sickening sense of mounting panic.

'Sorted *what* out?' she squeaked, her heart gathering momentum the closer he got.

'Us. What's been happening between us.'

He was dangerously close to her now, looking down at the faint shadow of cleavage visible above the tautly pulled towel.

'I don't know what you're talking about,' Melissa babbled hysterically. 'One minute you're accusing me of being a lunatic for having the occasional dip in the sea when you're not around, the next minute you're ranting on about *us*. I'm your secretary! You're my boss! I thought we understood one another!' She could feel herself almost on the verge of tears at his bewildering intrusion into her bedroom and cuttingly pertinent choice of conversation, given what she had spent the past hour brooding over.

'We do understand one another. Therein lies the problem.'

He raised his hands to her shoulders and began rotating the pads of his thumbs against the sides of her neck. Melissa emitted a strangled sound and fought a desperate need to sink to the floor, rag doll style. 'I always knew we worked well together, but it's only since coming here that I've realised how much further it goes between us.' His voice was low and smoky and sent shivers racing up and down her spine. 'And don't try to pretend that you haven't felt it, too.'

He had inclined his body forward so that his lips brushed her hair and his voice was barely audible. 'You've enjoyed all those accidental touches, as much as I've enjoyed doing it, feeling the charge running between us like an unstoppable electric current.' He blew into her ear and then his tongue flicked against her earlobe, squirmed into the delicate dip just above. Melissa moaned softly and bravely but ineffectively flattened her palms against his chest and attempted to push him away.

Instead of responding to the half-hearted pressure, he covered her hands with his, then raised them, one at a time, to his mouth so that he could flutter kisses on the tender flesh of her inner wrist.

'I've been wanting to do this for weeks,' he breathed shakily. 'In fact, I suspect that I may have wanted to do this for far longer than that.' One finger slipped a centimetre under the top of the towel. A few centimetres lower, Melissa's nipples pulsed into life, pushing against the rough cotton of the towel.

'No.' Was that a protest? To her own ears, it sounded like a feeble avowal of defeat!

He laughed softly under his breath. 'Why am I unconvinced by that?' His mouth found the slender column of her neck and she arched back to accommodate his nuzzling exploration of it, sinking back and feeling sweet relief when he picked her up and carried her to the bed.

'No, don't,' he rasped, when she moved to pull aside the

towel which for some reason she was still clutching in a rigor mortis grip. 'Let me. I want to savour every glorious moment of this. I've waited long enough.'

Her mind snagged on the *every glorious moment,* and she smiled a radiant, feline smile of pure satisfaction, moving sinuously against the sheets, her eyes half closed, her damp, unbrushed hair framing the small, smooth face so that she looked like a wild child.

He uttered a sound that was halfway between triumph and craving and knelt between her legs so that he could better see as he yanked down the towel, exposing her small, pointed breasts and the patch of soft, downy hair between her thighs. Thighs which she opened to accommodate his greedy, needy gaze, pleasure and passion filling her as his eyes darkened with hunger.

When he touched her, she could feel the burning urgency in him which he was trying to control, and the knowledge of that gave her a heady sense of power. She closed her eyes, every pore in her body attuned to the man towering over her. When she knew that he was stripping off his clothes, she felt a quiver of nerves, but kept her eyes firmly closed until he resumed his position between her legs, then she opened her eyes and feasted on the throbbing, jutting manhood that proclaimed his desire more fiercely than any words could.

With a purring smile, she raised her hands above her head, inviting him to touch her wherever he wanted and sizzling as his mouth clasped over one nipple and he began sucking at it, drawing it into the wetness of his mouth, while his fingers played with her other nipple, provoking the tight, brown bud into glorious arousal. As she squirmed against the sheets, her legs opening, the cool air from the air-conditioner caressed the inside of her thighs. She raised her legs so that her slender feet brushed erotically against his erection and with a groan he moved down to capture the honeyed moisture of her aroused with his tongue.

By the time she felt flashpoint nearing, his tongue had already invaded her most private parts. The throbbing bud had swollen but before she could quiver to orgasm, he raised himself and thrust into her, rhythmically and forcefully, over and over and over, a complete masculine possession that sent her senses spinning into orbit and filled her with the deepest, sweetest feeling that at last, things all made sense.

CHAPTER EIGHT

FROM behind the bedroom window, Melissa stood and surveyed the neat parameters of her garden with very little satisfaction. Summer should, by now, have been disposing of what had been a very lukewarm Spring. Instead, the days fluctuated between the promise of warmth and the spiteful deliverance of yet more rain. The coolest June, it was repeated on the weather reports every so often, since records began.

Behind her, her tan suitcase was packed although now that the taxi to the airport was imminent, she was torn by the certainty that the holiday which she had booked in a moment of maudlin self-pity, had been a very bad idea.

The past can never be revisited, she thought, staring out beyond the rectangle of the garden to the road. Melissa wished that she had had the wit to realise it a little earlier, like when she had found herself in the travel agency, scouting through brochures for warm holidays, pausing as a certain familiar sight accosted her eyes for a hotel, newly opened, in the divine solitude of the sea and forests of Trinidad. He must have paid the earth to have it included in the exclusive brochure at the last possible moment and just in time for the summer trippers.

She had stared at the picture, hands trembling, and thought, *So this is how it all turned out in the end.* Even more spectacular than her wildest imaginings. She remembered in those heady remaining weeks, when they had worked and played with abandon, that they had chosen the colour for the outside facade. A startling blue, the same colour as the sea, with white fretwork and wrought iron providing eye-catching con-

174

trast. Seeing it reproduced in the exclusive *Elegant Caribbean* brochure, glossy and enticing, had sent her shocked heart into immediate overdrive. It had also sent her mourning soul into wild temporary insanity that had seen her booking a week's vacation on the spot, using a different name for the hotel booking, *just in case.*

She heard the sound of the doorbell and when she focused her eyes on the road, she realised that the taxi had arrived. Her mind had taken flight and winged its way back into the past, as though it hadn't had enough of it over the past two and a half months. How much more was it possible to dwell on a past without collapsing from an overdose?

She grabbed the case, which was small and pleasantly light, and as she locked the front door, the full force of her stupidity hit her like a bucket of cold water.

Why was she going to the hotel for a holiday? What exactly was the point of *that?* She had spent the past three weeks convincing herself that the only way she would ever be able to deal with Robert was to revisit the spot that had been the site of all the cataclysmic changes that had happened to her, put the whole episode to rest, so to speak.

Now, in a flash, she realised that going back was only going to further her misery. She wouldn't *put thoughts of Robert to rest,* she would revive them, not that they needed much reviving anyway. She would spend an entire week wallowing in self-pity and grief. She would, she was now convinced, as the taxi trundled off to the airport, be surrounded by an invisible aura of unspeakable, harrowing depression that would probably frighten off the other guests. After all, what could be more off-putting for her fellow holiday-makers, out for a jolly, relaxing vacation, than the sight of a miserable, heartbroken woman sitting alone in a corner of the lounge glugging back rum and Cokes and trying to stave off a nervous collapse?

She rested her chin in the palm of her hand and peered out of the car window.

Whichever way she went, it all came back to Robert.

She wished to God that she could forget, but the minute she opened her eyes in the morning, she was instantly besieged by memories.

The sex, she knew, she would never forget and would never want to. Every minute, replayed in her mind, was to be savoured, as was the memory of how complete and fulfilled she had felt when his lips had touched her and she had felt herself blossom under his caresses.

Hard on the heels of those thoughts, however, were a host of others. Just conjuring up an image of him was like opening a Pandora's box.

She closed her eyes and recalled the plane flight back, when she had sunk into herself, already reerecting the defences she had willingly allowed him to demolish. He had slept through most of the trip back, which had been a blessing, and when he *had* tried to talk to her, she had clammed up and feigned exhaustion. After all, it *had* been a night flight and she *had* been tired.

When they hit England, everything happened so quickly that it had been possible, just, to ignore the increasingly impatient look smouldering in the depths of his eyes. When he had held her arm and demanded an explanation for her weird behaviour, she had taken refuge behind an apologetic smile and some mumbled excuse about a headache from the pressurised cabin of the plane.

'I just need to think about…what happened between us…' she had pleaded softly. 'Please, *please,* try and understand…could we talk about this next week? Give me the weekend to recover…'

He hadn't liked it, but he had grudgingly agreed. With his typical, forthright aggression, he had seen her delaying tactics as cowardly, but he hadn't pressed her and for that she had been grateful.

She doubted whether he would have been as accommodating if he had seen the thoughts scrambling through her head.

Forty-eight hours after they had said an awkward goodbye to one another at the terminal, he would have been all too aware of every thought. Every thought but the big, important one, because the word *Love* had been nowhere in the resignation letter waiting to greet him on the Monday morning.

It had been carefully constructed. It spoke coolly of the impossibility of ever working together, it contained enough thank-yous to strip it of any personal emotion whatsoever, and most importantly it implored that he accept the situation along with her most profound regrets and make no attempt to confront her face to face.

We were a little incautious and perhaps what happened might serve as a reminder of where lust can get someone, but I hope you will remember me on friendly terms as I shall remember you.

As an exercise in detachment, the letter had been beautifully worded. She had crept like a thief into the office on the Sunday, deposited it on his desk, had a final look around, cleared her few personal possessions from her desk, and left the way she had come, depositing her office key with a bemused Frank at the reception desk.

Her only consolation was that she was sparing herself further hurt by leaving as she did. Robert Downe didn't love her and not once had the word passed his lips. *Want* had been a frequent intruder in his vocabulary, but *wanting* and *loving* were world's apart and without the one, the other was, in the long term, unacceptable. At least to her.

She knew that he had wanted their affair to continue. He

had assumed that she would have no problem with that. The fact that it would, by nature of its foundation, be temporary, was something he appeared not to have considered.

When your heart's not involved the termination of a relationship becomes a formality, she had reasoned over the past two months, a hiccup that you can put behind you with no effort at all. She would be the only loser.

'Going anywhere nice?' the taxi-driver asked, eyeing her in the rear-view mirror.

'Nope. It's going to be a horrendous week and if I hadn't paid for the thing, I wouldn't be going at all.' That had silenced him, and she had slumped back into her repetitive, unwelcome line of thought.

It proved so tiring that she ended up sleeping a good deal of the flight away, only rousing herself when the captain announced that they were about to land in Barbados. Thirty-five minutes to go and they would be in Trinidad. As she blinked herself wide awake, she could anticipate her oncoming nightmare with depressing clarity.

By the time the plane landed and she found herself sitting in the back of one of the few taxis available for hire at the airport, she had resigned herself to her situation with a certain amount of fateful calm. The prospect of one week of unrelieved depression was beginning to feel masochistically satisfying, especially if she could convince her usually alcohol-free body to immerse itself in seven nights of splendid, helpful inebriation.

Unfortunately, by the time the long, winding drive was completed, and she had paid the taxi-driver, it was too dark to make out much of the outside of the hotel. The lights interspersed around the wide veranda circling the hotel were only able to give a tantalising glimpse of blue and white. Tables and chairs were informally dotted on the wooden deck and guests were milling around in shorts and T-shirts, drinking and chatting. There was something inescapably old-fashioned and sedate about the whole scene and Melissa thought that if Robert were here, he would be thrilled to see his completed work and its residents.

Inside was small but exquisite. She was efficiently welcomed by a beaming woman in her forties with impossibly white teeth and impossibly smooth skin and her bag was whisked away with such speed that she only had a brief glimpse of the decor before being shown to her room.

It felt strange and unsettling to be looking at the fruition of what had started out as a dream on a piece of paper.

Her mind seemed to stop totally at Memory platform and her eyes were blurring over with unshed tears by the time she hustled the porter out of the spacious, wooden-floored room. She would have her breakfast in her room in the morning. She *had* to. The thought of chatting politely with the other guests and skimming over the fact that she was intimately connected with the hotel was something she would have to work up to.

With the anticipation of a sleepless night, she was surprised, on hearing a gentle knock on her bedroom door, that she had slept like a log. It was eight-thirty and when she staggered drowsily out of bed and pulled back the curtains, it was to find the sun shining in all its glory.

'Breakfast, Miss James,' a local voice said, and she stuck on her dressing gown and gazed out of the window as the bustle of trays was heard behind her. When she heard the bedroom door click shut, she turned around.

The sight of Robert leaning against the wall by the door was shocking enough to make her rub her eyes. For a mirage, he looked remarkably real!

'Surprise, surprise.'

Mirages didn't hold conversations. Her legs felt weak and she half stumbled into the soft, comfy chair next to her.

'Breakfast?' He lifted the silver lid covering the plate, one hand still in his trouser pocket. 'Your favourite. Coconut bread, scrambled eggs, some cheese. Aren't you suitably flattered at the personal service?' He flashed her a hard, cynical smile while she continued to stare at him with her mouth half open, goldfish style. A goldfish that has suddenly found its bowl invaded by a piranha.

'Maybe not,' he mused, replacing the lid and strolling towards her, stopping en route to look through the window at the meltingly beautiful vista stretching down below. 'Why should you be?' He perched on the window ledge and gave her a long, withering look to which she could find no suitable response save for some more inelegant opening and closing of her mouth. Shock was still in total command of her vocal cords. 'You obviously weren't impressed by anything else about me judging from the way you vanished in a puff of smoke with no warning at all.' His jaw tightened and she watched, fascinated, at the rapid beating of the pulse in his throat.

'I can explain,' she croaked, a little wildly. Why he had taken this long to demand an explanation, she couldn't understand but next to her electrifying shock was a fierce, illicit thrill of setting eyes on him again, even under these circumstances. 'I thought…you do remember that I said…that I mentioned…I needed to think…I thought th-that it would be easier all…'

'Do you know how I felt when I found that miserable, unrevealing excuse of a note?' he bellowed, his dark eyebrows meeting in a thunderous frown.

Melissa gulped. *And how do you think I felt when I discovered that I'd fallen in love with you? Chipper? Overjoyed? Ready to rush out and start buying bed linen for our shared life together?* 'I would have told you…face to face…but…'

'You liar!' He advanced towards her and she pushed herself back into the chair.

'Why now?' she whispered, as he towered over her cringing form. 'Why have you decided to…were you here all along? Did you spot me when I arrived and thought that you might as well have it out…?'

He leaned over her, breathing heat from every pore, his arms like steel rods on either side. 'I couldn't believe what I was reading when I got that note. I had to reread the damn thing over and over. Look at it!' He took a crumpled piece of paper out of his pocket and flung it on her lap. 'Read it! Go on! Go on!'

She falteringly read the first line and a half and then dried up.

'I wanted to come after you,' he grated harshly. 'God knows, I wanted to break down your damn door and throttle you until I got a sensible answer out of you! Weeks in each other's company and…' He raked his fingers through his hair. 'But no way. *No way* was I going to hound you down. As far as I was concerned, you could take a running leap. The sea is full of fish. Positively *brimming over* with them!'

'So I'm sure you've snapped up one or two already!' Melissa was stung into replying. His face darkened as he lowered brooding, blue eyes for a few seconds before raising them to hers accusingly.

'As a matter of fact I haven't,' he threw at her. He walked towards the window and stared out while Melissa watched him compulsively.

'Why didn't you come and find me before?' she asked his profile. The disappointed accusatory tone of her voice left a sour taste in her mouth, but she knew that his lack of pursuit had hurt far, far more than she had expected. For the first week after she had left her job, she had daily expected him to show up on her doorstep, a hulking, angry figure of rejected male, if only to lambaste her with his contempt for her behaviour. In her head, she rehearsed a number of approaches she could take to his appearance on her doorstep.

As the days lengthened into weeks, she gradually and bit-

terly accepted that her absence in his life had simply not meant
enough for him to pursue her. He didn't' want to show her
his anger, he didn't even want to ask her what the hell she
thought she was up to, walking out of her job and leaving him
in the lurch when she was required by law to work a month's
notice. She had pitifully clung to the belief that he *must* get
in touch, if only to ask some boring, technical question to do
with work, but time had killed any such expectation.

'Give me one good reason why I should have.'

'Okay. Why have you sought me out *now?*'

He turned to face her fully, his face dark and glowering.
'Because…' he began. A look of hesitation darkened his face
and he flushed uncomfortably.

'I don't think you were here already and spotted me arriv-
ing,' Melissa said to herself. 'When the booking was made,
I specifically asked my travel agent to make sure that you
weren't around. I told her that you owned the place but I
wanted to be here when you weren't because we had been
through a bad patch and I couldn't face you…'

'Why couldn't you face me?' he asked quickly, and she
looked at him distractedly.

'Let me finish. *How* did you know that I'd be here? Did
you book your trip at the last minute? Is it just coincidence
that we're both here at the same time?' She had no idea what
to make of the surreal situation. She knew that she should
be enraged at his sudden appearance in her life just when she
had accepted that she would never see him again, but all she
felt was a soaring joy and satisfaction at seeing his face, a
frustrating, infuriating reaction that made a nonsense of all
the common sense mini lectures she had delivered to herself
on a daily basis for the past few weeks.

'You can't blame a man…' he muttered, folding his arms
and glaring at her perplexed frown. 'Most men would have
done exactly what I did…'

'What are you talking about?'

'I decided that I wasn't going to chase you down...I've never run behind any woman in my life before...' He raked his fingers through his hair and shook his head in frustration. He frowned and stared at the wall behind her. 'If you couldn't incorporate what we had going into life over here, then that was *your* choice. It wasn't my business to try and talk you out of it.'

'So why are you here?' Melissa repeated.

'Because none of it worked. I've spent every day thinking...about you...it's driving me to distraction. A week after you left...I...employed a private detective to follow you...'

'You what!'

'You heard me!' he rasped defensively, moving towards her. 'You were driving me crazy!'

'So now it's all my fault, is it?' She tried to feel insulted but a soft smile curved her lips and he fell to his knees to stare into her face. He picked up one of her small, slender hands and turned it over and over in his big palm.

'I was too proud,' he muttered. 'I knew that I'd fallen in love with you but I couldn't stand the thought of rejection and I was too proud to follow you and ask you what you felt, what I had meant to you...'

Fallen in love, fallen in love, fallen in love... When? Shouldn't she have been able to spot a man in love? She peered into his face to see whether he was joking, and when he returned her stare levelly, she whispered, in a numb voice, 'You mean it, don't you?'

'Every word. I fell in love with you. While I was going along my merry way, working hard and playing hard, I fell in love with you and I think, at the back of my mind, that's part of the reason why I went to Trinidad to put up the hotel. Some part of me wanted you so badly that I just wanted to *be* in the place where you'd grown up. I thought that I could somehow find the key to your soul if only I knew more about your past. You were so damned cagey! I wanted you to open up to me, long before we ended up on the island, and I was prepared to travel halfway across the world to try and unlock the door.

'If you're not ready for all this…I'm prepared to wait, but when I found out where you were heading, I knew that I had to get over here and finally have this all out. I couldn't live with the pain of being apart from you for a second longer.'

'Are you sure,' Melissa said gravely, while her spirit took flight and discovered Heaven, 'that all this has nothing to do with the fact that you can't find a replacement secretary?' She smiled slowly at him, her eyes brimming with the love she had dared not speak before and he returned her smile with a blissful one of his own.

'Which reminds me,' he said, kissing each of her fingers, 'there are a couple of things I can't find…'

'You should have called me earlier…'

'You should never have left me,' he returned with a sulky, little-boy grin. 'Fortunately, I have a solution for that…'

'Which is?' As if she couldn't guess!

'You'll just have to marry me, my darling Miss James…' He pulled one of her fingers into his mouth and sucked it until the sigh that came from her lips and the adjusting of her position had less to do with discomfort and more to do with her body wanting him to suck rather a lot more than one finger.

'Before I find speaking impossible,' Melissa gasped, as he pulled aside her bathrobe and delicately licked the raised, tight bud of her nipple, 'I'd better agree.' She ran her fingers through his hair and sighed with deep happiness, 'I love you, Robert Downe. I can't remember a time when…I didn't.'

And then she slipped forward in the chair, pulling apart her bathrobe entirely and succumbing to the sweetness of his mouth caressing every minute pore of her yearning body.

She would have this…today, tomorrow and forever….

EPILOGUE

'IT LOOKS different. Does it look different to you?' Melissa looked at the walls, the decor, the abundance of plants that seemed to be waiting patiently in their plant pots before staging a complete takeover of the foyer. She couldn't put her finger on *what* was different, but she knew that something was.

'It looks lived in,' the tall, dark man standing next to her said. 'Not so new and shiny.'

'A bit like you, in other words,' she said with a grin, and he bent to kiss the corner of her mouth, as though unable to resist the fleeting touch.

'What do you expect?' Robert asked, sighing elaborately, his hand pressed into the curve of her back, a strong, warm, deeply satisfying pressure that would never, she knew, lose its ability to thrill her.

Melissa didn't have to turn her head for the expression in his voice to bring a contented smile to her face.

'I do nothing but work!'

'You poor baby.' Melissa oozed amused sympathy.

'Pleasing three women isn't an easy task, even for someone like me, a man in his prime, at the peak of his physical prowess…and two of them don't even seem to appreciate my efforts!' In unison they glanced at the little figures lying in the double buggy in front of them. Identical girls, a little over six months and already, as he was fond of saying, particularly when holding them both close to his chest, showing every indication of being as stubborn and demanding as their mother.

'Oh, they do.' Melissa tousled the thatch of black hair that sprang with identical lushness from the tiny, exquisite faces. In reply, there was a whimper which never made it to a cry because Robert scooped up the grumbling infant, holding her out in front of him and inspecting her with the pride of a man utterly in love with the product of his virility. Bright blue eyes stared back at him and the lower lip wobbled, threatening to cry.

'This is your hotel,' he murmured, 'and your sister's…and you'll be coming here every year, at least once a year because your mother tells me that she prefers the weather over here to the weather in England.'

'That's not what *I* tell them,' Melissa said, with a gurgle of amusement, savouring this moment of shared intimacy in the darkness of the outside veranda, before they were spied by the zealous Vanessa at reception and ushered in with pomp and ceremony.

'And what, might I ask, *do* you tell them, Mrs. Downe?'

'Why, that their father's a sentimental dear, of course! Which is one of the reasons why I adore him… So much masculine virility concealing such a big, soft heart!'

'Keep your voice down, woman! Walls have ears, you know!' He paused and then tickled her ear with his tongue and whispered, 'But you're right about the masculine, virile part. Tonight, my darling, I'll show you just how masculine and just how virile your adoring husband is…'

Melissa chuckled and looked at him, meeting his eyes with tenderness, 'And the girls…?'

'Are under instructions not to disturb…' He sighed. 'I hope!'

MILLS & BOON®

Makes any time special™

Mills & Boon publish 29 new titles every month. Select from...

Modern Romance™   Tender Romance™

Sensual Romance™

Medical Romance™   Historical Romance™

MAT2